Blood Valley

Blood Valley

William W. Johnstone

PINNACLE BOOKS
Kensington Publishing Corp.
www.kensingtonbooks.com

Master Henry Joseph Wheeler
1212 Elm Street
Rock Springs, Wyoming
United States of America

April 17, 1925

My dear grandson Henry,

I was thrilled right down to my sock feet to get your letter of 12 April. For a young feller of thirteen years your handwriting is mighty fine indeed. Just goes to show what a little good school-learning can do.

You say your schoolmarm has taken you to task for spinning yarns to your friends about your old granddaddy and his adventures here in Wyoming back when she was still a territory. How I was a town marshal and kilt some bad men and such. It's been nigh on fifty years since that day when I rode into the town of Doubtful, looking for a hot meal, maybe a drink of whiskey, and a bed with clean sheets, and how my life was about to change forever.

A lot has been writ large about my exploits in Doubtful in those dime novels and western adventure magazines I see in the drugstores and such. Writ, I suppose, by some derby-wearin' double-shuffle thimble-riggin' New York dandies with typewritin' machines who probably ain't been any further west than the end of their peckers. Not one of them ever come close to gettin' the story right, nor did any of them ever see fit to ask me direct what really happened there in Doubtful.

So I take pen in hand now and will write it up my own-self, exactly the way it happened. You know, Grandson, that I never had much in the way of school or book learning, and could barely read nor write till your grandma Pepper taught me. So I'll put it down best as I can with the understanding that I ain't no Mark Twain—I sorta write the way I talk, as you'll see.

BOOK ONE

BOOK ONE

Chapter One

When I come off that ridge, there wasn't but one thought in my mind: hunt a hole and crawl in deep.

I didn't want to look behind me. I had a pretty good idea what I was gonna see. And that would be a good-sized posse with an already knotted rope. And the necktie party they had in mind was gonna feature me as the honored guest.

If hangin' was ever an honor.

I knew I should have stayed out of that little pissant town. Something warned me that I was lookin' at trouble. But I'd been paid off 'bout ten days back, up in Montana Territory, and I hadn't as yet found me a place to spend none of it. I had me six months' wages—earned hard winterin' in a line shack—and I had me a growlin' belly. I could smell that food a-cookin' in that cafe. Least I thought I could; might have been my imagination. I'd run out of grub a couple of days back and was so hungry I could have et the ass end out of a skunk. Well . . . almost.

I sat Critter on that little hill overlookin' the lights of town and ruminated matters around in my head.

I figured I'd passed into Wyoming Territory a few days back—not that it made no difference noways. I didn't have nobody waitin' neither behind nor ahead of me, and I sure wasn't on no schedule.

"What you say, Critter?" I asked my horse.

He just looked at me sort of mournful-like.

I give him his head and down that hill we went. He was as tired as me, I reckon, and lookin' for a warm stall and a bellyful of hay, maybe some corn if he was lucky.

The name of the town was Doubtful. That right there should have warned me off. Who in the hell ever heard of a town called Doubtful? But it looked to me a right nice-sized town, and nobody was shootin' at me. Yet.

The cafe was warm and sort of homey, the food was good, and the gimp-legged, scar-faced man served plenty of it. So after two plates of food and half a dozen cups of coffee, I just naturally headed for a saloon. I had my choice of three. I picked the closest one. Place was near'bouts deserted, except for a few hard-lookin' ol' boys playin' poker. I bought in. Second mistake of the evenin'.

I could tell after a few hands that I was bein' cold-decked, bottom-dealt, and palmed from the word go. Problem was, they was all so clumsy with it. And that made me mad; like they figured I had just rode in on a turnip wagon and fell off it.

I also noted that they was all wearin' two guns. And you don't see no average puncher packin' that much iron.

So I told them ol' boys, all of 'em, that if they wanted to play poker, why, that was fine with me. But the name of the game was draw, and that meant take the first five off the top and halt.

One of 'em asked me my name and I told him it was Cotton.

They all thought that was funny, all except for this feller dressed in a business suit standin' at the bar drinkin' him a beer and eatin' a hard-boiled egg from the platter.

I slipped the hammer thong off my .44 with my right hand and sorta grinned along with 'em.

If they thought Cotton was funny, I sure as hell wasn't gonna tell 'em my Christian last name.

Then this fat, ugly, young one asked if I was accusin' him of cheatin'. I told him the way he was comin' off the bottom with them pasteboards, it sure looked like it to me.

Then damned if he didn't call me a right ugly name.

Next thing you knowed, they was two of them ol' boys stretched out on the sawdust with holes in them. The air was filled with gunsmoke, the guy eatin' the egg had jumped behind the bar, and I knowed ol' Cotton had done screwed up again.

We just couldn't go no more. My big horse, Critter, was so bad tuckered that he was staggerin'. And I'd be damned if I was gonna kill my good horse over some tinhorn gamblers. 'Specially one that was as ugly as that fat one was.

Or had been.

I found me a stand of timber with a little stream runnin' through it, a sheer rock wall to the back, and a good field of fire to the front. I stripped the saddle off Critter and told him to take him a good roll and a rest.

"And keep your head down when the shootin' starts," I added.

You spend a lot of time with a horse, you get to talkin' to it. I used to try to sing to Critter, but ever'time I done that he bucked me off. I reckon he had him a tin ear.

Surely, it wasn't my singin'. But come to think of it, I did get blamed for stampedin' a herd one time when I was ridin' nighthawk. I blamed it on the weather, but the cook said my singin' sounded like a bear caught in a trap.

I listened to Critter take him a roll and a good long drink, then he got to croppin' at the grass. It was spring, with new grass, but this high up, it's liable to be warm and then an hour later, start snowin'. When he finished chompin', I picketed him and got back into position, my Henry at the ready, all full and ready to bark and snarl.

Damn, but I was tired. I wasn't much worried about nobody slippin' up on me. Critter was better than any watchdog I'd ever seen; he'd warn me. So I just put my head down on my forearm and closed my eyes.

Critter's soft nickering woke me up. I opened my eyes to a real pretty day. Sun shinin' and warm and lazy-like. I couldn't help wonderin' if this was gonna be my last pretty day, 'cause when I looked around, there was about twenty men sittin' on their horses about two hundred and fifty yards off.

I wished I had me a cup of coffee. I'm a coffee-drinkin' man, and I just hate to start the morning with no cup of coffee. 'Course, I didn't feel like *endin'* no morning with no cup, neither.

"You crazy son of a bitch!" a man yelled at me. I reckon he was hollerin' at me, wasn't nobody else around.

I kept my mouth shut and listened.

Wasn't much else I could do, boxed in like I was.

"You, there! Man who called hisself Cotton. We know you're down there in that holler. Ain't nobody gonna hurt you. We got a proposition for you, that's all."

I looked back at Critter, lookin' at me. And from the look on his face, he didn't believe the guy neither.

"Look here, now! Don't start no shootin', Mister Cotton."

Mister Cotton! Mighty damn formal name-callin' from a bunch of people who was fixin' to hang me.

I decided to give it a whirl. Damn near anything beats hangin'. I peeked out and squinted my eyes and spotted that feller who had been gnawin' on that egg in the saloon. "I hear you! What do you want?"

"That there was Jack Nolan you kilt back yonder in the saloon. The other one was his partner, the fat one. Name of Larson. Both of them was gunslingers."

I'd heard of 'em. Figured they was some better than that.

"Is that right? Well," I hollered. "They couldn't drag iron no better than they played cards!"

"You plenty fast, Mister Cotton. Might be the man we want. You want a job?"

"I ain't lookin' for one."

"We'll pay you a hundred a month and give you a place to stay."

A hundred a month! Hell, it'd take the average cowboy damn near six months to earn that much, unless they was drawin' fightin' wages. "What's the catch?"

"There ain't no catch! Damn, you shore are suspicious. How about the job?"

"What kind of job you talkin' about?"

I could see them talkin' amongst themselves up there on the ridge. They was out in the open, and I could probably knock two or three out of the saddle. But they wasn't actin' hostile, and I didn't see no one wavin' no rope around.

"We'll give you a hundred and twenty-five a month, Mister Cotton!"

"What kind of damn job are you jabberin' about, anyways?"

When he told me, I just sort of hunkered there in that holler and was stunned-like. I been a lot of things in my time, but this one took the cake.

I was still sort of not believin' it when they handed me the badge. Sheriff of Puma County, Wyoming Territory.

I looked down at the badge in my hand. "I thought there was supposed to be an election before someone got to be sheriff."

George Waller, the man who'd been chewin' on that egg, and who was the Mayor of Doubtful, and who'd just sworn me in, in a manner of mumbling, cleared that up right quick—sort of. "There was. We had it last night, right after you kilt them gunhands. Everybody that was in town voted for you. Congratulations, Sheriff Cotton. That is your rightful Christian name, ain't it?"

When I had to be, I was as good at mumblin' as he was. "One of 'em, yeah. How about the folks out in the country, the ranchers?"

"We rung the town bell," the scar-faced, gimp-legged cafe man said. "If they didn't hear it, that was their hard luck. We out-vote them anyways."

"Uh-huh. Well, am I supposed to handle the whole county by myself?"

"Oh, no!" the mayor said. "You can have up to four deputies. Problem is, nobody wants the job." He looked like he was unhappy he told me that.

"But that don't mean there ain't men to be had," the woman who ran a boardin' house piped up.

I took one look at her—and once a day would be plenty—and figured she'd know if there was a man to be had anywhere in the Territory. That woman, Belle something-or-the-other, was so ugly she could stop an eagle in a dive—just by lookin' at it.

I scratched my woolly head—woolly 'cause I ain't had a bath in two weeks—and done some thinkin'.

Now . . . I ain't never took myself to be no real intelligent fellow. My momma, God rest her soul, didn't have to hide me under no bucket 'cause of my brilliance. I can read and write and figger some . . .

"Sheriff . . . ?" George said.

"I'm thinkin'!"

. . . I can bust near'bouts any horse I ever tossed a saddle on, and I can ride and rope with the best of 'em. And, I got to admit, I'm more than passin' fair with a six-gun, too.

"You ain't thinkin' about backin' out, are you, Sheriff?" George asked.

"No, I ain't. I'm . . . *prayin'*, that's what I'm doin'."

"Let's all bow our heads, too," Belle suggested.

"Fine. Lemme get done with mine and then we'll talk some more."

They all took to mumblin', and I went back to thinkin'.

And, I got to say, I've ridden the hoot-owl trail a time or two . . . but not because I broke any laws. I'm just sort of a curious type, that's all. I wanted to see how the outlaws lived. According to them penny-dreadful books they was all glamorous. But I soon found out they lived mighty damned sorry, that's how.

"Hallelujah!" Belle hollered.

I like to have jumped out of my boots.

"Hush!" George said.

Before she took a runnin' a boardin' house, Belle must have had her a job callin' hogs!

Top hand. That's me. Cotton. I don't use my last name much. I ain't ashamed of it, I just figure Cotton will do. I've punched cows from Texas to Montana Territory. I been over the Bitterroot and seen the ocean. Took my breath away. Damn near as much as that place folks got to callin' the Grand Canyon. It's grand, all right. I seen it just after Major Powell come along in '69. But I got lost as a goose in there. Took me three days to find my way out. I don't talk about that much.

But this job. There was something about this here sheriffin' job that just wasn't shapin' up right in my mind.

I looked up. Everybody was lookin' at me.

"What happened to the last sheriff?"

"Uh . . . why, he up and quit," George said. I reckoned he knew I'd find out anyways.

"And the one before him?"

"He got roped and drug," the cafe man said.

"And the one before him?"

"He got kilt," Belle said.

Now I was gettin' down to the facts. "Who killed him and why?"

"Gunhands from the Circle L," the cafe man said. "Right out there in front of my place." He pointed. "They kilt him in a fair fight. And 'cause he was a coward and they knowed it."

"Baited him like you would a bull, huh?"

"Yes, sir."

I thought a mite longer. Now, if I could stick it out for a year, I could have me a right nice poke. By livin' close, I could gave a thousand. And that could get me started on a small spread.

I looked at that cafe man kinda hard. "I get my meals free."

"Now, see here! You et enough las' night for three people."

But George give him an eyeballin' and he closed his mouth. They probably figured I'd be dead in a month anyways. "Certainly, Sheriff," the mayor said. "That's fine."

"And I ain't buyin' my own lead, neither."

"That's perfectly understandable. Get them at my store."

Belle batted her eyelashes at me. Plumb sickenin'.

"Where do I bunk?"

George swelled up like a coon in the moonlight. "Right there." He pointed toward the rear. "Got you two nice rooms back yonder and a two-hole privy out back. It's even got a back-flap for better ventilation."

Belle giggled. Sounded like a rattlesnake caught in a tin bucket.

"OK," I said, "You folks got yourself a sheriff."

They all shook my hand and Belle puckered up. But I shook her hand too. She just grinned big and batted her eyes and then sashayed out to the boardwalk, her bustle a-jumpin' from right to left. You ever followed a cow? You know what I mean. With that rear end of hers, she didn't need no extra girth. Two ax handles wide as it was.

I stuck the badge in my pocket and began unpackin' my kit

and war bag. I was gonna have to buy me some new duds—mine was shabby-lookin'. Diggin' down in my war bag, I fished out my second gun. I seldom wore it, 'cause don't nobody but tinhorns and trouble-hunters and them lookin' for a reputation pack around two short guns. Well . . . maybe another type: lawmen totin' a big badge that makes 'em a handy target.

Walkin' over to Leonard Silverman's Emporium, I got me a better look at the town of Doubtful. It was some bigger than I gleaned at night. Two full blocks of stores on either side. Several saloons, couple of general stores, a hotel, leather shop, smithy, a dress shop—spelt with two P's and two E's; didn't look right to me—and half a dozen older businesses I'd have to look at closer.

Now, I reckon I did look like a saddle bum, but that wasn't no excuse for what happened next. I wasn't dressed up like no dandy. Old wore-out jeans and a shirt with the elbows ragged. My left boot had a piece of rawhide tied around it to keep the sole from flappin'. But I ain't never believed in makin' fun of other folks just 'cause they wasn't dressed to the nines.

I heard the riders, and they was comin' hard, kickin' up dust like a bunch of idiots and shootin' pistols into the air and whoopin' and hollerin'. And me? I was caught right in the middle of that street.

Must have been a dozen hands, and one woman. And that woman was ridin' astride. I've seen plenty of squaws ride that way, but never no white woman. It kinda come as a shock to me.

"Ride him down!" that woman screamed, for no good reason that I could think of. "Nobody stands in our way."

Now that made me mad.

I never could abide no one that thought he or she was so almighty big they could just run over other people. I have whupped more than two or three in my time.

Them ol' boys come a-foggin' straight at me. I stepped back, judged the speed of that lead hoss, and when he come even with me, I just reached up and snatched that redheaded young rider off the horse and flung him not-too-gently to the dirt.

The brand on the horse's hip that the horse's ass had been ridin' was Circle L.

The wind was knocked out of the cowboy on the ground, but them others had made the turn down at the far end of the street and was lookin' at me. That she-person sittin' astride had hate in her eyes that I could read from this distance.

Me? I just quick-stepped on across that street and was up on the boardwalk 'fore they could do anything more about it.

"Somebody get Rusty!" the woman yelled. "We'll deal with that saddle tramp later."

So now I was a saddle tramp. Well, hell, I'd been called a lot worse than that.

Leanin' against the support post of the awning over the boardwalk, I watched as the woman said something to a big gent on a midnight-black horse. He rode down my way, wheeled in, and sat starin' at me.

The gent was a big, handsome-lookin' man, and his clothes was expensive-lookin'. I say handsome, but his face was cruel-lookin'.

Real slow and dramatic-like, he dug in a pocket of his leather vest and hauled out a timepiece, smilin' at me as he clicked it open.

"Two hours," he said, clickin' the watch shut. "That's how long we're gonna be in town. And that's how long you got 'til you get roped and dragged. No saddle bum puts a hand on any Circle L rider."

"You the one who roped and drug one of the lawmen a time back?"

His eyes narrowed. I reckon he was tryin' to figure out how I came to know that.

"You're a nosy bastard, ain't you, saddle bum?"

I shrugged my shoulders. "Let's just say I'm the curious type. And you didn't answer my question, neither."

"Why should I waste my time talking to a tramp?"

"Hell, you come to me, not the other way around, remember?"

His face flushed up red and his eyes turned real ugly.

"You won't be near about as mouthy when I get through with you, punk!"

I laughed at him.

He wheeled around and left me in a cloud of dust.

He had him a big mouth, but he had the size to back it up, too. Looked to be about six feet, four, two hundred and thirty or forty pounds.

I spat in the street. I just wasn't all that impressed.

Chapter Two

Steppin' out onto the boardwalk, I checked my timepiece—the sun. In an hour's time, I'd had me a shave and a good hot bath. Had to dump the water three times 'fore I got clean. Before I done all the spit and polishin', I'd bought some new duds at the Emporium. If I was gonna be sheriff, I figured I'd best look the part.

I left my new suit and some shirts and britches at the Chinaman's place, and now I was all decked out in spankin' new duds, bandana tied proper around my neck. Them new boots felt good. 'Course my socks and long johns was new, too.

Socks fit fine, but that new underwear was just a mite itchy.

I went back to the office and hung that second gun on, left side, butt forward. I ain't as fast with it as I was my right-side gun, but I ain't been beat with it, neither.

It was a gambler's gun, meanin' the barrel was some shorter than my right-side .44.

Checkin' myself in the mirror—noticin' that I hadn't got no prettier—I gave my cowlick a lick and put my hat on. It was old, but I'd had Wong brush it off while I was wallowin' around in the tub out back.

From pure habit, I checked both guns, left the hammer

thong off my gambler's gun, pinned on the star, and stepped out onto the boardwalk.

Half a block down, I stepped into George Waller's general store. I have always loved the smell of a general store. The leather, tobacco, spices, and pickle barrel all mingled their smells together. I got me a cracker and a hunk of cheese and a pickle, munching on that while I waited for George to finish with a customer.

"Yes, sir, Sheriff?"

"Circle L man who rides a black horse. He's about as big as the horse. And he's got a big fat mouth."

"Ah . . . Sheriff . . . that's, ah, Big Mike Romain. He's the foreman at Circle L."

"Is that supposed to impress me? I can tell you *he* don't."

"Well, ah, no, Sheriff. Not at all. But Big Mike is a bad man to fool with. You've had trouble with Big Mike? *Already?"*

"That wild woman with him ordered her boys to ride me down. Then this Big Mike tells me he's gonna have me roped and drug. And the more I think on it, the madder I'm gettin'!"

"I don't blame you. Now you see what the good citizens of this town have to put up with, Sheriff. And why lawmen ain't lasted too long."

"You just never had the right lawman. George, you depend on the Circle L for a livin'?"

He picked up on my drift right quick. He smiled and shook his head. "No, Sheriff. This part of the territory is filling up with ranchers and farmers. We hired you to keep the peace. No one is immune from the law. No one!"

Fancy words. But I wondered if, when it got down to the humpin', would George and the others really back me up?

Belle had been listenin' from the open door. "That Mike Romain is nothing more than a brute!" She stamped her foot. Good-sized foot, I noticed. That foot-stompin' knocked a trace chain off a peg.

And I had me a hunch that Belle would like to hang a saddle on that "brute" and try to ride him.

Nodding my head at George and smiling at Belle, I took my leave. As I was walkin' up the boardwalk, I heard Belle say, "Oh, what a handsome man, Mister Waller. I think I'm going to swoon."

I picked up my pace, not wantin' to be around if she did come down with the vapors. It'd take a mule team and a pulley to get her back on her feet.

Walking to the Wolf's Den Saloon, I pushed open the batwings and stepped inside, pausing for a second to let my eyes adjust to the sudden dimness. I walked to a table and sat down, my back to the wall.

The place had hushed somewhat as I walked, my big spurs jingling. All had taken some notice of the badge on my shirt.

And Big Mike's eyes had narrowed considerable.

"What'll it be, Sheriff?" the barkeep called.

"Beer."

The beer was cold and good and I knocked back half the mug. Setting the mug down on the table, I said, "'Bout two hours ago, there was this big-mouthed, overbearin', candy-assed son of a bitch who told me he was gonna rope and drag me. Well . . . here I am."

Man, that place got so quiet you could hear a fly fart!

Folks started movin' chairs back, out of the line of fire. Big Mike had stiffened when I called him that name, as any man with any pride would have done. Now he turned to face me, his face ugly with hate.

"You might not like me, Sheriff," Mike said. "But my mother was a good woman. I'll not have her name slurred in such a manner."

I took my time thinkin' about that. "All right. It ain't your momma's fault what you turned out to be."

That really pissed him off.

"You . . . !" He strangled on his anger.

"But the big-mouthed, overbearin', candy-ass stands," I said.

He was so mad he was tremblin'.

I looked around for the woman who'd ordered me rode down. She wasn't in the saloon. Might be hopes for her yet . . . but I kinda doubted it, considerin' the company she kept. There was a lady in the saloon, however. But I figured her for the owner, way she was all decked out in satin with her petticoats showin'. She was kinda familiar to me, but I couldn't quite place the face.

"Git him, Rusty!" a cowboy said.

The cowboy I'd jerked out of the saddle and dumped in the street stepped forward. Another one of those two-gun types, hung low and tied down. Matter of fact, I'd noticed that nearly all the Circle L boys was wearin' two guns, and they all had a salty look about them . . . like maybe they was drawin' fightin' wages.

But the cowboy called Rusty had kind of a different look about him—like maybe he didn't really like what he was doin'. But the pay was good, so he'd try it.

Now he wasn't so sure about it.

I stood up, the thumb of my right hand restin' on my belt buckle, the fingers just inches from the butt of that gambler's gun.

"Let Rusty take the bum, Mike," a puncher said.

Mike smiled. "I guess you've got first dibs, Rusty. He did dump you in the street."

But Rusty didn't appear all that eager. Not that he was afraid, for I didn't believe he was. I think he was just a pretty good ol' boy who'd got caught up in a bad deal.

"You realize I can put you in jail for bracin' me, don't you, Rusty?"

Mike sneered at me. "That badge supposed to make you a big man, saddle bum?"

"No. But it does make me the law."

Everybody in the place, except for the lady and Rusty, thought that was real funny. That woman kept starin' at me, like she was tryin' to figure out where she'd seen me.

"Sheriff," she said. "Did you ride for the Hilderbrant outfit up in Montana Territory a few years back?"

"Yep," I did not take my eyes off of the cowboy named Rusty.

"Thought it was you. I seen you brace them three Reno Brothers in that boomtown just south of the Little Belt Mountains."

"Yeah. Knowed I'd seen you somewheres."

All them hardcases in the room was listenin' real close.

"I helped take up the collection to bury all three of them boys," the woman added softly.

Any steam that Rusty might have built up left him a hell of a lot quicker than it come to him. His face suddenly got sweaty and he come up out of that gunfighter's crouch, his mouth hangin' open.

"You better shut that trap, cowboy," I told him. "Flies is bad for this early in the season."

His mouth closed with a smack.

"Your name Cotton?" the woman asked.

"Yep."

All of a sudden there was a lot of ol' boys lookin' in ever' which direction . . . not at me. Like I said, I wasn't unknown when it come to gunslickin'. I just never made no big deal out of it.

"Heard of you," Big Mike said. "But I think I'm better."

"One way to find out."

But Mike was real careful to keep his hands away from his guns.

I killed my first Injun when I was ten years old, a Blackfoot, if I recall right. A whole bunch of 'em was tryin' to bust into our cabin, and the west wall was mine to protect. I killed my first white man when I was about thirteen. He was tryin' to steal our milk cow. Fever got my folks shortly after that. My brothers and sisters was farmed out to neighbors, but I took off, and I been on my own lonesome hustle ever since. I reckon I have picked up the name of gunfighter, but it wasn't nothin' I went lookin' for.

Rusty looked like he was comin' down with something terrible contagious. He backed up, his hands relaxed, palms up.

"Take him, Rusty!" Big Mike shouted. "That's an order."

"Hell with your orders! You want him so bad, you take him. Come to think of it," the redhead said, "I ain't never seen none of your graveyards."

"You insolent yellow pup!" Mike slapped him, the blow knocking the smaller man to the sawdust.

The kid had sand, I'll give him that. He come up off that floor and took a swing at Big Mike. 'Bout like a gnat tryin' to fight a mosquito hawk. Big Mike hit him once, a hard straight right, and Rusty hit the floor and didn't move.

Big Mike dug in his pocket and tossed a handful of silver coins to the floor and on Rusty. "Let's ride!" he barked. Then looked at me. "I'll see you around . . . Sheriff."

That "Sheriff" bit was greasy. "Yeah, I imagine you will, Romain. 'Cause you gonna screw up, and when you do, I'm gonna put your big ass in jail."

"You'll play hell ever doing that!" he blustered.

"Then I reckon I'll just have to shoot you, Romain. Why don't we settle it now?"

"Mike!" a woman squalled. I recognized the squall. The same woman who wanted me rode down.

"Saved by a woman. You're a lucky man, Romain."

That got next to him. I really thought he was gonna jerk iron. But he just turned his big butt to me and walked out, his punchers trailin' along behind him.

Kneeling down by Rusty, I noted that he was gonna have a shiner for a few days.

"I'll get him a beefsteak," the woman said. "Couple of you boys haul him up and sit him over there."

The barkeep leaned over and dumped a pitcher of water on the puncher. Sputtering and shaking his head, Rusty sat up, allowing the boys to drag him to a table and sit him down.

I got me another beer and one for Rusty. The woman—she introduced herself as Mary—brought a beefsteak out and Rusty held it to the side of his face.

"How old are you, Rusty?" I asked.

"Twenty." He grinned and I liked him immediately. "And for a minute there, Mister Cotton, I didn't think I was gonna get much older, neither."

"How'd you get tied up with Circle L?"

"Signed on to shove beeves around. Then the word come down about six months back, that anyone who wanted to ride for the brand had best be ready to fight for it. Some left, I stayed, figuring the fightin' wages would come in handy." He shrugged his shoulders. "I was gonna quit come payday anyhow."

"How good are you with them hoglegs?"

"Better than average, I reckon. But not near'bouts in your class."

"You ain't worried about what people's gonna say?"

"'Bout me backin' down?"

I nodded.

"Hell, no! I'm alive!"

I returned his grin. "That's your money layin' over yonder on the floor."

Mary got her swamper to pick up the money. He laid it on the table and Rusty shoved a dollar at the old man.

And I liked that gesture. Even though the old swamper would surely spend it on rotgut.

"What are you gonna to do now, Rusty?"

"I don't know. Drift, I reckon. When Big Mike fires some-one, it ain't wise to hang around. Only two I know of that's still around is De Graff and Burtell. They pretty salty ol' boys. Mike's got this hang-up about ropin' and draggin' folks."

"So I heard. How much was he payin' you at the brand?"

"Fifty and found."

"I'll give you seventy-five and one meal a day and a place to bunk."

His eyes widened. "Doin' what?"

"Totin' a deputy's badge."

His grin was infectious. He stuck out his mitt and I shook the work-hardened hand. "You done hired yourself a deputy, Sheriff."

"Who's this woman that was ridin' with Mike Romain?"

The middle of the afternoon, next day. Rusty had been sworn in by George Waller, and we'd spent some time cleanin' up the office and findin' out where things was. It had been quiet so far. We'd made a visit to all the businesses and introduced ourselves. Now we was relaxin', sittin' on a bench in front of the office, talkin'.

"I thought you knew."

"No."

"That's Joy Lawrence, A.J.'s daughter. She and Wanda Mills think they's queens of the valley."

"Circle L and Rockinghorse that big?" I hadn't had the time to ride out and inspect for myself. Something I needed to do.

"I should say! They're two thirds of the Big Three, as they're called around here. Circle L, Rockinghorse, and the Quartermoon. Matt Mills owns the Rockinghorse, Rolf Baker owns the Quartermoon. One lies at the western edge of the county, one to the north, and the other to the east."

"And lots of little spreads caught up in the middle, hey?"

"You got it, Sheriff. Between the three of them, they must control close to a million acres. But don't nobody really know for sure. You see, the nesters and small ranchers is stringin' wire. They want to know *exactly* what they own and so forth. Lawrence and Mills don't want that. They want free access to the water like they've always had. But the Quartermoon ain't bad. Baker ain't pushin' for no more land or water; he's got the best water and graze of 'em all. But Rockinghorse and Circle L . . ." He shook his head. "There's gonna be a lot of blood spilt."

"And just the two of us standin' in the way of it, Rusty."

"I give that some thought last night, Sheriff. I shore done it."

"But you still here."

He grinned. "I like it when things get to jumpin'."

I laughed at him. It was the same old story, and I'd been caught up in similar situations before. Some people get a lot, and they want more, and they get to feelin' that they're kings. It had been that way up in Montana Territory when I'd been ridin' for Hilderbrandt. Ol' boy name of Williston had him a big spread and got power mad, shovin' and killin'. He just had to have more land. He finally got his wish when he braced that ol' salty dog, Hilderbrandt. Williston got him six feet more land. That was right after I dropped them Reno boys.

"I heard about them Reno Brothers," Rusty said softly. "I heard they was real fast."

"They wasn't fast enough. Well, one of 'em was, I reckon. He beat me to the draw but he put his first bullet in the dirt. Rusty, how come the sheriffs don't last long in this county?"

Rusty grunted. "I hope you ain't thinkin' that I had anything to do with any of that mess, Sheriff."

"I don't. George Waller said you was a good boy that just turned briefly down the wrong road."

"Good way of puttin' it, I reckon. The lawmen? Well, one

of them was ambushed. Another got roped and drug to death. Next one quit. Another got killed. And so on. Why? 'Cause Mills and Lawrence don't believe no law applies to them. Or none of the hands. You see, Sheriff, the range of the Big Three spreads kinda makes a half circle on the top of the county, connectin'. Man, you oughtta see the main ranch houses of Lawrence and Mills—them folks live like kings and queens!"

"So they've been here a long time?"

"Lawrence and Mills and Baker was the first white men in this area. To settle, I mean. I think Preacher might have been the first white man to roam around here."

"I heard of him."

"You know Smoke Jensen?"

"Not personal. But I seen him work one time. That's the fastest man with a gun anywhere. Left hand or right hand."

"So I heard. Anyways, Baker and Mills and Lawrence come in as young men. They all married at about the same time. All their kids is about the same age."

"This Joy . . . she playin' with a full deck?"

Rusty laughed. "She's just natural mean, Sheriff. Just like her brother, A.J. Junior. They're spoiled and they're cruel. They ain't never wanted for nothin'. And Junior is fast with a gun, remember that. He's good. But he likes to hurt people— 'specially women. He's raped more than one."

"Why hasn't someone hung the bastard?"

"Between the two ranches, Rockinghorse and Circle L, Sheriff, they can mount a hundred and fifty men."

"Guess that answers my question."

"Mills and Lawrence had them kids tutored, the teachers brung in from overseas, French and English. Baker's wife was a well-educated lady herself, with money of her own. She taught her own younguns, Pepper and Jeff. They right good kids."

"Pepper's a girl?"

"And how! Just lookin' at her makes a man wanna go run rabbits and howl at the moon. I know, I done some howlin' myself one night."

"She must be a sight to behold."

"Purtiest thing you ever seen in all your life, Sheriff, and Big Mike wants her bad. Goes courtin' her. But she won't have nothin' to do with him."

She come up a whole lot in my eyes with that statement.

Rusty said, "Now then, right in the middle of that half circle I tole you about is the fly in the soup. Maggie Barnett and Jean Knight. Their husbands was kilt fightin' the Circle L and Rockinghorse—nobody could prove it, but ever'body knew who done it. That happened some years 'fore I come down here. So them gals, they just up and joined spreads and formed the Arrow band. Little spread; 'bout seventy-five thousand acres. And them two gals is tougher than wang leather, let me tell you that right now. And cuss! Lord have mercy!"

"How do they ride?"

Rusty rolled his eyes. "Astride. Plumb indecent. The Arrow hands ain't young, by no means, but they're salty ol' boys. And Miss Maggie and Miss Jean can ride like men, work like men, and shoot just as good as any man."

I looked up and down the main street. At the far end was a church. At the other end, a schoolhouse. And in the middle, three saloons. The Wolf's Den, the Dirty Dog, and stuck back, almost in an alley, was Juan's Cantina.

"Odd to find a Mex joint this far north."

"Sheep to the south of us," Rusty explained. "The sheep-men gather at the cantina. The crews from the Big Three gather at the Wolf's Den. The smaller ranchers and nesters gather at the Dirty Dog. Small ranchers and farmers are bandin' together for protection. First time I ever seen that."

I thought for a moment. "What is today?"

"Friday, Sheriff. Box social night at the school. Dancin' and all that, too."

"Like you bid on lady's dinner boxes?"

"Yep."

"Lots of folks turn out?"

"Near'bouts ever'body in the whole area. Some left at dawn just to get here. I've only been to a couple of them. Punchers is said to be too rowdy for the good folks."

"Is that a fact?"

"Yep."

We both grinned at that.

"I just might make that social tonight, Rusty."

"Should be interestin', Sheriff. Big Mike never misses one."

The buckboards started rattlin' in about four-thirty that afternoon, a lot of them trailed by heavily armed outriders. I didn't think they was there 'cause of Indian trouble. It'd been four years since the Little Big Horn fight and the following Injun wars. There was still a right smart amount of Injuns around, but this area was so populated, Injuns mostly stayed away. The Crow, Blackfeet, Flatheads, and Cheyenne was north of us, mostly up in Montana Territory.

No, I had me a hunch that all this gun-totin' didn't have nothin' to do with Injuns.

I said as much to George Waller. Rusty had wandered off somewhere.

"Yes, it's coming, Sheriff," he admitted. "The lid could fly off the pot anytime."

I shoved my hat back and stared at him. Must have made him uncomfortable. He fidgeted some and said, "The cattlemen want the sheep out. Sheepmen say they're staying. Two of the Big Three want the nesters out. Nesters say they're here to stay."

"And the Arrow spread?"

"Right in the middle with prime land. Good graze and good water. Circle L and Rockinghorse want that land bad."

Was that it? Was that all this was about? For sure, men have died for less. The lust for power does strange things to people sometimes.

I nodded at George and walked out to the boardwalk.

Strangest damn town I'd ever been in.

Takin' my time, I walked the boardwalk toward the schoolhouse, tippin' my hat and smilin' at the ladies, noddin' to the menfolk.

"Coming to the social tonight, Sheriff?" a man inquired, friendly-like.

"I'll be there."

Walkin' on up to the school, I seen a gaggle of womenfolks spreadin' tablecloths out on long made-up tables. They was a-gigglin' and a-carryin'-on like they do. They give me the once-over and some of 'em started whisperin' amongst themselves and sneakin' looks at me.

I done a quick about-face and got the hell gone from there.

Tell you the truth, womenfolk make me nervous. A sashayin' and a-twitchin' around. And you don't never know what they're thinkin', neither. Give me a good horse and a good gun anytime. A dog is right nice to have around, too. A man can depend on them. And a good watch. I wanted me a good watch—one of them gold railroad watches, with a nice fob.

Matter of fact, I seen some watches down at Waller's Store. Come payday, by God, I'll just get me one.

Walkin' back, I stopped midtown and stared at the comin'-up parade. There they was, comin' in east by north, so it had to be the Circle L and Rockinghorse bunch. My, but they was makin' a grand entrance. Like some of them. East Injun Pootentoots I'd read about. I wasn't real sure what a Pootentoot was, but I figured it was somebody who thought more of hisself than other folks did.

I had to take me a second look to see for sure if that was the same woman that'd hollered like a whoor to have me run down day before. It was. But this time she was sittin' in a surrey, and she was all gussied up in a fancy gown and was a-twirlin' a little pink parasol.

I leaned agin' a post and watched the parade. Best shot I'd seen since I was a kid up on the Yellowstone and old lady McKinny got her dresstail caught in the door one windy day. Took it plumb off. She wasn't wearin' nothin' under the gingham neither. I never saw such a sight in all my nine years of livin'. I run home and told my pa and he like to fell down he was laughin' so hard. I told Momma and she whupped me.

Took me years to figure that out.

That older man sittin' beside Joy—he wasn't that old, maybe forty-five—that had to be her pa, ol' A.J. hisself. I wondered it the J. stood for Joy. If so, his middle name was as strange as my last name.

And there was Big Mike, sittin' up on that big black of his, lookin' like hell warmed over.

And then I seen the outriders, and knew right off that the hundred and twenty-five I was gettin' was some short.

Gave me sort of a funny feelin' in the gut.

Rusty joined me by the hitchrail. "You know any of 'em, Sheriff?"

"Most of 'em. And there ain't a one there that's worth a damn for nothin' except gunslingin'."

And I was speakin' the truth. There was Lydell Townsend, Tanner Smith, Dick Avedon. There was the Mex gunfighter, Sanchez, riding a horse with a Rockinghorse brand. Jim Reynolds, Hank Hawthorne, Joe Coyle, Little Jack Bagwell, Johnny Bull, and Tom Marks. There was some others that I couldn't right off hang a name on . . . except Trouble-Hunter.

I named off all that I personal knew.

Rusty, he said, "That one on the bay, that's Waldo Stamps, the Texas gunhawk. Clay Dundee on the paint. Behind him is Fox Breckenridge, Ford Childress, the Arizona gunhand. And that's the German, Haufman."

"The fat one; the back-shooter?"

"That's him. See that close rifle boot? That's a .44–.40, and he's dead right with it."

"So I hear."

"Them other ol' boys is just as good as any of 'em, but they just ain't got no public name, as yet."

"Rusty . . . what in the hell is goin' on around here? Do you know?"

The passin' parade had slowed down some, waitin' on the second buggy to catch up, I reckon.

"All sorts of rumors, Sheriff, from gold to oil. But I think all that is just talk to cover up a range war."

"Yeah, that'd be my guess, too. When did all these gunslingers start showin' up around here?"

"Well, Rockinghorse and Circle L has always had a few gunhands on the payroll . . . more to protect the kids than anything else. But about a year ago, that's when Mills and Lawrence really started hirin' on gunhands."

"And that's when the lawmen started goin' down, huh? How many . . . four?"

"Something like that. Four's right, I think."

The second buggy come better into view. An older man and a pretty young woman. "That Wanda Mills and her pa?"

"Yeah. The second queen of the valley."

"Where's the mother of them gals?"

"They hardly ever come into town. They don't associate much with the lower classes. 'Sides, I don't even know if they're around here; they might have gone off on some trip. They're always goin' here and yonder."

"Must be a terrible burden for them ladies to have to bear."

He looked at me to see if I was serious, then he grinned. "Yeah, plumb awful load to have to tote around."

For some reason, the passin' parade of highfalutin' folks had stopped, the fancy surrey with Joy and her pa was right in front of Rusty and me, and ol' A.J. was givin' me a good hard once-over.

I had stepped down to stand by the hitchrail with Rusty.

"You there!" A.J. hollered, and the tone of his voice made the short hairs on the back of my neck tingle. "Get over here. I wanna talk to you."

"Your legs broke?" I called, some louder than was needed, but I wanted ever'body to hear.

Man, ol' A.J. puffed up like a spreadin' adder, his face high-colored like a wild berry.

There was a hard poundin' of hooves and a young man on a fine-lookin' red horse was glarin' down at me. The family resemblance was strong, so strong that this had to be A.J. Junior. Twenty-one or so years old, and no little feller neither.

And damned if he wasn't wearin' two guns. I never in all my life seen so many men who fancied two short guns.

I smiled real friendly at the young man. My, but he was all slicked up. Fancy silk shirt and handsome vest. Tailor-made britches and hand-tooled boots. He sure cut a fancy figure.

And then he had to open his damn mouth. Kinda ruined my image of him.

But I kept smilin'.

"When my father orders you to do something," squirt said to me, "you will, by God, do it!"

Pushiest bunch of damn folks I ever did see. Sorta put a damper on my right friendly smile.

"Sonny," I said, "you best run along now, 'fore I jerk you off that horse and have to teach you some manners . . . like your pa and ma should have done a long time ago."

Joy took to fannin' herself like she was comin' down with the flashes, or something, and ol' A.J. blustered.

"How dare you!" ol' A.J. squalled.

Young Junior looked like he was gonna have a heart attack.

Behind me, a woman said, "Junior sure needs it, Sheriff, and I'd give a double eagle just to see you do it."

"And I double her offer," a young man said.

I didn't know who was sayin' what, 'cause I wasn't about to take my eyes off Junior.

"Let's pass the hat for the Sheriff," somebody hollered. "Put the money right in here, ladies and gents."

"I think I'll just kill you!" Junior hollered, then grabbed for iron.

Chapter Three

I been blessed with good coordination near'bouts all my life. I'm a shade under six feet tall, but I weigh more than most people would guess, and I'm uncommonly strong, with a lot of hardpacked muscle in my arms and shoulders.

You wrestle beeves all your life and you get that a-way.

And I'm quick . . . real quick. I wintered with a China-person one time; got to be real good friends with him. He taught me a different way to fight, and taught me concentration.

He told me what it was he was teachin' me, but damned if I could ever pronounce it. He used to get so tickled at me tryin' to talk China-talk he'd just roll over and fall out laughin'.

So when Junior grabbed for iron, I just reached up and snatched him off that horse and gave him a little midair help towards a water trough. He landed face-first, full length, and sank like a rock.

Through it all, I heard Rusty ear back the hammer on his .44 and say, "First man to grab iron, I put lead in Mike Romain."

"And I'm standin' behind the deputy!" That same young man's voice said, the one who doubled the ante of the woman, "Backin' the law."

I didn't have time to see who else was with me in this

squabble. 'Cause ol' A.J. was hollerin' and squawkin' things like, "Intolerable," and "Out-rageous!" Joy and Wanda was actin' and soundin' like a bunch of guinea hens, and Junior was comin' up outta that hoss trough, mad as a hellfire and brimstone preacher with a sore throat.

Junior had lost his pearl-handled pistols somewhere between saddle and hoss trough, and his pretty duds was all messed up and smelly. He was cussin'! His momma would have washed his mouth out with soap! Then he took a swing at me.

I poleaxed him with one big hard fist and he dropped like a ripe tomato off the vine, down, but not out.

Reachin' down, I got me a handful of wet silk shirt and hauled him to his feet and give him a little shove toward the jail. I say little shove, he musta tripped or something, 'cause he went down face full in the dirt.

"You're under arrest," I told him. "Threatenin' the life of a peace officer and disturbin' the peace."

And his pappy started hollerin' like a hog caught up in barbed wire.

"I'm going to faint!" Joy squalled.

"Good!" I yelled. "Maybe that would shut you up!"

That really got Ol' A.J. riled up.

"Watch my back!" I yelled over my shoulder, and never stopped walkin' and shovin' Junior, who had him a dirty face and a bad case of bleedin' and busted mouth.

"You cain't do this to me!" Junior hollered, squishin' along in his water-filled, hand-tooled fancy boots.

"Looks like he's doing it, Junior!" that woman who'd mentioned something about a double eagle laughed. I guessed it was her.

I locked up Junior and went back outside. A.J. was out of his buggy—Joy hadn't fainted as yet—and was standin' on the boardwalk talkin' with the gent who'd been earlier pointed out to me as Lawyer Stokes. A.J. was flapping his arms and hollerin'.

"You there, Sheriff!" Stokes hollered.

I pushed through the knot of horses. "Get these horses off the street and stabled or reined down! Or I'll stick the whole bunch of you in jail for blockin' a public road."

Now I didn't have no idea if that law—or any other law, for that matter—was on the town's books. But it sounded good, and it got results.

I met Johnny Bull's eyes. He nodded at me and said to a rider, "He means it. We could take him, but he'd kill half a dozen of us before we did." To me, "Some other time, Cotton."

"I'll be around, Johnny."

The street cleared, the riders breaking up and moving out.

"Sheriff!" Lawyer Stokes shouted. "I demand you release young Lawrence and that you do so immediately."

"And I demand that you git your face outta mine 'fore I put you in jail for interferin' with a peace officer." Good thing I'd read that book on law that time, one writ by some Englishman named Blackstone, I think he was. Cowboys that can read will read anything; bean-can labels, five-year-old newspapers, mail-order catalogs . . . even the Bible when times get desperate.

I told Rusty, "You get over to the office and find that bond sheet, get the dollar amount for Junior's charge. Write it up and then daddy can come up with money and get his big-mouthed kid out of the calaboose." I looked around, "OK, folks, show's over. See you all tonight at the social."

The townspeople, all of them grinnin', began movin' out.

A man held up a heavy-lookin' hat. "I'll bring this by your office, Sheriff. And it was worth every penny, believe me."

"Will you listen to me, Sheriff?" Lawyer Stokes hollered. I looked at him. He was so mad he was shakin'.

Then he made the mistake of grabbin' my arm and jerkin' me back, spinnin' me around.

I poleaxed the lawyer and dropped him to his butt in the horse-droppin's.

"Yuk!" Stokes said, then put down his hands and stuck both of them in piles of manure.

"If your nose gets to itchin'," I told him. "I'd suggest you scratch it with your knee."

That young woman was laughin' so hard she was leanin' up agin' a buildin' for support. And from what I could see, she was sure some fine-lookin' filly.

"Rusty! Come put Stokes in the bucket and charge him with battery on a peace officer. Set his bond, too."

"Outrageous!" A.J. yelled.

"You want to go to jail, too?" I asked him.

He closed his mouth.

"You get five dollars for every arrest you make, Sheriff," George Waller said.

That got my attention, 'Way things was goin', I'd have that spread and all stocked, too, 'fore summer was out.

Howsomever, 'way I was fast makin' enemies, I just might not live to the end of summer.

Stokes was sittin' in the dirt, in the horse shit, on his butt, his mouth all swole up. Rusty helped him up, just a tad rough, and marched the lawyer off to the jailhouse.

A few punchers had returned to the street.

"Clear the street!" I hollered. "And do it right now."

Man, that street cleared so fast you could fire a cannonball up it and not hit nothin'.

Turning, I looked at the woman who'd thought it all hysterically funny. She met my eyes, and like them writers say in them dime novels, my ol' heart went . . . *bong!*

She was about five foot, two inches tall. Robin's-egg-blue eyes, hair the color of wheat. Heartshaped face. Figure that was . . . well, it was!

Somebody ought to write a song about five foot two and eyes of blue. Be a right catchy tune, I bet.

I took my hat off and took a step towards her. The toe of my boot caught on the lip of the boardwalk and I fell forward. I grabbed her and she grabbed me and together the two of us kept me from falling down.

Plumb embarrassin'! But she sure did feel nice, though.

She thought it was right funny. Personal, I didn't see the humor in it.

My eyes bugged out when I seen the contents of that hat. More than two hundred dollars in there. I wanted to keep the Stetson, too, but the owner balked at that.

Jeff Baker, Pepper's brother, sent around a boy with two double eagles for me.

All in all, it was turnin' out to be a pretty nice day.

The lawyer and Junior had been bonded out, both of 'em madder than hell. Shadows was beginnin' to creep around the town as me and Rusty got dressed for the social. I'd bought me a new suit and had the Chinaman press it to get the shelf marks out. My boots was blacked and I was all decked out in a new shirt with a little string tie. My face was patted down smelly-good with Bay Rum. I strapped on my guns and pinned on my badge.

A little boy stuck his head into the office.

"Sheriff?"

"That's him with the big feet," Rusty said with a grin.

I give him a look that didn't have no effect a-tall and took the envelope from the boy and give him some money for a sarsaparilla drink. The kid ducked out of the office.

Careful-like, I tore off one end of the envelope. A double eagle rolled out. I grinned like a schoolboy as I read the note. Pretty handwritin'. *My box is wrapped in red. White bow.* It was signed Pepper.

Rusty was peerin' over my shoulder. "Lord have mercy!"

"Mind your own truck!" I careful folded the note and

tucked it away in my pocket. I'd save it; that was the first letter I'd ever got in my life, posted or otherwise.

Rusty wouldn't let up. "Man! Pepper Baker's had suitors lined up from the Sweetwater to the South Fork Shoshone. But she never give none of 'em the time of day."

"Yeah? Well, maybe she ain't never met no one quite like me."

"Yeah," he agreed with a grin. "I'd shore go along with that." He drew back and looked at me. "There must be somethin' there, but damned if I can see it. You look like a lost calf in a snowstorm."

"Well, you shore ain't got nothin' to brag about. I never seen so many freckles."

We insulted each other for a time then walked outside, laughing.

"Take the other side of the street, Rusty. We'll make rounds and then meet up at the school."

I might not be no great shakes as a lawman, but I was gonna give it all I had.

Steppin' into the cantina, I nodded to the barkeep, a big rough-lookin' Mex with a bushy moustache. He didn't look like he was too thrilled to see me, but he also knew there wasn't nothin' he could do about it.

"Just makin' rounds, barkeep," I assured him. "No trouble."

He nodded his head and relaxed a mite, putting his hands on the bar to show me they was empty. I took a casual look around the place.

The clothing and the low-heeled boots and clodhopper shoes of the men told me that most were farmers and sheepmen. Walkin' around the room, I introduced myself, usually sayin' something like, "If you got a problem, don't hesitate to come to me with it. I'm here to enforce the law, fair and equal."

They liked it, I could tell that. Whether they believed I'd actual follow through on it was something else agin.

It was dusk when I stepped out of the cantina and walked to the hotel, Doubtful Lodgings. It was a weird town.

The Dirty Dog and the Wolf's Den was quiet. I think my actions of the past two days had put a damper on things. Them that hunted trouble had seen that I wasn't goin' to kowtow to no one, and there just wasn't no backup in me.

Steppin' into the hotel, I walked up to the night clerk, a young man with slicked-back hair, parted smack down the middle. I spun the register and noticed, among the people that had registered that day, two names that caught my attention— Black Jack Keller and Pen Castell.

Both of them was hired guns, and among the best. They come real expensive, so I'd heard.

I pointed at the names. "These two gents, they still in the hotel?"

"No, Sheriff. They partook of our special dinner menu and then stepped across the street to the saloon for a drink and cards. They seemed like very nice gentlemen. Their manners were impeccable."

I blinked at that. Impeccable sounded like something you wouldn't want on you. "Yeah. They're just dandy fellers."

On the boardwalk, I waved at Rusty and walked over to join him, telling him about Pen and Black Jack. He whistled softly.

"Top guns, Sheriff."

"And fast. I seen 'em work up near the Oregon/Washington line. Little town in the Umatillas. Don't never sell 'em short. They're among the best. Things is heatin' up, Rusty."

"I wonder who hired 'em?"

"I don't know. Was that feller who backed you up this afternoon Jeff Baker?"

"Yeah. Pepper's brother. He's a square shooter, all the way."

"I figured as much. Let's take the Dirty Dog first, then we'll ease on over to the Wolf's Den."

The Dirty Dog was filled with the crews from the smaller ranches around the area, and they seemed to be a friendly, easygoin' bunch. But I noticed that they was, to a man, all packin' iron, some of them with an extra six-shooter tucked behind their gunbelt. That was not a good sign.

"Wouldn't have taken a month's pay to miss that show this afternoon, Sheriff."

"Yeah," another said. "That kid's been achin' for something like that to happen. He's been ridin' high, wide, and rough for a long time."

"You be careful, Cotton," an older cowboy told me. "That kid's bricks ain't stacked jist right."

"I know you?" I looked him up and down.

"I know you. I was ridin' for the Twisted River brand down on the Big Sandy when you braced them rustlers that night—'member?"

"Oh, yeah!" Rusty was all ears, leanin' close. "They run off part of that herd we was pushin' north and stole one of my horses. Sure."

"What happened?" the barkeep asked.

"We planted the two rustlers that braced Cotton," the cowboy said quietly.

I noticed a puncher leavin' out just then, turnin' in the direction of the Wolf's Den. But then, maybe he was just headin' for the privy.

The older puncher said, "He's a sneak and a snitch for Big Mike. Thinks we don't know it."

I chuckled. "Good way to feed wrong information."

The puncher just grinned.

Me and Rusty could both feel the hostility when we pushed open the batwings and stepped into the Wolf's Den.

Place got real quiet. Big Mike Romain was standin' belly

up to the bar, nursin' a beer. Johnny Bull was on his right and Little Jack Bagwell to his left. Man enjoyed some fine company, to be sure.

Rusty stood at the end of the bar closest to the door while I ambled around the place. I met every eye that would meet mine. And I was thinkin' that to my knowledge, this many top gunslicks had never been gathered in one place at the same time.

Other than a cemetery.

And neither of them thoughts was real comfortin', to my way of thinkin'.

I nodded at the gunfighters that I knew personal well. They returned the unsmilin' nod and that was the extent of our happy fellowship.

I'll admit, I was some relieved to be out of that place and walkin' up toward the schoolhouse.

Rusty must have read my mind. "You got anyone in mind for additional deputies, Sheriff?"

"I don't know no one to even mull over. You got any ideas?"

"Matter of fact, I do. 'Member I tole you about them two punchers I rode with, Burtell and De Graff?"

"Yeah."

"They're livin' in an old line shack north of town. They're good boys, both of 'em."

"Tell me why they got fired."

"They didn't. They quit. They didn't like what was happenin'. Big Mike said he was gonna run 'em both out of the county. That was tried a couple of times, but they're still here."

"Gunhands?"

"No. Just punchers. They pro'bly better than average with a short gun, but they ain't real fast. They will make their first shot count, though."

"Hell, that's half the fight. Some of the fastest guns I ever seen usually put their first shot in the dirt. You ride out in the mornin', fetch them boys into town. Lemme talk to them."

At the schoolyard, it was all lantern-lit, the lanterns hung from ropes, with fancy streamers a-danglin' ever' which-a-way. The adults were sippin' punch and the kids was playin' and runnin' around and havin' fun. The boys was pullin' the girls' pigtails and the girls was pretendin' they was all upset about it.

And it made me kinda sad. This type of gatherin' sometimes does that to me. Here I was, twenty-eight years old, I think, give or take a year, and I'd never had nothin' much to speak of. I'd been driftin' for a good many years. Oh, I'd seen the country, all of it west of the Big Muddy, but the feelin' of belongin' to someone . . . that was something I'd never known. Don't get me wrong; I love the high lonesome. I like the smell of a wood fire and the cool mornings and the feelin' that there ain't another human person within a hundred miles of you.

But . . . well, you can't think about that too much or too often. Tends to get a body down.

These folks now, all happy and gay, they had that feelin' of belongin'. And it showed. Oh, many of them didn't have all that much, cash-wise, but they had somebody.

Well, hell! You know what I mean.

And then I seen Pepper. That brightened me up real quick . . . in one way. And yet, in another, it produced a feelin' that I never recollected havin' before. Kind of a warm, gooey sort of feelin'.

I shuddered like a big shaggy buffalo and walked around the yard. Rich gal like Pepper Baker wasn't gonna have nothin' to do with a two-bit cowboy turned sheriff like me.

But she did send me that note.

There was three guys with a fiddle and guitar and squeeze box, and they cranked it up for dancin'. That left me out in the hog-waller, 'cause when it comes to fancy footwork with a female, I got two left feet. So I just stood around lookin' like a lonesome hound dog while Pepper danced every dance. And I couldn't help but wonder how Big Mike felt about that . . . him havin' her all staked out, at least in his mind.

Pepper took a break from her dancin', leavin' a lot of disappointed men standin' around lookin' glum. Damned if she didn't walk straight up to me. I took off my hat when she come up.

"Put your hat back on, Sheriff. You might catch a chill out here."

She stood lookin' at me with them blue eyes, and that syrupy feelin' sort of oozed over me again. I really didn't know what to make of it. Least that's what I kept tellin' myself.

"Enjoyin' yourself, Miss Pepper?" I managed to ask. Least I hadn't tripped over my feet yet again.

"I'd enjoy it more if I knew why you haven't ask me to dance."

"I never learnt how! You get me out there on that flat and you'd have sore feet for a month."

"Well, at least you're honest about it. I better warn you, Sheriff . . . what is your name? I'm not going to call you Sheriff forever."

"Cotton."

"Just . . . Cotton?"

"Just Cotton."

She smiled, a mischievous look creeping into her eyes. "You wanted by the law, Cotton?"

"Oh, no, ma'am!"

"Well, if I leaned rreeaall close," she said softly, "would you whisper it in my ear?"

With a sigh, I agreed.

She leaned close, Rreeaall close. I could smell the flowery

perfume she was wearing and the clean scent of her hair. I whispered in her ear.

I knew what she was gonna do. Ever'body does the same thing.

She started gigglin'. Really had to struggle to keep from bustin' out laughin' and drawin' a lot of attention to us. She put her little hand on my arm and kind of guided me along, out of the lamplight. I got a little edgy about that.

"That really your last name, Cotton?"

"Sure is."

"But Cotton is not your real first name? Surely not!"

"Yes, ma'am, it sure is. My daddy had a funny sense of humor."

We stopped under a tree. The lights and the whoopin' and hollerin' kids and the music and the gaiety seemed to be far away. It was kind of a nice feelin'.

She leaned against the trunk of the tree and fanned herself with a little hanky. "I declare," she whispered. "I do believe I've gotten too warm dancing."

I was gettin' a little warm myself.

I got a hell of a lot warmer when she undone the top three buttons of her dress and fanned her pale skin with that little hanky. It was just a damn good thing I didn't have no chaw of tobacco in my mouth. I'd have swallowed it for sure.

I looked in ever' direction there was except the . . . upper part of her. "You, ah, was gonna warn me about something, Miss Pepper?"

She laughed softly. "So you can be trusted, too, Sheriff," she said. Kind of a strange thing to say, I thought. "Mike Romain would have had me raped by now." She buttoned herself back up. "Forgive me?"

"Sure. I, ah, kind of enjoyed it, tell you the truth."

"That's good. I was beginning to think that you were made of stone."

"Far from it, ma'am."

"Would you please stop calling me ma'am!"

"Yes, ma'am."

She laughed and took my arm. "Come on, let's walk back. Tongues are wagging now. Cotton, I . . . may have set you up for trouble. If so, I'm sorry. I simply cannot abide sharing my box with that Mike Romain another time."

There was two ways to take that, but since I figured her for a nice lady, I elected for the fried-chicken side of it.

"Big Mike has made up his mind that I'm the woman for him. No one else will bid against him."

"Why?"

"They're afraid of him. He's crazy."

"I didn't figure his wagon was loaded full. And you want me to bid agin' him, right?"

"Yes." I could feel her eyes on me in the darkness. "For more than one reason, Cotton."

I could see my ranch fadin' away into the distance, 'cause if it took all that was in that hat, I was gonna have a taste of Pepper's box. "I'll go as high as the traffic will bear, Pepper."

Her eyes had kind of a frightened look in them. "No one has ever gone over ten dollars."

"I got a hunch this one will."

She reached into a pocket of her dress, a real pretty gingham dress; not fancy like the gowns on Joy and Wanda. She reached down and took my hand, pressing something into it.

Several double eagles.

"Now, ma'am . . . !"

"No," she said, a final tone in her voice. She gave her pretty head a toss. "If you're brave enough to bid against Big Mike, on my behalf, the least I can do is pay for it. Don't worry, my mother came from a very wealthy family back east. Old money. And I have money of my own. Besides, we're doing this with Father's permission and blessing."

"Figurin' anybody else might get stomped or killed, but Big Mike should have more sense than to brace the sheriff?"

"You're quick, Cotton."

I wasn't really sure what she meant by "old money." I guessed that meant she was rich.

All kinds of suspicions jumped into my head.

She looked up at me in the dim light from the lanterns. "You don't trust me, do you?"

Before I could reply, and if I had done it, I'd a probably stuck my foot in my mouth, she said, "You're different, Cotton." She smiled. "And kind of cute, too, in a range-rough way. And you're not afraid of Big Mike, or . . . anyone, or so it seems. Cotton, you're either a very brave man, or a fool. Time will tell where that takes the both of us. Now please walk me back. The bidding will start in a few minutes."

Big Mike and some of his boys was all lumped up together, and they give me some hard looks when they spotted me and Pepper. I just smiled at them all and tipped my hat to Big Mike.

That made him so mad he looked like he was fixin' to swell up and explode.

The little band had stopped playin' and some fellow that I didn't know stepped up on the raised platform and announced that the biddin' was about to get underway, and it was all for a good cause and all that.

I was very conscious of Big Mike's eyes on me as the biddin' got underway. Pepper had joined up with her pa and ma and brother. I didn't know where Rusty had gotten hisself off to, but I figured he was close by.

Like most of these socials I'd been to, and that wasn't all that many, all the gents pretty well knew in advance how to identify what box they wanted to bid on, and it was almighty easy to tell who was sweet on who.

I'd spotted Pepper's box right off, and it was comin' up next.

I let Big Mike open the biddin' with a two-dollar call. Then I upped the ante to five.

He looked at me, and the expression on his face was anything but nice to look at.

Big Mike went to ten and I went to fifteen. Rusty come up beside me and said, "Pepper's daddy tole me to stand by with these in case you needed them." He shook his fist and I heard some coins rattle.

"I can't figure this, Rusty."

"I can. You're an honorable man. You ain't got no sense, but I reckon Pepper can't see that." He grinned hugely.

"Fifty dollars!" Big Mike squalled.

"Sixty." Man, that crowd was some kind of dead quiet.

I chanced a look down and Rusty opened his fist. Close to a hundred dollars in coin.

I shook my head.

"Seventy-five!" Big Mike yelled, anger plain in his voice.

I looked at him. Even across the yard I could tell his face was flushed.

"One hundred dollars," I called. "Ought to be a piece of apple pie in there for that bid," I said with a grin.

A few of the ladies laughed. I'd find out what they was laughin' about shortly.

Big Mike whirled around, facin' me and glarin' at me. "By God, I'd like to see the color of your money, Sheriff!"

"Oh, I got it. And if you don't believe that, then I reckon you'd be callin' me a liar." With my right hand, I swept back my coat, exposin' the butt of my .44.

Big Mike stepped away from the crowd, droppin' his hands to his guns.

"Sold to the sheriff!" the auctioneer screamed, puttin' an end to what might have been a shootin'. "Next box!"

"Goddamn you!" Big Mike hissed at me.

"You sure are a sore loser," I told him.

"I'll knock you down to size someday!" he warned.

"Yeah? Well, you a big feller all right. I never knowed shit come stacked that high."

Man, he turned about five different shades of red. He took a step toward me. A.J.'s voice stopped him.

"No trouble here, Mike. There is always another time."

I didn't think Mike was gonna pay any attention to his boss's words. He was so mad he was shakin'. Finally he turned around, shovin' both men and women out of his way. He stomped off into the night.

A.J. looked square at me. "You're a fool, Sheriff."

"What I am, is hungry. How about you? Ya'll gonna stick around and join in the festivities?"

"I do not wish to associate with ruffians and common trash . . . like you!" Joy said, giving her head a toss.

A.J. and Joy, Matt, and Wanda all trooped off, heads held high.

I looked around. Lydell Townsend was lookin' at me, a grin on his face. He shook his head and wandered off.

"With them gone, now we can all have some fun!" a man shouted.

The biddin' started again.

"You made a bad enemy, Sheriff," the voice come from my left side.

It was Pepper's brother, Jeff, and he was smilin' at me. "Yeah, I reckon so."

"I'm sorry to hear you're hungry, Sheriff."

"Why?"

"Well, let's just say I hope you have an iron stomach. My sis can't fry chicken worth a damn!"

Chapter Four

I'd et worse. Just don't ask me where or when. It might have been that winter I got snowed in early up near the Musselshell and cooked a coyote. Up to this point, that was the awfullest food I ever tried to eat.

Pepper was tryin' to keep from laughin' at the expression on my face. "You don't have to eat it. I'm really a good cook. . . . I just can't fry chicken."

I wanted to be real tactful, so I didn't say nothing.

She covered her mouth with a hand, stiflin' her gigglin'.

I laid that drumstick down on a napkin and half expected it to walk off. I wished it would. "Pepper, would you like to stroll down to the hotel dinin' room and have supper?"

She laughed, and it was a nice laugh. "I sure would. I'm *hungry!*"

We walked over to her ma and pa, with her proddin' me along, like a kid goin' to the woodshed for a hidin'. She introduced us. They seemed like real nice people, and it was then that I knew what she had meant about old money.

Rolf and Martha Baker had that quality that comes with breeding. Just like with cows or horses. It wasn't nothin' that stuck out obvious-like, but it was sure there.

"Thank you for standing up to Big Mike, Sheriff," Martha said. "Pepper cannot tolerate that animal and neither can we." She indicated her husband. "You're the first person who's had the courage to bid against him." She smiled—looked like she wanted to bust out laughin'. "It didn't take you and Pepper long to finish eating."

I got it then. Pepper had fixed that awful chicken deliberate— for Big Mike. "No, ma'am. Not long."

But my mind was workin' hard. Out here in the west is where a man saddles his own horse and kills his own snakes. Yet, this man, Rolf Baker, owner of one of the three biggest spreads in the Territory, and a wealthy man to boot, somehow lacked the sand to stomp a snake named Big Mike Romain. It just didn't make no sense to me.

And I knew that he knew I was wonderin' about it.

I looked Rolf Baker direct in the eyes. "Where's all your gunslicks, sir?"

He smiled thinly. "I don't hire gunhands, Sheriff. My men can all use guns, of course, but they're hired as cowboys."

"That's good to know, sir. The only gunhawk I ain't seen around here is Clay Allison, and he'd probably be here if he wasn't in prison."

Agin, he smiled. "As is Wild Bill Longley and John Wesley Hardin, and a score of other men who fancied violence over order and decency. The West is maturing, Sheriff. Slowly."

Was he tryin' to tell me somethin'? I didn't know. But he was right. Law and order was comin' to the woolly west . . . but it was almighty slow in gettin' here. And when it did get here, with all the lawyers and fancy words, something big and grand and simple but workable would vanish with its comin'.

"Does the coming of law and order make you sad, Sheriff?" Martha asked.

"Kind of. If the lawyers is gonna be all like Stokes."

"Stokes is a pompous ass!" Rolf said, with some heat in his voice.

I agreed with that. "Law and order and gentle folks would be a grand thing. But in this part of the world, that's gonna come only after the gunsmoke is blowed away."

"I fear you are correct, Sheriff. Well, anyway, you and Pepper had best go have your dinner." Another sign of class. Out here, it's called supper. "Pepper's fried chicken is, at best, unpalatable."

I wasn't real sure what that word meant, but if it meant that chicken couldn't be et, I'd be the first to agree.

Pepper could stow away the grub as good as any cowboy I'd ever seen. We'd talked on the walk to the dinin' room, and chatted while we was waitin' for the food to be brung us, and it was good food, but conversation while we was eatin' was sparse. She was a rancher's daughter all right. Eatin' was serious business, with no time for talkin'.

With a twinkle in her blues, she looked over at me. "I told you I was hungry."

I showed a bit of tact by not agreein'. Hungry! She ate like a just-woke-up grizzly. "You gonna have a long ride back to the ranch tonight."

"No, we're staying in town. With Doctor and Mrs. Harrison. Have you met them yet?"

"Not yet. I hope I don't on no professional basis."

Over coffee, which she loved as much as I did, she brung me up on the gossip. And she confirmed Rusty's suspicions about a range war. Her dad and the ladies at the Arrow brand was tryin' to stay out of it, but it didn't look good.

She told me about the nightriders that struck ever' now and then, burnin' people out and killin'. And nightriders was something that I just didn't hold with.

I walked her to the doctor's house, met Doctor Harrison, and said my good nights.

Standin' there, alone with her on the porch, she smiled at me, and I got that gooey feelin' agin. But I might have been comin' down with the collywobbles, or something.

It was Monday mornin', 'bout an hour 'fore dawn, when the hammerin' on the front door woke up me and Rusty. I answered the door in my long johns, my pistol in my hand.

Couple of farmers, by the way they was dressed. And a sooty, smoky smell was lingerin' around them.

"Nightriders, Sheriff," one man said, his voice filled with weariness. "They hit the Simmons place. Killed Broderick and burned him out. Can you come take a look?"

"Rusty, you know where that is?"

He tossed me my britches. "Yeah." He was buttonin' up his shirt. "'Bout ten miles out, to the northwest. Close to the Circle L spread."

Buttonin' up my britches, I asked the men, "You wanna stay here and rest, or ride back out with us?"

"We'll go with you, Sheriff."

We could smell the charred wood long before we come up on what was left of the place, and that wasn't much. It had been a little two-bit nester outfit. But what pissed me off was that the nightriders, and I hate them all, had shot the cows and mules and hogs.

In the light of God's dawn, it was pretty pathetic.

A wore-out lookin' woman in a wore-out dress was standin' over the blanket-covered body of her husband. Half a dozen towheaded boys and girls gathered around the woman, the youngest clingin' to her skirts and squallin'.

She told me her story in a flat, tired voice.

I just felt sick at my stomach. Glancin' over at Rusty, I

could tell the scene had touched him just as hard as it done me. It just wasn't right; it just flat wasn't right.

They'd come out of the night just after midnight, she reckoned. They was about twenty or so nightriders. Big, brave men all, I thought, a sour feelin' in my stomach. I hate all nightriders for they're all cowards at heart. Hooded, menacing shapes that appear out of the gloom—but never alone, by themselves. That's why any person with a lick of sense despises them.

They almost never have the sand to face a man one on one, totally alone. They might agree to meet a man one on one, but then they'll show up with some buddies, as witnesses, they claim. That means that if they start gettin' the crap beat out of them, their "witnesses" will jump in and haul their ass out of the fire, so to speak.

Her husband had grabbed up his shotgun and run out to meet them—a foolhardy thing to do, but hell, I'd have done the same.

I lifted the scorched blanket and eyeballed the man. He was a mess. Those big, brave riders had pumped what looked to be twenty or thirty rounds into him. Then someone had leaned down and shot the man right between the eyes. The powder burns were plain on his bloody forehead.

"They shot him down right in front of the kids, Sheriff. And then they grabbed up and tooken Marie with them."

"Who's Marie?"

"My oldest girl. She's just turned sixteen."

"Can you describe any of the men? Any of their horses? Just give me something to go on—anything?"

She didn't know a thing. "I didn't see no brand left or right flank, Sheriff. I'm sorry."

"Course, we all know who they was, Sheriff," one of the men said.

"Yeah. I know. But provin' it is gonna be something else."

"They rode towards the northeast, Sheriff!" Rusty called, lookin' at tracks. "Right over yonder is the edge of Circle L range. They pro'bly rode right into a herd to cover their tracks."

Noddin' my head, I looked around. The damn nightriders hadn't left nothin'. They'd deliberately trampled over the new-plowed garden, shot the animals, then torched the house and barn. It was just a miracle that none of the little kids had been killed.

Brave men all.

The woman touched my arm. I met her sad-lookin' eyes. "Will you find Marie, Sheriff?"

"Yes, ma'am." I spoke around the disgust that filled my throat. "I'll find her."

I found her. Naked, raped, and dead from a broke neck. She'd been a pretty girl, even with the ravages of poverty touchin' her young face.

I felt like pukin'!

I found her patched and torn nightgown, lyin' off to one side. And from the looks of her, more than one man had taken his pleasures with her.

Lookin' up at the sounds of hooves, I seen two punchers ridin' my way. Slippin' the thong off the hammer of my .44, I waited, then relaxed when I could make out the brand. Arrow.

"Jesus Christ!" one of the cowboys said, lookin' at the body of Marie.

I knew that badge or no badge hangin' on my shirt, I'd better start talkin' and do it swift. 'Cause messin' with a woman in the west was the fastest way I knew of to get your neck stretched.

One of them punchers done got his rope out.

I told 'em who I was and what had happened, so far as I knowed. They was as disgusted as me about it.

"I don't like nesters and barbed wire," one said, "but this

is awful. I'll go get Miss Maggie and Miss Jean. We'll bring a buckboard." He wheeled his horse and was gone.

I took the slicker off my saddle skirt and gently covered the naked girl. I felt some better when that was done. It just wasn't decent, her layin' there with no clothes on.

"Them was good folks for nesters," the Arrow rider said, dismountin'. He plopped his hat back on his head. "I knowed them all. And that there was a good girl. The woman know who done it?"

"She has suspicions, just like me and you. But provin' it is something else."

He made a low sound in his throat. "Yeah, ain't that the truth?"

He introduced hisself as Ben and we shook on it.

Both of us done our best not to look at the slicker-covered body with the bare feet stickin' out.

"Ben, what's your opinion of what's happenin' around here? If it's an upcomin' range war, why? Nesters and barbed wire?"

Barbed wire had been slowly workin' its way west since first being introduced back in the early '70s. Personal, even though I could see where it might serve some purpose, I didn't like it. All kinds of barbed wire was being strung . . . and people was gettin' killed for doin' it.

I still carried the scars on me from where I'd gotten all tangled up in it once. And I mean . . . once.

"Strictly personal opinion, Sheriff?"

"Have at it."

"I think Lawrence and Mills want to be kings of this area. I don't think it's nothin' but greed. Pure and simple."

Maybe that was all there was to it. Maybe they'd just gotten so big and powerful, they believed they was kings. "I was sorta ruminatin' about gold or maybe oil . . . ?"

Ben shook his head. "There might be enough gold around here to fill a tooth. As for oil, I don't think so. I ain't never seen none of it. And I been around here a long time."

"It's just hard to believe that anybody as rich and powerful as Lawrence and Mills would sink so low as that." I pointed to the dead girl.

Ben spat on the ground. "It'll get worser, Sheriff. Believe it."

I believed it.

Maggie Barrett and Jean Knight come ridin' out with the buckboard. They was gals in their mid to late forties, I'd guess, and they rode astride, just like a man. Each of 'em had a six-gun belted around their waist and a rifle in the saddle boot. They looked like they knew how to use the weapons, too. And would.

I met them look for look. "I'm Maggie and that's Jean." She jerked a gloved hand toward the other woman. "And you're the new big, bad sheriff, huh?"

"I don't know about the big or bad, ma'am. But I'm the sheriff."

"You're mighty young," Jean said. "But you got a hell of a reputation behind you, Sheriff Cotton." She let her eyes drift to the slicker-covered body. "And what are you aimin' to do with the sorry son of a bitch who done that?"

"More than one, ma'am. I aim to find them, arrest them, try them, and then hang them."

"And if their names are Mills or Lawrence or Romain . . . ?" She let that trail off.

"They pull their britches on same way anybody else does, ma'am."

She stared at me. She was still a handsome woman. Twenty years back, she'd been beautiful. "I think you'll do, Sheriff Cotton. I think you'll do to ride the river with. If," she added drily, "you live that long."

Them gals personal loaded Marie into the buckboard, and none of us men standin' around was too unhappy 'bout that.

Rusty had joined me and Ben, and then some Quartermoon punchers come ridin' up. Lookin' them over, I seen what Rolf Baker had meant the other night. They wasn't none of them no slick-backed gunhawks, but they was rough through and through, and I'll take that kind of man over a gunsharp any time, hands down.

All of 'em give me the once-over, takin' in my butt-forward, left-hand .44.

They done some low cussin' and growlin' about what had happened, and one of them said he made a damn dandy noose.

"It'll be done legal-like," I heard the words come out of my mouth. "They'll be no gawddamn vigilantes ridin'. Sometimes, they're just as bad as nightriders."

Kinda surprised me, but after I said that, they all just quieted down.

While waitin', I'd done some circlin' on foot, tryin' to come up with just one track that stood out. About my fifth try, I found one.

A horseshoe had been worn or chipped to form a V on the left side of the shoe.

"Rusty, Ben, you Quartermoon boys!" I called. "Come over here and look at this."

I pointed out the track to them.

But none of them had never seen it before.

I glanced at Ben. "You busy?"

"Not to speak of. What's on your mind, Sheriff?"

"You know two ol' boys name of De Graff and Burtell?"

"Hell, Sheriff!" he protested. "They couldn't have done this. They . . ."

I waved him quiet. "I never said they done nothin'. I want to talk to them 'bout bein' deputies. Can you find 'em and have 'em meet me in town?"

"Consider it done, Sheriff." He was on his horse and gone.

I mounted up.

"Where are we goin', Sheriff?" Rusty asked.

"To wherever this track leads, Rusty. Let's ride."

We was on Circle L range, and we all knew it. And no one amongst us would have bet against where that track was gonna lead. And it done it, sure as shootin'.

It was mid-morning when we rode up to the great house. House! It was a damned mansion. Looked as out of place on the range as a turd in a punch bowl.

And it made me mad. It was some unreasonable, and I knew it, but it done it anyways. I was thinkin' about them poor nesters back yonder, burned out with not even a pot left to piss in—the nightriders had even burned the privy—and here was this palace . . . where the tracks of the nightriders led straight for.

All that was mingled in with the sight of that dead girl, raped, and neck broke.

I just got mad!

I rode straight up to the front of that house and looped Critter's reins around the hitchrail and stomped up the steps onto the porch. I commenced to poundin' on the front door.

One of the Mex servants seen me and run back into the rear of the house. I kept on hammerin' on that door until ol' A.J. hisself jerked open the door.

"What is the meaning of this . . . outrage?" he yelled at me. "Git out here!"

"I beg your pardon, you . . . you saddle bum!"

Jerkin' open the outside door, I grabbed mister bigshot by the shirtfront and hauled him out, then I shook him like a hound dog with a rabbit in its mouth.

Wanda Mills must have been visiting over, 'cause she and Joy run to the door, looked out, and then started squallin' and jumpin' up and down and makin' more noise than a fire drill at a loony house.

Ol' A.J.'s head was bouncin' back and forth like a puppet.

I shoved Mister Hotsy-Totsy down in a porch chair and told him, very quickly, what had happened.

Big Mike and about a dozen other hands come a-runnin' over. Rusty shoved the barrels of a Greener under Big Mike's chin and said, "First one reaches for iron, I blow your fat head off!"

Rusty eared back the hammers, both of 'em, on that sawed-off, and Big Mike's eyes got to lookin' like saucers.

Jerkin' A.J. to his feet, I shoved him down the steps and toward the corral and barn. The rest followed, Joy and Wanda blubberin' and snortin' and flingin' snot ever' which-a-way.

On the way over, I showed Mister A.J. the tracks of that horse we'd been trailin'. His face turned white as a fresh-washed petticoat.

It was some rash on me and Rusty's part, for if Maggie and Jean and some of their hands hadn't a showed up, me and Rusty just might have ended up lookin' like that cheese that's full of holes.

But show up they did, along with some Quartermoon boys, all of 'em ridin' escort to the buckboard carryin' the dead girl.

I was right proud to see them all.

By this time, the grounds was full of Circle L riders, most of 'em gunhands, or at least drawin' fightin' wages. And they was ready to earn their money, too.

The Arrow and Quartermoon boys circled the yard.

"Rusty," I said. "Find that horse with the marked shoe." I kept an eye on Big Mike while Rusty started lookin'. Mike was so mad his face was all mottled lookin'. But he kept his hands away from his guns. I sorta wished he would try to grab iron, and I think he knew it.

It didn't take Rusty long to find the horse. He led him right into the yard and I checked the shoe. There it was, the V standin' out plain as egg on your face.

I looked at A.J. and then at Mike. "You're both under arrest."

"On what charge?" Mike hollered. "That horse don't prove nothing!"

"Orderin' the murder of Broderick Simmons and aidin' and abettin' them who done the killin'."

Well, that wound up Joy's key agin, and she and Wanda tuned up and commenced to squallin'.

Jean and Maggie was both smilin' kind of grim-like.

"You'll never make it stick, Sheriff," A.J. said.

"Maybe not," I told him. "But I'm sure gonna give it all I got."

"You're a fool!"

As time would tell, I did come out of it lookin' kinda foolish, but it did accomplish one good thing: it lined up the smaller spreads directly on my side.

Chapter Five

My, but it was a grand sight, for as long as it lasted, that is. Me and Rusty had tied A.J. and Big Mike's hands behind them and boosted them up into the saddle. Only I give A.J. too much of a boost and he fell plumb over the other side of the horse. I 'spect it hurt when he done a belly-flopper on that hardpacked ground. He squalled something fierce about it.

"I'll sue you!" A.J. hollered, wallowin' around on the ground.

"Hell, I ain't got nothin'. Go ahead and sue me."

We finally got everybody mounted and commenced to head for town. A.J. and Big Mike give us all a pretty good cussin' on the way in. My, my, but for all of A.J.'s gentility and suaveness, he sure knew how to string together some mighty bad words. And that way of ridin' was none too comfortable for them, neither. Big Mike fell off his horse twice. And that was a sight to behold. Come to think of it, he done some pretty fair country cussin', too.

Joy and Wanda had some hands hitch up a buggy and they followed us, in the drag, both of them varyin' between cryin' and cussin'. Them gals weren't no ladies, neither, let me tell you that right off the bat. I never heard such nastiness come out of a woman's mouth. Kinda makes a feller's faith in womanhood quiver a bit.

The whole town turned out to see A.J. and Big Mike get put in the pokey, not all of the onlookers pleased to see it.

De Graff and Burtell was waitin' in the office when I come inside, pushin' A.J. and Mike ahead of me. George Waller was in the office, too.

"You approve of these ol' boys bein' deputies?" I asked.

He did.

I looked at them. "You boys wanna wear a badge?"

De Graff, he said, "Beats hell out of starvin'." Then he looked at A.J. "And cuttin' out an occasional steer for food." He grinned big.

"Goddamn thief!" A.J. hollered.

"Hush!" I told him. "Swear 'em in, George."

He done it, all to the background noises of A.J. and Mike cussin' and Joy and Wanda blubberin' and squallin'.

Then I locked up A.J. and Mike. Man, but they was hot under the collar.

I'd ordered the body of Marie to be taken to Doctor Harrison's office for an official opinion on the cause of death—not that it mattered much to Marie—and to verify that she'd been raped, too.

"Rusty, you and De Graff and Burtell make damn sure nobody breaks our prisoners out. I'm goin' down to Doc's place."

De Graff just smiled and jerked a Greener out of the rack on the wall and broke it open, loading the sawed-off shotgun with buckshot. Like Rusty had said, they was both men to ride to the river with.

I got a lot of congratulations on the walk down to Doc's office, all mixed up with some pretty dark looks from the Circle L and Rockinghorse riders. There must have been forty or fifty of them ol' boys in town, all of them all geared up and ready for trouble.

I seen Pepper and her ma as they come into town in a buggy, driven by Rolf Baker. Half a dozen Quartermoon riders flanked the buggy, her brother Jeff among them. And while those Quartermoon riders might not have been hired guns, I could tell by the way they conducted themselves they knowed what to do with them guns.

Looked to me like the town of Doubtful might be gettin' awful interestin' pretty quick.

But I hoped not too interestin'. It don't take a fellow long to start thinkin' like a lawman. Just hang a star on. They make dandy targets.

Steppin' into Doc Harrison's office, I seen right off that the doc was mad as hell. He was kinda white around the mouth and his fists were clinched tight shut.

"Tell me what you can, Doc. And keep it simple, please."

"The girl was horribly used, Sheriff. She was not only raped, but violated in an unnatural manner as well. It's the most disgusting thing I've seen in all my years of practicing medicine."

I didn't know what in the hell he was talkin' about. But I wasn't gonna show my ignorance by askin' him to explain. If it was that disgustin', I didn't want to know noways. So I just nodded my head and pretended I knew what he was sayin'.

"Cause of death?"

"Her neck was broken. Bruises on the throat indicate it was done deliberately. By someone with enormous strength."

Big Mike popped into my mind. Or Junior. Both of them looked to be strong as hell. "Well, I know the family ain't got no money for no fancy burial, Doc. I'll ask around for contributions to help out."

"I'll handle the arrangements with Martin Truby's funeral

parlor. I should imagine the mother is too disconcerted to be of much assistance at this time of grief."

"Uh . . . yeah! Right. Dis-concerted. That's her. See you, Doc."

Steppin' onto the boardwalk, I wondered who I might ask what dis-concerted meant.

Damn, but it's hell to be ignorant.

Back at the office, I was pleased to see that both De Graff and Burtell had armed themselves with Greeners. They's lots of tough ol' boys who'll face a man with a six-gun in his hand but damn few who'll stand up to a sawed-off shotgun— 'specially when that shotgun is loaded with ball bearings and nails and pieces of scrap iron. One time, I seen an ol' boy cut slap in two catchin' both barrels of a Greener in the belly. It was not a sight I was likely to ever forget.

A.J. and Mike had stopped cussin' and hollerin'. I stepped back and looked in on them sittin' on their bunks. Lawyer Stokes had been sent for.

"What's the bond for our charges, Sheriff?" A.J. asked. First time I could remember him ever callin' me Sheriff.

"That's gonna be up to the judge. Barbeau's been sent for."

I said that with a bad taste in my mouth, for I'd been told that Judge Barbeau was a personal friend of both A.J. and Matt Mills.

Both A.J. and Big Mike smiled at that, and I had me a sinkin' feelin' in the pit of my stomach that the rumors about Barbeau was true.

"So that means the judge will be here sometime in the morning?" A.J. asked.

"I reckon so. If he can get his lard-butt up on a horse, that is." I'd been told the judge was rather portly, as George put it. Fat-ass.

"Well, Sheriff!" A.J. was all smiles now. "You don't object if we have our meals sent in, do you?"

"Nope. That's about the only way you gonna get fed."

"That's very good of you. Since we've missed lunch, why don't you just step over to the cafe and order us something to eat?"

I was still laughin' as I closed the door leadin' to the rows of cells. Big Mike and A.J. had started cussin' again.

Neither Joy nor Wanda was nowhere to be seen, and I was thankful for that for more reasons than one. There was some day-old beans in a pot and a half loaf of yesterday's bread.

Guess what A.J. and Big Mike had for lunch?

"Outrageous!" A.J. had squalled. "Prisoners in the territorial prison get better food than this!"

I didn't pay him no mind.

The novelty of A.J. and Big Mike bein' in the pokey had wore off some when I stepped back outside. But the mood of the town had changed, I could sense it. It was an ugly, tense feeling in the air.

I had left Rusty and Burtell back in the office, De Graff was makin' rounds with me. He carried his Greener.

He was quiet for a time, then said. "Trouble's brewin', Sheriff."

"Yeah. I feel it. We'll stay out of the Wolf's Den. Ain't no point in us eggin' nothin' on. That's what A.J.'s gunhands want us to do."

"Sheriff? You ever heard of Jack Crow?"

"Yeah. He's supposed to be the best gun west of the Mississippi. But I ain't never seen him. Can't tell you what he looks like. Why?"

"Rumor has it he's on the way in."

I glanced at De Graff. The man was about medium height and stocky, lookin' to be in his mid to late thirties. Both he and Burtell were about the same height and build; both of them appearing to be quiet and steady men. Not gunhands, but the type of men who would back a fellow up and make the first shot count. Both De Graff and Burtell were western-born and raised, both of them comin' from a little town down in Colorado.

But Jack Crow, now that was something else. Jack Crow had built himself a reputation over the years as a tough, vicious gunfighter. Nobody had ever beat him to the draw. And he come real expensive. And when he left out of a place, two or three people was dead.

The description of Jack Crow was vague, only one thing remaining constant—he dressed in black and rode a black horse.

I wasn't lookin' forward to meetin' Jack Crow.

"You heard anything else about Crow?" I asked De Graff.

"Just that he's definitely on the way here with the promise of big money."

I nodded, thinking. I knew from talkin' to folks that Burtell and De Graff had been cowboys all their lives, ridin' for the brand and loyal to it . . . except for the last brand. I asked De Graff about that.

He was silent for a moment, the only sounds the striking of our boots on the boardwalk and the jingle of our spurs. "Mills and Lawrence is evil people. There ain't no goodness in neither of 'em. They'll do anything to take control of the area. Anything. They're both power-crazy, and I don't know what changed 'em. Maybe they was always thataway and me and Burtell couldn't see it. But we just couldn't take no more of it."

"But they got everything now!"

"Seems thataway, don't it? You or me or Rusty or Burtell, hell, most people, we'd be happy with just a little-bitty portion of what they got. But they want it all. And they're bound and determined to get it, anyways they can. And I'll tell you something now, Sheriff. Judge Barbeau is gonna cut A.J. and

Mike a-loose. He's done it before, and he'll do it this time. Bet on it."

"That's the feelin' I get."

We stopped in the mouth of an alleyway, off the boardwalk, after first checkin' the alley for any trouble-hunters. It was clear. But over across the street, leanin' up agin' a hitchrail, was a young man I'd seen ridin' in with Jim Hawthorne, and he had trouble written all over him.

De Graff had spotted him, too. "That punk's gonna try us, Sheriff."

"Yeah. But not us—just me. It had to come sooner or later."

Out of the corner of my eyes, I seen Rolf Baker and Pepper, standin' in front of a store. If something was going down, at least they was out of the line of fire.

The punk kid across the street, wearin' two guns, tied down low, called out, shoutin' a terrible ugly name at me. I stepped out of the alley, into the street, facin' the kid, still a pretty good distance between us.

"Go on back to the saloon, boy!" I told him. "I got no quarrel with you."

"What's the matter, Sheriff?" the young man yelled, grinnin' at me, his hands clawed, hovering over his gun butts. "You scared?"

"No, boy. I ain't scared of you." I took a couple of steps toward him.

"I'm just as good as Jack Crow!"

I doubted that, but I still wasn't afraid. Maybe I don't have enough sense to be afraid. But I think it's thisaway with anybody who's handier than he ought to be with a short gun. Everything just sort of narrows down in your field of vision. You know they's people watchin' but you really don't see nobody except the man you're facin'. Time seems to pause for the draw. And you can hear the slightest sound, from far away.

"The sheriff's a coward!" the young man hollered, laughing.

I took another couple of steps toward him. Since I'd brung A.J. and Big Mike to jail, I'd been wearin' my right-hand .44 without the hammer thong, just a-waitin' for something like this to happen, knowin' in my heart it was soon comin' at me. And here it was.

"You're bracin' an officer of the law, boy. You're in trouble from the git-go, don't you know that?"

"I just figure I'm facin' a tinhorn who ain't got the guts to draw!"

"You wrong, boy," I said quietly.

"Jack Crow's gonna have a long ride for nothin'," the kid hollered, "'cause when he gits here, you gonna be dead!"

There it was again. Jack Crow. Looked like he was sure on the way in. I took a breath and two more steps. "You're wrong, boy." My voice was just loud enough for him to hear. "Get on your horse and ride on out of here. I'm givin' you a chance to live. Take it. Think about your momma, how this is gonna bother her."

"I figure she'll be right proud of me, Cotton. After I kill you, I'll have me a name that's worth something."

"It'll be on your tombstone, boy. That is, if you got the greenbacks in your pocket to have one stuck up over you. But chances are, two days after you're planted, won't nobody even 'member who you was. What is your name, anyways?"

"They call me the Cheyenne Kid!"

They? I wondered who "they" was. Probably a name the kid hung on hisself. I never heard of no Cheyenne Kid.

People left and right of both of us had cleared a path, gettin' out of the way.

The kid's face was all sweaty and I knowed he was scared. It was a tolerable pleasant afternoon, with a nice breeze fannin' the valley.

I took another step toward him; the distance was just about

right. But I didn't want to kill him, even though I knew in my guts that a killin' was only seconds away. The kid wasn't gonna back down. His kind was all over the west. Punk trouble-hunters, lookin' to make a name for themselves.

Problem was, the kid didn't realize that most of his kind was already rotting in some lonely, windswept, and mostly not-cared-for boot hill.

And there wasn't no marker to tell the world how stupid they'd been.

I could feel the breeze touchin' my face, real gentle-like. Soft cool invisible fingers from off the still-snowcapped mountains that surrounded the huge valley. It just wasn't no good day to die . . . if there ever is a good day to die.

Then the ugly, naked picture of young Marie entered my mind, and it turned me as cold as a cave full of ice. And I knowed I was gonna kill this punk facin' me. That's the way it is with me; it just comes on me sudden-like.

I took another step in the street. "You ride for what brand, boy?"

"The Circle L!"

"You draw fightin' wages, punk?"

"Yeah!"

"Then fight, goddamn you!"

The Cheyenne Kid didn't even clear leather. I put two slugs in his chest, the dust poppin' as the lead hit him. He staggered backwards and sat down on the edge of the boardwalk, his guns slidin' back into leather as numb fingers released the butts.

Then he just sort of sighed and fell over to one side, on his face. His boots—and they was all tore up, the holes in the soles plain to see—kicked a couple of times as death took him wingin' into the dark unknown.

Walkin' across the street, I stood over him, my .44 in my hand, and it was cocked and ready to bark and snarl.

The Cheyenne Kid was dead.

I looked up at a grim-faced knot of Circle L gunhands. "He's your buddy, you take care of him. Get him off the boardwalk."

I wondered which one of these men had egged the kid on to try me? I knew it had to be one or several of them.

Little Jack Bagwell looked at me. "You some better than I recall, Cotton."

I lifted my .44, the muzzle pointed at Jack's belly. I could see him suck in his gut at the same time his mouth opened, pullin' in breath. His eyes turned a little scary.

I let the hammer down easy and enjoyed watchin' the look on Little Jack's face as I lowered the .44 and broke it open, punchin' out the empties and reloading. I deliberately let the brass fall onto the Cheyenne Kid's body.

"You ride for the Circle L, Jack?"

"Yeah."

"Then you personal take care of the Cheyenne Kid's body, Jack. And that ain't no request. You get my drift?"

"Mayhaps I don't wanna do that?" Some of his bluster and bullshit had returned.

I just grinned at him. "You wanna try me, Little Jack? Come on."

He met me stare for stare.

Everybody heard the hammers bein' eared back on De Graff's Greener. And it wasn't no real pretty sound. He had crossed the street and was standin' to my left, in the center of the boardwalk, that sawed-off pointed at the knot of gunslicks.

At a distance of no more than six or eight feet, that Greener would have killed or maimed half the men crowded on the boardwalk facin' me. Then Johnny Bull put an end to what might have been a field day for Martin Truby's funeral parlor.

"We'll take care of the body, Sheriff," he said, kind of quiet-like.

"Fine. Now you all just clear the boardwalk."

Don't get it wrong, these men I was facin' wasn't scared of me nor De Graff. They just knowed a bad situation when they seen one. They'd brace me, sooner or later, probably one on one, for that was their style. All except for the German, Haufman, that back-shootin' bastard. It was just that this wasn't no good time for any more gunplay.

But, as it turned out, none of the gunfighters had to do nothing with the body of the Cheyenne Kid. Doc Harrison came a-pushin' through the crowd to check the body.

He pronounced the Kid dead. Martin Truby was right behind Doc. Truby found ten dollars in the Kid's pockets and said that would bury him, but not nothing fancy. He couldn't buy no mourners for ten dollars; not and plant the Kid in no box. I suggested he take the Kid's guns; they looked to be in pretty good shape. They was Peacemakers, but not the fancy engraved kind. They'd bring about fifteen dollars, new. Truby settled for the guns.

The gathered-around crowd began to break up, the men mostly headed for the saloons to jaw about the killin'.

Truby, he covered up the Kid with a sheet and him and another man, his helper, I reckon, hauled the body up off the boardwalk and toted it to a black wagon, layin' the Kid gentle-like in the back. I kicked some dirt over the bloodstains on the boardwalk and for the first time, began to relax just a bit.

Tell you the truth, I was just a bit concerned about Jack Crow. I was uncommon quick with a short gun, but I wasn't in Jack Crow's class. He was, unquestioned, the best around . . . anywheres. Jack, he had more than forty kills to his credit—if that's what you want to call it—and he never once had let the other guy get lead in him.

Truby, he was talking to me: ". . . what should be put on the marker, Sheriff?"

I was conscious of Pepper's eyes on me, standing about twenty feet away, with her pa.

"That the Cheyenne Kid should have stayed home with his momma, plantin' potatoes."

I turned and walked away.

Chapter Six

It come as no surprise to anyone when that lard-butted Judge Barbeau cut A.J. and Big Mike loose.

A.J. said he'd tried to tell me that the horse with the chipped shoe had wandered up on Circle L range and some of his punchers had just brung it in.

"How do you explain all them other tracks that led straight from the burned-down house to your house?" I jumped up.

"Order in the court!" Barbeau beat his wooden mallet on the table.

"That don't answer my question!" I fired back.

The judge, he was in the middle of what he called "admonishin'" me, when I just got up and walked out of the makeshift courtroom.

His voice stopped me at the door.

"I can and will hold you in contempt of this court, Sheriff!" he shouted.

I turned and smiled, but it wasn't no pleasant smile. "You don't have to do that, Judge. I got enough con-tempt for this court for the both of us, I reckon."

Pickle-barrel-butt turned beet-red as the crowd began applaudin' me. I walked out the door.

Ol' hog-butt, he was hollerin' and bangin' his wooden hammer on the table. I just kept on walkin'. I needed me some fresh air. Smelled like cover-up in that courtroom.

Later, I stood on the boardwalk in front of the office and watched as the Circle L and Rockinghorse crews rode out of town, A.J. and Mike up amongst 'em. Neither one of them give me a second look as they rode out.

But Joy and Wanda did.

They was in a buggy, and both of them cussed me as they rode by. I tipped my hat and smiled at them. Then they was gone in a dust cloud, the matched horses high-steppin'. Them horses had more class than the gals.

One of the men who rode in with Judge Barbeau come up to me.

"Don't take this the wrong way, Sheriff, but if I was you, I'd hightail it out of this part of the territory. You've made some bad enemies . . . including the judge, I might add."

Funny thing for him to say. "I thought, from readin' a few law books, that the judge was supposed to be impartial?"

The man, he just shrugged his shoulders.

"What side are you on?" I asked.

"I ain't on no side. I'm paid to act as bailiff and bodyguard for the judge. But I know a bad situation when I see one."

"Yeah? I imagine if you've spent much time around that big-butted judge, you've seen more than your share of bad situations."

He wouldn't reply to that. I stared him down until he cut his eyes away from mine. "You know what I think? I think if things was to get too hairy around here, the U-nited States Marshals just might perk up their ears and take some notice. What do you think about that, Mister Bailiff?"

He smiled. "Probably. But first you'd have to get word to them, wouldn't you? Think about this, Sheriff: there's no telegraph here, two stages a week, one road in, and one road out. I'd give that some thought."

Then he walked away, leavin' me ponderin' over what he'd said.

Miss Pepper come up to me, steppin' dainty-like down the boardwalk. "I could have told you what was going to happen with A.J. and Mike, Cotton. The judge knows his cake is iced on just one side."

I looked sharp at her. "He gets money from Lawrence and Mills?"

"So the talk goes."

"That's agin' the law."

"But first, Cotton, you have to be able to prove it."

"Yeah." I told her what the bailiff/bodyguard had said.

"My father says that wherever Haufman goes, somebody gets killed—shot in the back. But I imagine you know that. And my brother tells me that some gunfighter named Jack Crow is coming in."

"Yeah, you're right about Haufman. And about Jack Crow, I guess."

She put a small hand on my arm. "You ride careful, now, Cotton."

Here come the goo agin. It was a right nice feelin'. I never had no one much give a damn about me. At least, not since I was left alone, years back. I looked deep into her blues, and the feelin' was like I was standin' with my boots filled up with molasses. "Miss Pepper, I been fairly careful about my back trail for a good many years."

"Be extra careful."

"You reckon it would be all right with your pa if I was to come callin'?"

She smiled at me. "I would think so. I'd certainly like that."

"Well . . . if I ever get some time off, I'll surely do that."

"I'll be looking forward to it."

"Mayhaps a picnic would be fittin'?"

"Yes. That would be nice. Let me know, and I'll prepare some food."

I must have looked sorta queer at that remark, for she laughed and said, "Sandwiches, Cotton. Not fried chicken."

I grinned at her.

She said her farewells and walked off, that part of her sashaying. It was a right interestin' sight, producin' some other feelin's to go with the goo.

I stepped careful-like back into the office.

Rusty, he said, "What you holdin' your hat down there for?"

"Shut up!"

Seemed like damn near the whole valley turned out for the double funeral. Everybody—except for them partial to the Rockinghorse and the Circle L—had contributed to father and daughter's plantin'. And it was a nice funeral.

Nice, as far as funerals go. Lots of sad singin' and slow walkin'. And some professional mourners come in from the next town, and they added a right nice touch to it all.

They could sure moan.

The Reverend Sam Dolittle got a bit carried away and I could tell he was one of them preachers who was in love with the sound of his own voice. Took him more'un an hour of shoutin' to convince the angels to come down and personal take up Miss Marie and her pa and escort them to the Pearly Gates.

I was damn near ready to do some shoutin' of my own, if they'd just hurry up and git here. No slight agin Miss Marie intended.

Truby, he done it up fancy, rollin' out his two black death-wagons, pulled by matched horses. And then ever'-body walked along behind the hearses, after the services. Them paid mourners, they really got to moanin' and carryin'

ryin' on as we walked to the graveyard. They sure earned their money.

Marie's momma, she took it hard, naturally, but she held up tolerable well until the pine boxes was lowered into the ground, then she fainted.

It was just a sad day, and it got to me, and I could tell it got to Rusty and Burtell and De Graff just as hard. Nobody with any sense likes to see no decent person took into the darkness that young, that savage, and for no real reason.

After the graveside services—and Reverend Dolittle preached *another* sermon on the mount—we was walkin' back to the office, Pepper was with her family, when De Graff pretty well summed up the sad day.

"Pisses me off," he growled. "It just ain't right."

My smile was very thin-lipped. "Let's go get us a beer," I suggested.

The boys, they picked up on that real quick-like, addin' some hard smiles of their own.

"Like at the Wolf's Den?" Rusty asked.

"Seems like a nice enough place." I slipped the hammer thong off both my .44s.

The others done the same.

"I'll open the dance, boys. Then we'll see who wants to pay the fiddler."

Readin' the brands at the hitchrail, the saloon was filled up with Circle L and Rockinghorse riders, probably some of them punchers, the most of them gunhawks. And I wasn't in no real peachy mood after the services, you can believe that.

One drunk Circle L rider stumbled out of the batwings just as I was steppin' through. He run slap into me and stumbled, fallin' on the boardwalk.

He was young, and drunk, and cocky.

"Get on your horse and get the hell out of town," I told him. "If I see you agin today, I'll toss you in the pokey."

He got to his feet. "You and who else?" he snarled at me.

I knocked him plumb off the boardwalk with a short left hook. He landed hard in the dirt, on his butt.

"Put him in jail, De Graff."

De Graff, he jerked the puncher up and marched him off, bleedin' from his big mouth. We waited on the boardwalk until De Graff got back.

Then we all stepped inside the Wolf's Den. And it wasn't a real friendly bunch that greeted us.

Wasn't on no signal from me, but my crew separated as soon as we was inside and our eyes had adjusted to the dimness. De Graff, he had picked up a Greener at the office, after tossin' the puncher in the pokey. De Graff, he favored them Greeners, and I was right proud that he did. At close range, makes one man the equal of six.

The Wolf's Den, it got real quiet, real quick-like.

I ordered me a beer from a suddenly very nervous barkeep and took me a long pull. Settin' the mug down easy on the bar, I looked around. Miss Mary wasn't in sight, and I think the barkeep would have preferred to be near'bouts anywheres else but where he was.

"Nice service today, barkeep," I told him, raisin' my voice so all could hear. "I understand why you didn't come, your job and all, but I think it takes a real heathen to sit in a saloon and suck up booze and party rather than pay last respects to a nice kid and her hardworkin' pa who died in a real nasty way."

"You ain't welcome in here, Cotton!" the voice came from the rear of the saloon, and to my right.

Cuttin' my eyes, I studied the man. I'd seen him around over the years, man who called hisself Jackson Ford. I understand that back in Ohio he'd called hisself Matthew Ramsey, 'fore he killed a woman and had to hightail it out west.

"Yeah? Well, I can understand why you wouldn't want to

come to the funeral, Ford. Dead girl and all might bring back some memories you'd rather not recall—right?"

Ramsey/Ford, he glared at me and mouthed a silent ugly word. But he didn't speak it out loud.

Haufman, the back-shooter, was sittin' by hisself, his back to a wall. Haufman was not a real friendly sort, always by his-self . . . either that, or nobody wanted to be seen with the jerk.

"Ve did not know der young lady, Sheriff," Haufman said, his speech heavily accented. "Zo vhy should ve attend der funeral?"

I turned slowly, my thumb hooked into my gunbelt, my fingers touching the butt of the left-hand .44. "Just common good manners, Haufman. But then, I reckon if you work for skunks, some of the smell is gonna hang on you, right?"

"Schwachsinnig!" he growled at me. Sounded like a mean dog.

I didn't have no idea what he called me, but I figured it wasn't very nice. "If you're gonna call me names, make it in English, blockhead!"

Haufman, he dropped his eyes, refusing to look at me. But his face was flushed. Haufman wasn't no gunhand. He could probably use a short gun, but he favored back-shootin' with a rifle. From deep ambush. The piano player had stopped his playin' when we entered.

I turned to hide a smile, that and to deliberately turn my back to the room full of gunslicks. A plan was takin' shape in my mind. But I also knew the plan could easily backfire on me.

"You know," I spoke to the room, my back to them. "I just can't help but think about that poor widder woman, with no husband and all them kids to feed. What you all reckon that poor woman is a-gonna do now?"

Nobody said nothing.

"Well . . . I think it would be kinda nice if somebody was

to take up a collection to help that lady out. . . . How do you boys feel about that?" I turned to face the crowded room.

Rusty, he was grinnin' like a kid locked up in a peppermint store.

"I think a singin' would be nice too," De Graff growled.

"My, my!" I said. "What a grand idea! Yeah, sure. Sort of praisin' the Lord and helpin' them two souls on their way to the Pearly Gates. How does that sound to you boys?"

My eyes touched Johnny Bull. There was a twinkle in them. Oh, he might kill me if he ever got around to bracin' me, but for now, he was findin' the whole thing sort of funny. Johnny and me had never really been enemies. And we'd even rode a few miles together, now and again.

Lookin' around, I could see a few of the real gunhawks thought it funny, too. But most didn't like it worth a damn . . . or me, either. And some, like Haufman, wore looks of pure hate on their faces.

Behind the piano, the man wearin' a derby hat all cocked back on his head was looking a tad green around the mouth. "You!" I called to him. "You know any Christian songs?"

He gulped a couple of times. "Yes, sir!"

"Then play one!"

He started playin' something that wasn't familiar to me, but it did sound sort of religious.

I picked up the tune and started hummin' along . . . sounded kinda like a one-lung bullfrog with a bad case of the sore throat.

Johnny Bull, he laughed at my singin', but he commenced to hum right along with me, grinnin' all the time. He was enjoyin' it!

But the others wasn't.

The piano player ended the tune and turned a sweaty face towards me. "How about 'Rock of Ages,' Sheriff?"

"That's a good one. I know some of that one. Play it. And this time," I looked around the room, "ever'body's gonna join in."

That 88 player, he give them keys a long rip and set to it. Man, you never heard such a ragged bunch of voices in all your life. But them that was hesitant about singin', why they just looked at De Graff with a Greener in his hands, then at me and Rusty and Burtell, and they all lifted their voices in joyous singin' to the Lord, just like their mommas had taught them.

After that was over, we sang "Washed In The Blood" until the windows was rattlin'.

A crowd had begun to gather on the boardwalk, and it was growin' in size.

Then Big Mike come a-pushin' and shovin' through the crowd.

"What in the goddamn hell is going on in here?" he shouted.

"You hush up that blasphemous talk, you heathen!" I yelled at him, turning to face him, my right hand poised over the butt of that .44. "We're havin' an after-the-service service. A-praisin' the Lord and a-helpin' that girl and her pa find their way through the Pearly Gates."

"Have mercy and praise the Lord!" Johnny Bull laughed, slapping his hands together. "Only thing we ain't got is no eatin' on the grounds."

"I got some hard-boiled eggs!" the barkeep blurted.

"Well, bless it and toss it over here," Johnny called.

"Bless it?" the barkeep said.

"Yeah!"

The barkeep looked at the tray of eggs. He picked one up and said, "Bless this here egg and them that is about to partake of it." He tossed the egg to Johnny.

Big Mike now, he wasn't no fool. It didn't take him long to size it all up. There in that room was about thirty-five or forty of the saltiest gunhands to be found anywhere, and they had all been shoutin' out Christian songs.

"A Christian singing?" Big Mike said, no small amount of amazement in his voice.

"Yeah," I said, grinnin' at him. "Ain't that sweet of these ol' boys? Don't you think their mommas would be right proud of them? Don't you want your mommy to be proud of you, Mike?"

"No, by God!" Jackson Ford yelled, jumpin' up and knocking over his chair. "I'm gonna kill you, Cotton." He give me a good cussin'. After all that nice Christian singin', I figured the Good Lord didn't appreciate that, not one little bit.

Then he grabbed for iron.

I let him get that hogleg all the way clear of leather before I drew. It was a mite showboaty on my part, but I wanted these ol' boys to know that Cotton was just as good or better than anyone there a-lookin' on.

I shot Jackson twice, once in the gut and once in the chest. He sort of stumbled back agin the wall and slid down, his gun rattlin' on the dirty floor.

I looked for the piano man. He was a peekin' out from under the lip of the piano. "Git up on your stool and play that one about Jesus calmin' the stormy seas. I was always partial to that one."

"I ain't believin' this," Big Mike mumbled.

I looked at him. "And you join in, too."

Now there was a big crowd outside, pushin' up close to the windows, peerin' in. Pepper and her pa was among them.

Big Mike was hot, all right. Man, he was so mad he looked like something out of a child's nightmare. But he was in a bind, and he was smart enough to know it. He knew all them folks outside was listenin' to every word said.

I raised my voice so them outside could hear it plain. "You

mean, Mike, that you wouldn't sing a Christian song in memory of that poor little girl and her pa? I can't believe that a fine, upstandin' citizen like you, or that you claim to be, wouldn't sing a song for them unfortunate folks now on their way to heaven."

Big Mike looked at the piano man, and when he spoke, his voice was full of disgust. "Play it!" he growled.

And then we sang. We calmed the stormy seas and then we sung a couple of Charles Wesley's hymns . . . I 'specially liked that one about "Jesus, Look Upon A Little Child."

And then I passed the hat.

Actually, I passed Big Mike's hat. I asked him, real solemn-like, if he would be so kind as to take up the collection for Marie and her pa. Please? Man, he turned about four kinds of red.

"I'll return your hat to you." I said. "And bless your heart, Mike."

What he said to me was mostly unprintable. Except for, "Keep the goddamn hat!" Then he hollered for his riders to clear out! Back to the ranch.

Johnny Bull, he kinda dragged his feet to be the last Circle L hand out. He stopped by me at the bar and said, "I didn't have nothin' to do with what happened to that girl, Cotton."

"I believe you. That wasn't your style, Johnny."

And it wasn't his style. Johnny Bull was a stand-up, look-you-in-the-eyes-and-shoot-you sort of fellow. He was a hired gun, yeah, but of them all, Johnny had him a queer sense of decency about him.

"I enjoyed it, you know that? I really did, Cotton. Took me back years, back to when I was just a little boy."

"Yeah. Me, too, Johnny."

"See you, Cotton."

"See you, Johnny."

The Circle L boys were gone, but there was still some

mean ol' boys in that barroom, them that was ridin' for the Rockinghorse brand. And now I knew who was hired on to who.

Still sittin' in there was Pen Castell, Ford Childress, Fox Breckenridge, Waldo Stamps, Dick Avedon, Hank Hawthorne, Sanchez, Joe Coyle, and Tim Marks.

I figured me and the boys had stretched our luck 'bout as far as it was gonna stretch. "Thanks, boys," I said. "The widder Simmons will sure appreciate your gesture." I lifted the heavy hat—Mike had him a head about the size of a hot-air balloon—and walked outside.

"You like to live dangerously, don't you?" Pepper asked me, her blues darkened from concern, I reckon.

I shrugged. "Sometimes."

"I'll be waiting for you to call on me, Cotton. And make it soon."

"I'll sure be there." To George Waller, "Will you tell Mister Truby he's got hisself another customer?"

But Truby was already hot-footin' it up the street. Little fellow was quick after a shootin'.

I walked over to Juan's Cantina and stepped into the beery dimness. A bunch of clodhoppers had gathered there after the funeral. I dumped the contents of Mike's hat onto a table.

"One of you boys see that the widder Simmons gets this, please. It was give by some with a guilty conscience and by some who didn't have nothin' to do with what happened durin' the nightridin'."

One of the men who'd come to the office to fetch me that tragic morning stepped over and slowly counted the money, stackin' it up, and it come to a right smart amount. Lookin' up at me, he said. "It'll sure come in handy, Sheriff. We thank you."

"Thank me when I hang them that done it." I thought about

that. "Or shoot them," I added. "That's Big Mike's hat. He don't want it back. One of you can have it."

A farmer got up, got the hat, and walked off towards the back, to the privy, unbuttonin' his overalls as he walked. I had me a pretty good idea what he was gonna put in that hat.

And it wasn't his head.

Chapter Seven

Steppin' out of the office, I took a deep breath and smelled pure spring in the air. And I knowed that for the most part, except for the real high-up places, the winter was gone for this season.

The smell of wildflowers was soft in the early morning air; a whiff of sage drifted to me, the odor of cedar and the sharpness of fresh-cut pine was all mingled in.

One week to the day had passed since Marie and her pa had been planted. A week of peace in the area.

But I wasn't kiddin' myself, I knew that peacefulness wasn't gonna last. I'd heard reports that the Circle L and the Rockinghorse brands were hirin' more gunslicks and were stockin' up on ammo. I figured when it did bust loose, all hell was gonna break loose from it.

I had gone callin' on Miss Pepper, and we had us a picnic, with food that was fitten to eat this time around.

I was kinda gettin' used to and likin' that gooey feelin'.

When I brung Miss Pepper back to her house—and it wasn't no palace like the Circle L mansion, just a big house with a homey, lived-in look—she'd kissed me . . . right on the lips, right there in front of God and ever'body.

I felt that goo changin' to quicksand. And I knew I was in trouble.

But then, I've always been partial to trouble.

Out of that quiet week's time, I'd spent three days of it just ridin' around the area, gettin' to know the lay of the land and some of the people.

People like Walt Burton, who ran a small ranching operation. People like Pete Taylor and Lee Jones, who also were small ranchers. There was a couple of farmers who ran some mighty big operations, Bob Caldwell and Bill Nelson. And lots of other men who was either farmers or ranchers or sheepmen. They all sized up to be pretty decent, hardworkin' people.

Unlike a lot of them who've spent most of their lives on the hurricane deck of a horse, shovin' beeves around, I never objected much to sheep; I reckon that's 'cause I've seen where and how sheep and cows can get along.

There's always been plenty of talk about what sheep do to the land. Some of it is true, some of it ain't. If sheep are moved properly, they don't do no permanent damage to the land, and the sheep-people I'd seen in the valley seemed to know what they was doin'.

I met some of the sheep-tenders, Basques they was called. Seemed like nice enough folks, but kinda suspicious of me at first. But then, maybe they had good reason to be. I doubt if they had many good memories about comin' face to face with cowboys.

I'd hauled down a box-load of books, most of them on the law—found 'em in a wooden box stored at the office—and had taken to readin' at least an hour a day. I even took one with me when I went ridin' over the area. I'd read while I took my noonin'. There was a book by Shakespeare there. It was interestin', but it was hard readin'. Just didn't make a whole lot of sense to me.

I took to them words written by Lord Byron, though. I

mean, I really took to it. I toted that little book with me all the time, in my saddlebags. I liked them lines that went: Let us have wine and women, mirth and laughter, sermons and soda water the day after.

That man, he knew what he was talkin' about, seems to me.

I mentioned Lord Byron to Pepper, and she seemed right impressed; said she had a book by some fellow name of Tennyson—another Lord—and said she'd loan it to me. When I come back to the office one afternoon after my roamin' around, there it was, on my desk.

She had underlined a passage, with pretty blue ink, and dated it. The date was the first day we'd seen one another. The line went: Such a one do I remember, whom to look at was to love.

I was sure glad none of the deputies was in the office when I read that. I turned as red as the lantern on a whorehouse door.

The peacefulness ended that mornin' I stepped out of the office and tasted the summer. A Rockinghorse puncher come foggin' up the street and slid to a halt in front of me, standin' on the boardwalk.

"Rustlers hit us last night, Sheriff. Took about a hundred head, mostly young stuff. Mister Mills asked if you'd come out quick."

He wheeled and was gone 'fore I could say anything to him.

I left Rusty in charge and took De Graff with me. We headed north of town, the towering mountains pullin' us along, always in sight, lonely and far-off. We crossed the Arrow range and, about halfway through, come up on Miss Maggie and Miss Jean.

We howdied and shook—just like men—and I explained what all I knew. Miss Jean, she spat on the ground and snorted, real unladylike.

"Sure, Sheriff. Sure they had rustlers. Fifth, sixty gunhands roaming around the spread, with that many more punchers, and rustlers are gonna run off some cattle? I don't think you believe that any more than I do."

That thought had occurred to me, and I said as much. "But I still got to check it out. I have me a hunch the tracks of the missin' cattle—if there is any missin' cattle—is gonna lead straight to a small rancher's spread."

"Maybe you ain't as dumb as you look," Miss Maggie said. "I been hopin' and prayin' that something like this wouldn't happen. But I guess the Good Lord wasn't listenin' to me."

"What do you mean?"

"Way I figure it, you can bet that puncher come into town after you, losing after the so-called rustlers was found and shot, or hung. And if I'm wrong, I'll kiss your horse's . . ."

De Graff, he like to have swallered his chew when she finished tellin' what part of my horse she'd kiss. Critter, he looked plumb uncomfortable about the whole thing.

I said my fare-thee-wells and we headed out towards the Rockinghorse spread. Lookin' back over my shoulder, I seen them gals takin' their horses toward home. I had me a hunch they was gonna gather up some of their boys and meet us later.

De Graff, he agreed. "Them women embarrass me," he added.

"Take a powerful strong man to handle either one of them ladies."

"Several around here has tried. Come away lookin' like they'd been wrestlin' bear all night and facin' a breakfast or armadiller meat. One of 'em wandered around for days, mumblin' to hisself. I heard he joined the monkhood and swore off sex forever and always."

Laughing, I asked, "Men still come a-courtin' the gals?"

"Oh, yeah! Them that either crave excitement or ain't got good sense. They fine handsome-lookin' wimmin, still. Miss

Jean got to battin' her eyes at me 'bout three years back. I went to Canada for the summer."

"You're kiddin'!"

"No, I ain't neither!"

I got to laughin' at the sorrowful expression on De Graff's face.

I stopped laughin' when we come up on the sight. There was a whole bunch of Rockinghorse riders gathered around a tree. Two bodies were hangin' from a limb, an older man and a young man, scarcely more than a boy. Another young man was layin' on the ground, all shot to hell and gone, part of his face blowed away.

Joe Coyle, the gunslick, was lookin' at me.

"Mornin', Sheriff. We found the rustlers. Them's the cattle bunched up over yonder." He pointed.

"Yeah." Pitiful thing was, I couldn't do a thing about it. Horse thieves and cattle rustlers was usually hung on the spot. That's just the way it was.

The two hung men hadn't had their necks broke proper, they'd strangled to death danglin'. Their faces was all swole up, tongues stickin' out, all purple-lookin'.

"You' found 'em with the cattle?" I had to ask it, all the while knowin', or at least suspectin', that the man, and what looked to be his sons, had been set up for a hangin' and shootin'.

"Why, sure, Sheriff!" Tim Marks said. "We just wouldn't snatch up some innocent person and hang 'em!" He done his best to look insulted.

It just didn't come off. I knew that Tim Marks had sold his sister to white slavers workin' out of San Francisco some years back. Tim Marks was as sorry as a man could get.

I eyeballed him. "Seen your sister lately, Tim?"

He sulled up like a 'possum caught in lantern light and shut his mouth.

"Who's the dead people?" I asked De Graff.

"Father and his sons. Name's Farris. He run a small ranch that borders on the Rockinghorse range. Over yonderways." He pointed.

I had taken to carryin' a small notepad in my saddlebags, so I got it out and, with the stub of a pencil, wrote down all the so-called facts of the case. It took me awhile, writin' not bein' all that easy. "Cut the bodies down and tie 'em acrost their saddles," I told Coyle. "We'll take 'em into town."

Them gunhands, they didn't like that idea, so the regular punchers for Rockinghorse did it. Them drawin' gunslick wages, they just sat back and watched it all.

'Bout that time Miss Maggie and Miss Jean come ridin' up, with a half dozen of their hands with them, all of 'em ready for a fight.

Miss Jean looked at the bodies draped over and tied to the saddles. She shook her head in disgust. "Farris," she said to no one in particular. Then she looked at me. "Just like I told you it would be, Sheriff."

Joe Coyle glared at the woman, "What the hell is that supposed to mean, lady?"

One of the Arrow hands started to step down. She waved him back. "Easy, Jesse. I can stomp my own snakes." She looked at Joe. "What it means, gunhand, is this: Me and Maggie told Sheriff Cotton that this is what he'd find when he got out here. And that you and your scummy crew probably set the whole damned thing up, bein' the lowdown, yellow-livered cowards that you are."

Joe, he turned as red as the sun goin' down. First time I ever heard of Coyle not knowin' which way to jump. I mean, he couldn't challenge a woman to step down and jerk iron . . . that was damn near unheard of.

Well, there was Martha Jane Canary—better known as Calamity Jane. She rode astride and packed iron. But even Belle Starr, the ugly she-devil, she rode sidesaddle . . . most of the time.

"Well . . . well . . ." Joe stuttered. "Lady, you cain't talk to me like that!"

Dick Avedon grinned. "Shore 'pears to me like she done it, though." Dick, he got a big laugh out of that.

"Well, you wrong, lady!" Joe said. "We caught this bunch fair and square with the stole cows and we hung 'em high. All 'cept for that one." He pointed to the kid with half his head blowed off. "He jerked iron and we shot him."

Dick, he was lookin' at me, smilin' kinda funny-like. He knew that I knew they had set these men up and shot them and hanged them just as cold as a rattler strikes.

"Yes, you sure did shoot him," Miss Jean said drily. "About twenty-five times from the looks of him. You big brave gunhands must have been powerful afraid of that young man."

Dick, he stopped smilin'. That remark pissed off *all* them hardcases.

I decided it had gone on long enough, so I stepped between the Arrow and the Rockinghorse. "That's it! It's over. You Rockinghorse boys ride on back to the ranch. Shove them cows with you. Miss Jean, Miss Maggie, take your hands and go on back to work."

I thought for a minute she was gonna blow up on me. But finally she smiled, real slow-like, and nodded her head. "All right, Sheriff. Looks like you do have things under control. See you around. Come on, boys—let's ride!"

We watched until both brands was clear out of sight, and then strung a lead-rope on the dead-carryin' horses. We rode slow-like back towards Doubtful.

De Graff, he was oddly silent. I looked over at him, wonderin' what was the matter with him. Finally, I asked.

"I ain't got no problem, Sheriff. But you sure as hell do."

"Me!"

"Yeah." He grinned. "Miss Maggie likes you, and I think

Miss Jean does, too. And boy if that ain't touble on a cyclone level, why . . . I'll kiss your horse!"

Critter, he'd had just about enough of people who wanted to kiss on him . . . either end. He swung his head and bared his teeth at De Graff.

"Just kiddin', horse!" De Graff said, then looked at me. "Damned if I don't think he's got as much sense as I have."

"More."

It was noon when we rode into town. Folks started comin' out of the houses and the stores to stand on the boardwalk and look at us as we rode past slow.

We stopped in front of Doc Harrison's place and he come out to see what all the commotion was about. He looked quick at the bodies and then at me. I told him what had gone down, the Rockinghorse side of it.

"That's ridiculous!" he snapped. "Farris was no thief. He ran a completely honest operation and everybody knows it."

"Yes, sir. I 'spect he was an honest man, and his boys, too. But them Rockinghorse riders say they caught 'em with the stole cattle, and Farris and his boys can't rise up and talk to tell no different story, now can they?"

The Doc, he looked hard at me. "What do you intend doing about this . . . outrage, Sheriff?"

"Nothin' I can do, Doc. You know as well as me that hangin' a rustler or a cow thief is still as yet legal out here."

Doc Harrison mumbled something about livin' in the dark ages where law and order was concerned. Then he strung together a line of cusswords that would do any drunk puncher up proud. I never even knowed doctors and such knew them words.

I didn't know what to say, so I kept my mouth closed, and just let the Doc run hisself out of cusswords.

"I'll take these bodies on down to Truby's, Doc. Then I

reckon it's up to me to break the news to the Widder Farris. He was married still, wasn't he?"

"Unfortunately, yes, he was. But I should imagine Jean or Miss Maggie is already with the bereaved."

I knew what that word meant. Least he hadn't flung nothin' at me like that dis-concerted thing.

Just to be on the safe side, I rode over to the Quartermoon spread and asked Miss Pepper if she'd like to ride over to the Widder, Farris's with me. I wanted them astride-ridin' females to know I was about halfways taken.

Mister Rolf, he shook his head at my tellin' of the news. "I worry about you, Sheriff. This valley is going to run red with blood before long, and you're going to be caught up right in the middle of it all."

"That's part of my job, Mister Baker. And I ain't never backed away from a job yet."

"Yes," he smiled grudgingly. "You do have a bulldog tenacity about you. It's a very admirable trait, to be sure."

I mumbled something. Hell, I don't know what it was he'd just said!

"But," Mister Rolf said, "my daughter is quite smitten with you. And I'm rather fond of you myself, and so is Martha. We would not like to see you hurt . . . or killed," he added grimly.

I didn't wanna appear like I was bein' smartalecky, but gettin' killed wouldn't thrill me all that much, neither.

'Bout that time Pepper come out and we pulled out. I'd left Critter at the spread and drove a buggy, with Pepper sittin' close beside me. Sittin' that close, I was proud I'd taken me a good bath the night before over to the Chinaman's place.

We'd been gettin' chummier and chummier as the days drifted by, and both of us knowed something was gonna happen between us . . . so we had taken to bein' real proper with each other.

Last time we'd embraced and kissed, both of us had started a-grabbin' hold of things that was best not grabbed a-hold of by two people who wasn't hitched proper. Unless the female was a soiled dove, that is. Then it didn't make no difference what a feller grabbed a-hold of. Or got grabbed.

But Miss Pepper wasn't no soiled dove, and I was bound and determined to treat her like a lady . . . whether she wanted to be treated thataway, or not.

Lots of men think that a woman don't have no awakenin' feelin's like a man. I always figured that for bulldooky. They got feelin's that are sometimes stronger than a man's Not that I was no expert hand when it come to women, I wasn't. But ever since Mary Lou Robinson took me in her pa's barn one Sunday afternoon and commenced to show me the difference between boys and girls, I been plumb amazed at how inventive womenfolks can get at times.

And damned demandin', too!

I recollect one time down in . . . Miss Pepper, she picked that time to look at me.

"Why, Cotton! You're actually blushing!"

"Am not!" I knowed I was, but damned if I was gonna admit it.

"You are too."

"It's the sun, that's all."

"Crap!" she said daringly. I give her a dark look—a woman could get *too* bold. "Cotton, if you got any darker, you'd pass for an Indian. Come on!" She tickled me in the ribs and I about dropped the reins. "You can tell me."

"Pepper, now, you better quit that stuff. You remember where it got us last time."

"I rather enjoyed it. Didn't you?" she teased, leanin' closer and blowin' in my ear.

I tell y'all, sometimes it's hard to remain a gentleman.

"I bet you were thinking of another girl, now, weren't you?"

Reckon how she knew that? "As a matter of fact, I was thinkin' of a girl I knowed back in grade school."

"Oh. Well. I see. Were you enthralled with her, Cotton?"

"I was plumb *amazed* at some of her."

"What an odd statement."

"I guess so. Pepper, is there some land for sale around here? Maybe an established spread that somebody wants to unload for a fair price?"

"Yes." She smiled at me, her blues twinkling. "Are you planning on staying, Cotton?"

"I been thinkin' about it."

She touched my arm. "I hope you never leave."

There come the goo again.

Sure enough, Miss Jean and Miss Maggie was already at the little Farris spread.

The cowboy who was told by Miss Jean that she could stomp her own snakes was standin' outside by the corral when we pulled up.

"That's the foreman at Arrow," Pepper told me, "Jesse Bates. He was a cavalryman during the recent . . . unpleasantness between the States. He rode for the Gray. An officer, I believe."

The unpleasantness? One hell of a war, if you's to ask me. But I figured he'd been in the Army; that would account for the way he sat his saddle.

She said, "He's a good man and a good person. And quick with a pistol, too."

And that was good to know, too. "All them Arrow hands I seen shaped up in my mind to be some pretty salty ol' boys."

"They'll fight," Pepper agreed. "Just as will the men who ride for my father and brother. They're not paid gunhands, but to a man, they're loyal to the brand. Most of Father's hands have been with him a long time. He only hires others when they have to make a drive, and sometimes during branding."

Pepper introduced me to the tall foreman and we howdied and shook. He sized me up while I was doin' the same to him. I got the feelin' that this Jesse Bates would be rough as a cob if a man was to push him. And I could detect just a hint of suspicion or wariness in his eyes as he give me the once-over. But I didn't take no offense at it, it was a natural thing to do.

When damn near every man you seen was packin' iron, it's a good thing to know how the other man carries hisself. And hell, he didn't know, really, what side I was on. But without his sayin' it out loud, I could tell he'd heard of me down the line.

He might have even taken a trip or two down the hoot-owl trail before settlin' down. Lots of men have.

"The missus is takin' it pretty hard," Jesse said. "And the regular hands Farris has workin' for him is talkin' up trouble. They're over to the bunkhouse. You'd better talk to them. Sheriff, see if you can settle them down. They're all good cowhands, but up against the Rockinghorse gunslicks, they won't have a chance."

That made sense to me. I liked a man who knowed when to fight and when to back off and ruminate on the matter facin' him. Although I sometimes jumped right in without thinkin'. I knew how Farris's men was feelin'. I'd been there a time or two.

Pepper with me, I spoke to the widder woman. There was a whole passel of females in the house with her. As soon as I tipped my hat and stayed a respectable time, I got the hell out of there. I just wasn't no good when it come to consolin' folks after a death. Pepper stayed with the women and me and Jesse strolled over to the bunkhouse.

Sure enough, them hands was cleanin' guns and fillin' up belt loops with .44 rounds.

To a man, they give me some fairly bleak looks.

"You boys plannin' on startin' a war all by yourselves?" I asked.

"Law won't do nuttin'," one hand said sourly. "So I guess that leaves it up to us, right, Sheriff?"

"The law *cain't* do nothin'," I told him, holdin' my temper in check. Not something I'm real good at doin'. But this hand was speakin' out of anger and frustration, and I knowed it. Wasn't no personal slight agin' me. "You boys know how it is out here, just as good as me. Sure, it was a setup, I know that. And if I thought it'd do any good, I'd arrest all them that done the deed. But Judge Barbeau would just cut them loose. There ain't no evidence to prove the Rockinghorse bunch done wrong. Think about it from the law's side."

They had stopped war-preparation and was lookin' at me, listenin'. And I knew I'd better say whatever it was I was gonna say right. "It's spring, boys. The Widder Farris needs you here. There's cattle to be brung in, shifted to the high country. Cuttin' and brandin' to be done. She can't do that by herself."

I could see that they agreed with me, but they was men with men's feelin's. They'd been struck at, and now they wanted to strike back. But I knew they didn't have a snowball's chance in Hell of comin' out of it alive.

"Now, look boys . . . it's gonna come down to a war. You know it, and I know it. But now ain't the time for that. What you all have to do is get organized, get together. Little ranchers, farmers, sheepmen . . . you all got to start pullin' in double harness. You got to get strong. You got to be able to back up your beliefs with more than mouth. And more than that, you got to start bein' real careful not to let none of these high-paid gunslicks pull you into tryin' to match 'em on the draw. I figure that's comin' next. You boys followin' me?"

"Makes some sense," an older hand said. I figured him for the foreman. "Keep talkin', Sheriff."

Jesse Bates was leanin' up agin' the bunkhouse wall, lookin' at me. But this time, there was a different light in his eyes. All the earlier suspicion was gone from his face.

"Maybe you boys can't match the Circle L and the Rockinghorse with gun-speed—damn few men can—but if all of you got together, all thinkin' alike, you'd have them outnumbered." I waved a hand. "Four men here, two there, six over yonder—it starts to add up then."

"I got to agree with you," a puncher said. "But I dearly hate that gawddamn barbed wire them nesters is stringin' around the valley."

There was a low mumble of agreement with that. The day when farmer and rancher was goin' to get along real nice was still some years away. But maybe it could start right here in this valley. It was worth a try.

"I hate it worser. I got tangled up in it once. But the wire is here to stay, and we're all gonna be seein' more of it. You can't blame a nester for wantin' to protect what he planted."

We talked some more, and I could feel the fight slowly leavin' out of the hands. I was feelin' some better when me and Jesse walked back to the corral to wait for the women to come out of the house.

Miss Jean, Miss Maggie, and Miss Pepper soon joined us.

Jesse, he jerked a gloved thumb at me. "The sheriff, he pulled the fuse outta the dynamite. The hands is calmed down right smart." Briefly, he explained to the women what I'd said about bandin' together for strength as well as protection.

I was conscious of all them women lookin' at me real close.

Pepper looked at me and smiled. "So you can not only use a gun with the best of them, but you're a peacemaker as well."

I grinned. "You reckon that's why a Colt is called a Peacemaker?"

Chapter Eight

The mood of the town, at least the biggest portion of it, was ugly after the double-hangin' and the shootin' of the young man. And folks were, for the first time, openly choosin' up sides.

Me, I was glad to see that part of it. Now, when it come down to the nut-cuttin', I'd be able to know who was lined up solid behind who. Helps relieve that itchy feelin' you get in the small of your back.

And folks was definitely makin' their choices known, and they wasn't makin' no bones about it, neither.

It surprised me some, although later thinkin' on it, it shouldn't have, but Miss Mary at the Wolf's Den lined up square behind the Circle L and the Rockinghorse crews. The man who ran the gun shop, he was with them, too, as was the man who owned the livery stable and the lumber mill. It just kinda crisscrossed the street, back and forth. But more was on the side of peace than was on the side of Mills and Lawrence.

The funeral was a right nice one. But me and the boys skipped the church services. I just couldn't sit through another of the Reverend Dolittle's long-winded sermons. I knowed a preacher once who liked to say that more souls was won in the first five minutes and more souls lost in the last five minutes of preachin'. I figure that preacher knowed what he was talkin' about. He kept them talks of his short and to the point—'specially when there was eatin' on the grounds. He didn't like for the fried chicken to get too cold.

Course, he never ate none of Miss Pepper's chicken, neither.

The fellow who run the little weekly two-page paper—*The Doubtful Informer*—he come out squarely on the side of law and order, runnin' some pretty hot pieces about men who think they're better than other folks and who think they're above the law. Bernard Pritcher was his name. He was a feisty little feller. I went to see Mister Pritcher.

"Mister Pritcher, I'm right proud you run this here article in the paper, but don't you think you could have calmed 'er down just a mite? The way I see it, you just about called A.J. and Matt lowdown sons of bitches. I mean, you're settin' yourself up to get burned out or shot or something awful."

"Young man, the pen is mightier than the sword."

"Say what?"

Pritcher, he adjusted his glasses and took a deep breath. *"Hinc quam sic calamus saevior ense, patet,* Sheriff."

Only thing I understood out of that mess was the word Sheriff. I didn't know whether to ask him if he was sick or to haul off and slap the piss out of him for cussin' me. "Did you just swaller a bug or something?"

He smiled. "No, Sheriff. Let me explain. Cervantes said . . . you are, of course, familiar with Cervantes?"

"Oh, hell, yeah! Holed up one winter with him up near Fort Peck."

Pritcher laughed. "Very funny, Sheriff. You have a wonderful sense of humor."

"Yeah, that's me. One laugh after another."

"Cervantes said, 'Let none presume to tell me that the pen is preferable to the sword.' But then Robert Burton wrote what I just quoted you. The pen worse than the sword. Then in *Riche-lieu*, act two, Bulwer-Lytton wrote the line, 'The pen is might-ier than the sword.'"

"Do tell?"

"Yes. Sheriff Cotton, I am not afraid of hooligans and row-dies. I firmly believe that the truth shall make you free."

"Yeah? I'll tell you something else it'll do, Mister Pritcher. It'll get your ass killed sometimes, too."

"Poppycock and balderdash, Sheriff!" he hollered. "The people are guaranteed a free press. And I shall ring loudly the bell of freedom and liberty."

The little man was workin' up to a full head of steam. I wanted to cut him off 'fore he topped the grade. "Mister Pritcher, are you any kin to the Reverend Sam Dolittle?"

"What? Why, no. Why do you ask, Sheriff?"

"Just curious. Listen, can you print something up for me?"

"Certainly."

I handed him the paper I'd printed the words on and he read it quick. "Will I be allowed to correct the spelling. Sheriff?"

"Oh, sure. And word it different if you want to. I just want folks to be able to understand it."

"Oh, they'll understand, all right. It's free of charge, Sher-iff." He smiled. "I want to see the faces of the Circle L and the Rockinghorse hoodlums when they read this."

"For a fact, they ain't none of them gonna be too happy about it."

"Did you OK this with the town council?"

"Sure did. I just left George Waller's place of business."

"That's all I needed. The posters will be ready in two days."

"Thank you."

Me, I went courtin' Miss Pepper. I figured, and figured right, that when I started havin' them notices tacked up all over the big valley, I was gonna be plenty busy.

NOTICE—THESE RULES GO INTO EFFECT
RIGHT NOW

NO SHOOTING OFF GUNS IN THE TOWN OF
DOUBTFUL.
NO GALLOPING HORSES IN TOWN.
NO HORSE RACING IN TOWN.
REIN YOUR HORSE IN FAVOR OF PEOPLE
WALKING IN THE STREET.
VIOLATORS WILL BE JAILED AND FINED.

Me and Rusty and De Graff and Burtell, we spent one whole afternoon tackin' up them notices all over the valley. The boys didn't mind it none, anything they could do from the hurricane deck of a horse was all right with them.

Then we sat back and waiting for the action to get started.

It was just after breakfast, and we was sittin' in front of the office when Rusty poked me in the ribs. "Look who's gonna be the first ones to test the new rules, Sheriff." He pointed up the street.

A.J. Junior and two hands from the ranch was just comin' into view, turnin' their horses onto the main street of town.

"You reckon they've seen the signs?" De Graff asked.

"They've seen 'em. They ain't blind. We plastered them signs all over the valley. But them two with Junior?" I couldn't make neither of them out. Only way I recognized Junior was his horse.

"I don't know 'em," Burtell said, squintin' his eyes. "But I can tell from this distance that they're hardcases."

As they come closer, I silently agreed with Burtell. 'Cause I knowed both of them ol' boys. The gunhand ridin' the dun was Ike Burdette. The other was Dave Tunsall. Both of them Texas gunfighters; and both of 'em mean as snakes.

I shifted my chew and spat into the street. Then I informed the boys who they was.

Burtell, he had just finished rollin' him a smoke and lickin' it closed. He lit up just as Rusty said, "I heard of 'em both. But I can't believe just the two of them are here to start something."

I shook my head, not takin' my eyes off the three riders. "I don't think so either. I think they're in town to test the waaters."

We sat on the chairs and benches in front of the office and watched as Junior and his escort rode slowly by.

"Mornin, Junior!" I called out cheerfully. "Nice day, ain't it?

Junior, he give me a look that silently told me where I could stick my right friendly salutations. That'd probably be uncomfortable, too.

"Mornin', Dave, Ike!" I called.

Them Texas gunfighters, they knew me, but they looked at me and kept on ridin'. Plumb unfriendly of them.

"Surly bunch of bastards!" De Graff said.

"Hope y'all have a nice day in town!" I called. "And behave yourselves, too," I added, pushin' just a little bit.

None of the three paid much attention to my words. Just kept on ridin' and turned and reined in at the hitchrail in front of the Wolf's Den. They disappeared into the batwings.

"Do we amble on over there with 'em?" Rusty asked.

"Nope. I ain't gonna push no more as long as they behave themselves. Time's gonna come for shootin' soon enough.

"Well, right yonder is young Hugh Mills," Burrell said, noddin' his head towards the other end of the long main street.

I looked. I'd seen Young Hugh a time or two in town. He was a surly-lookin', pouty-mouthed, always-sulled-up young man. But my, my, he had him two of the fanciest short guns I ever did see. Wore 'em low and tied down. And I'd heard that he could use them, too.

If I was to work at it real hard, and I'd have to work at it, 'cause I never was one to envy much on other folk's possessions, I could surely covet them guns of Young Hugh's. They was a matched set of Peacemaker .45's, engraved and ivory-handled and restin' in embossed leather holsters. Lordy, but they was some fine!

That set would cost the average cowpoke a good three months' wages, or more.

"I heard he can use them guns," I said.

"Yes, he can," De Graff answered me. "He's uncommon quick. And just like Junior, he's spoiled, uppity, and about half nuts. Last year, Hugh rode down a young Mex boy who was out tendin' sheep. Just rode him down and trampled him to death. He's a bad one, Sheriff. And unpredictable."

"No charges brung agin him for the death of that boy?"

"Sure. But Judge Barbeau cut him loose," Rusty told me. "Hugh told the judge that he lost control of his horse. It was an accident."

"Somebody ought to shoot that judge," Burtell spoke aloud everybody's feelin's. He looked at the two men with Hugh. "Anybody know them two with him?"

"The one on the right is called Bitter Creek," I said. "The other one is known as Tulsa Jack. I think his real name is Wolcott. They're both quick with a gun."

And I silently wondered how many more gunslingers was gonna show up in the big valley. Place was beginnin' to look like a convention spot for killers.

I cut my eyes as George Waller come rushin' up the boardwalk. He was all in a sweat for this early in the day. He was movin' like a man with a powerful message to deliver.

"Sheriff!" he panted. "Injun Tom Johnson checked into the hotel late last night. The situation is just simply getting out of hand."

"Yeah," I sat still, mentally digestin' the news of the gunfighter called Injun Tom. He got his name 'cause he preferred squaws over white women. Rumor had it that Injun Tom had fathered a whole tribe of younguns over the years; and I didn't doubt it none. Injun Tom was a bad one, too . . . just bad through and through. And ugly! Lordy, Tom was ugly. It was said he was so ugly his momma had to tie a piece of salt meat around his neck to attract flies.

Gettin' to my feet, I said, "You boys mind the store. Me and Rusty's gonna move around some."

Walkin' up the boardwalk, Rusty said, "Reckon when Billy the Kid is gonna show up? Damn near ever'body that is somebody with a short gun is already done arrived." He shook his head. "And the worst of 'em ain't made it yet."

I knew who he was talkin' about. Jack Crow. I wasn't lookin' forward to his arrival.

"I hear that Billy's gone plumb bad now that Tunstall and McSween's dead."

"So I heard. He's gone to stealin' horses and rustlin' cattle. Somebody'll get him."

"Somebody always does. There's always somebody just a tad better with a gun, or just plain lucky."

"I heard his friend Pat Garrett is now sayin' that Billy's no good."

"He ought to know, I reckon. I seen Pat a couple of times when I was down south on a cattle buy. I hear he's gonna run for Sheriff of Lincoln County."

"Do tell? I thought he was a lawman all along."

"Naw. Last time I seen him he was tendin' bar at Beaver Smith's saloon at Fort Sumner."

"Well, I'll just be damned! Stories do get started, don't they? Next you gonna tell me that Billy wasn't raised up by the Apaches."

"Where'd you hear that? Billy was born in New York. He didn't come west 'til he was about thirteen. Didn't kill his first man 'til a couple of years ago. '77, I think it was."

"Ain't that something? I read in one of them penny-dreadful books that he was toted off by 'Paches and raised up with 'em."

"I read where I rode with the James Gang, too, Rusty. But I ain't never set my eyes on Jesse or Frank. And ain't never been to Missouri, neither."

"I read that same book," Rusty said solemnly. "That's what I was thinkin' about that day I braced you over at the saloon. Sheriff, you got one hell of a reputation."

I didn't reply to that, for my eyes had found yet another hardcase leanin' up agin' the front of the Wolf's Den. "See that ol' boy over yonder, Rusty?"

"The stranger by the batwings?"

"Yeah. That's Pete Clanton, the Montana gunhand. And wherever Pete goes, you can bet Bob Clay ain't very far away. Them two is close; first cousins, I think." I give out with a long sigh.

Place sure was fillin' up in a hurry . . . with the wrong kind of people.

"What's the matter with you? 'Sides bein' in love, that is?" Rusty grinned. "And havin' Miss Maggie and Miss Jean with the hots for your body."

I didn't deny the love bit. But I ignored that last bit. "'Way my luck's been runnin' here of late, the third member of that nasty little group will probably be hangin' around close by, too. If so, I gotta arrest him."

"You know this third person?"

"You've seen dodgers on him. His name is Al Long."

Rusty whistled softly. "'Deed I have, Sheriff. He's 'posed to be snake-quick."

"Yes, he is. And there he is."

Rusty followed the direction of my eyes. "The man wearin' the buckskin shirt?"

"That's him."

"Who's the man standin' beside him?"

"All I know is Nimrod. Far as I know, he ain't wanted for nothin'. That anybody can prove, that is."

"Nimrod? Didn't he kill that rancher over in California?"

"Was accused of it, so I heard. But it was a fair fight, so-called. The rancher just wasn't no gunhand, that's all."

"How you gonna handle it, Sheriff?"

"Only one way I know to handle it. Get the women and kids off the boardwalks, Rusty. There's gonna be a shootin'. I'll wait 'til you get things clear 'fore I make my move."

Boardin' House Belle come tippin' up the boardwalk and batted her eyes at me, then stepped into a store. As if I didn't have enough on my mind without her makin' eyes at me.

Now, I wasn't gonna brace Al Long purely out of civic responsibility . . . although that did have something to do with it. The bottom line was that three-thousand-dollar reward on Al's head. And I aimed to use that money to stock my ranch.

Rusty, he was movin' quiet-like but swift up and down the boardwalks, clearin' the area of folks. Al, he still had his back to me, jawin' with some other hardcases. I didn't want no innocent people to get hit by stray bullets, and that happened a hell of a lot more times than people care to talk about.

I looked up at the second story of the Wolf's Den. A couple of soiled doves waved at me. I motioned them to get down and they done it.

Must have been a slow night for them gals to be up and about this early in the mornin'.

Just as I was about to step out into the street and holler for Al to give it up or drag iron, the fanciest hearse I ever did see come a-rollin' into town. It was deep polished black with glass sides—covered now to prevent breakage durin' transport—and lots of silver on it. Then I 'membered that Truby, he told me he had ordered one from a funeral parlor down south of us. The undertakers who'd sold it was named Harder and Stiff. That was an odd enough name for undertakers; but down in Cochise County, Arizona Territory, there was a funeral parlor run by two men called Ritter & Ream.

And then I got to thinkin'. Who was gonna be the first to ride in that fancy death-wagon . . . me, or Al Long?

But you can't dwell on stuff like that for very long . . . gets to be depressin'.

I checked the street, both sides, up and down, and it was clear. Steppin' off the boardwalk, I called out.

"Al Long!"

Al, he spun around, facin' me, his hands clawed, over his gun butts. He peered hard at me. "Cotton? Is that you, kid?"

"Yeah, it's me, Al."

"I was told you was up in Montana."

"I was. But now I'm here. Sheriff of Puma County. You're under arrest, Al. Stagecoach robbin', bank robbin', train robbin', and murder. Give it up, Al."

He laughed at me. "And face a rope? That ain't no choice at all, Cotton. 'Sides, I don't think you're as good as your reputation."

"One way to find out, Al."

"Damn sure is, kid!" Then he grabbed for iron.

I was faster. But as he jerked iron, he ducked to one side and my slug whined off a horse trough. His bullet tore the hat right off my head. I stepped back and held off shootin' for fear I'd hit some onlooker standin' in a store a-gawkin'. Long, he popped up in an alleyway and fired just as I jumped to my left. His slug thudded into the building behind where I'd been standin'.

Al, he fired again, and again he missed, his slug bustin' out a window of the store.

I heard Boardin' House Belle give out a whoop that would put an Apache to shame and then she hit the floor. I could feel the vibration clear out in the street. I hoped to hell she wasn't dead. It'd take two teams of carpenters a full day to build a box big enough to hold her.

Not to mention a dozen hernias on the men havin' to tote it with her in it.

The lead really started flyin' and whinin' around my head as Al opened up with both pistols. But the street was wide and Al, while bein' fast, wasn't no real good pistol shooter at long range. Regardless, I done some rollin' and come up behind a fire barrel full of water. Gettin' to one knee, I cocked back and let it bark. One slug hit Al in the chest and the second one caught him in the shoulder. He was hard hit, but a long ways from bein' out of it.

Al, he staggered up to his feet and reached around behind him. I knowed that trick of his; he carried a third gun stuck down behind his belt, in the small of his back, under his buckskin shirt.

"You son of a bitch!" he cussed me, blood leakin' out of his mouth. "You've killed me. But you ain't gonna be hoss enough to stop my brothers."

"Drop your gun, Al."

"Hell with you!"

I waited until his pistol was in plain sight and he'd jacked the hammer back, then I shot him right between the eyes. He just sat down on the edge of the boardwalk, his head slumped between his legs, the pistol slippin' from dead fingers. He sat there, dead as a hammer.

Rusty, he come runnin' up just as Burtell and De Graff come up from the other side.

"Get the photo-grapher," I told Burtell. "I want pitchers to show the U.S. Marshals."

Injun Tom had stepped out of the hotel, standin' watchin'. Tunsall and Burdette and Bitter Creek and Tulsa had come out of the saloon to see the action. Injun Tom, he smiled— even that didn't do nothin' to improve his looks—and held out his hands, palms up, showin' me he wasn't takin' no part in nothin'. Yet.

I nodded at him and turned to face the men on the boardwalk in front of the Wolf's Den, across the street. They wasn't makin' no moves to join in, but I'm a right suspicious man at times.

"Clear the street or I'll have to figure you're all partners of Al Long!" I called out. "And we'll have us a slaughter right here and now."

De Graff and Rusty was carryin' Henry rifles and they levered them. Them gunhands turned and walked back into the saloon.

Oh, they wasn't afraid. It just wasn't the right time.

A big crowd started gatherin' around. Truby, at the direction of the picture-takin' man from the studio, stuck a board behind Al Long to prop him up. Truby used a piece of string to tie Al's head back, then plopped his hat back on his head. The hat hid the twine, but left the hole in Al's head showin', the blood leakin' out.

The photo man, name of Langford, set up all his fancy equipment and began poppin' and puffin' up smoke takin' pictures of Al. 'Bout that time Doc Harrison come up. He waited until Langford was donē, then he inspected the body, officially proclaimin' Al was dead.

I duly noted the time in my little notebook and had the Doc sign it and date it, all legal-like and proper.

Leo Silverman, he come out of his store, wipin' his hands on his apron. "You can show him off in my window, Martin," he told the undertaker. Leo leaned over and sniffed at Al. "Until he starts turnin' ripe, that is."

Truby looked at me. I shrugged my shoulders. "Suits me." But I could tell the Doc, he didn't like the idea at all.

But that's the way it was back in the wild and woolly days. Most folks wanted to take a glance or two at dead outlaws. The ladies would go "oohh" and "aahh" and get all flustered and act like it offended 'em—with everybody knowin' it didn't. And the men would puff up and say something like, "He got what he deserved." There just wasn't a whole hell of a lot in the way of entertainment in small western towns.

I went through Al's pockets and found enough to bury him

decent—even if, when Al was alive, he wasn't decent. I give the money to Truby and he give me a receipt for it.

I took ever'thing else of Al's, stickin' his personal belongings in a bag that I'd give to the U.S. Marshals. Then I sent Burtell ridin' south to the telegraph office to wire the Marshals.

Boardin' House Belle, she came waddlin' out of the store and batted her eyes at me a time or two. "What a brave man you are, Sheriff," she gushed. "So . . . *manly!*"

Then she went trippin' off up the boardwalk.

"I do believe Miss Belle has taken a fancy to you, Sheriff Cotton," George Waller said.

I wasn't fixin' to reply to that. "George, how come Doubtful don't have no telegraph office? It's the biggest town in the county."

"The poles have been up for some time. But every time wire is strung, somebody pulls it all down."

"Why do a damn fool thing like that? Is it Injuns doin' it?"

Bernard Pritcher come walkin' up just in time to hear me. "Certainly it is not Indians. Certain . . . *types* in the valley prefer to remain isolated from the rest of the world . . . and that is the truth."

"Meanin' the Circle L and the Rockinghorse bunch?" I asked him.

"But of course."

"But that don't make no sense to me at all, Mister Pritcher. Why do a damn fool thing like that?"

"Sheriff," Pritcher said, puffin' up. It was lecture time agin. "The Circle L and the Rockinghorse led the drive to stop Doubtful from becoming the county seat. It's still in contest, but it looks like we are going to be the seat of county government. Now then, as isolated as we are, if a crime of some heinous nature was committed, before you became sheriff, by the time outside authorities got here, witnesses would have either changed their minds, or would have disappeared. We have a system of feudal barony here in the valley, Sheriff Cotton."

Now, I didn't know what in the hell he just said, and from the look on Waller's face, he didn't neither.

But we both nodded our heads.

And with my head hangin' out bare, that reminded me that I needed a new hat. That .44 slug from Al's gun had tore the top plumb out of my good hat.

Pritcher, he walked off.

"Foodal *what?*" I asked George.

"Hell, don't ask me! Pritcher gets on them wordy rips of his and cain't nobody understand what the hell he's talkin' about."

"North end of the street," De Graff said softly.

I looked, then give out a long, slow sigh. Then I cussed under my breath in case they was ladies within range.

"What's the matter, Sheriff?" Waller asked.

"The Springer Brothers. Dan, Clemmet, Sid, and Barry. They must have just come up from New Mexico way. Last I heard, they was workin' the Lincoln County Wars."

"Are they bad hombres?"

"Between the four of them, they've tallied more than a hundred kills, and that's con-firmed. So yeah, I'd say they was some bad."

Waller, he turned a little green around the lips. "And did I hear that man you just killed say something about his brothers, Sheriff?"

"You sure did. Luther, Stan, and Cledus. Three of the most no-good men who ever hauled on a pair of boots. But they're quick with a gun."

De Graff, he done some head-figurin'. "You know, Sheriff, just figurin' all these hardcases is gettin' paid, say, seventy-five dollars a month—and some of them is gettin' more than that—I've counted forty or more gunslicks. That's . . . well, damn close to thirty-five hundred dollars a month in wages for them alone. Not even the Circle L and the Rockinghorse can keep that up for very long."

"But maybe long enough to see their plans come true," I spoke with bitterness on my tongue.

"And their plans are . . . ?" George Waller asked.

"First off . . . to see us dead!"

Chapter Nine

As soon as Burtell got back from the telegraph office, I gathered the boys around me in the office and laid it out to them. Way things was shapin' up, I figured they ought to have a choice, and I give them one.

"I wouldn't hold it agin' none of you if you all was to quit, boys. You ain't gettin' paid enough to put your butts on the line. The way I see it, we're soon gonna have more than fifty gun-fighters in this valley. It can't do nothin' 'cept get worser."

"And you Sheriff?" De Graff asked. "What about you?"

"I'm gonna stick it out. But then, I never did have no sense to begin with. You boys can drift; find yourselves a nice peaceful job of work punchin' cows around."

They all laughed at that, and I joined right in. Believe you me, there wasn't nothin' peaceful about bein' a cowhand. If a man wasn't fightin' rustlers and Injuns, he was fightin' rainstorms and tornaders, eatin' dust twelve hours a day, and beans and beef three times a day. At times, it got plain wearisome.

And if he was lucky, he was gettin' thirty-five dollars a month for it.

Rusty, he got up out of his chair and walked to the window, starin' out at the street. Without turnin' around, he said, "I been seein' me a little gal out in the country. Her pa has him a right nice farm. And I've had my eyes on a little piece of ground down south of here, 'bout twenty miles out. I want that ground. It could easy handle five hundred head of cows; raise me some horses, plant a garden. I figure I got me a stake in this town. So I ain't leavin'."

Noddin' my head, I said, "Your choice."

De Graff, he shifted his chaw around and looked square at me. "I like the idea of bein' a lawman. The right kinds of folks look up to you. Sorta look to a man to help them. I believe with this badge," he pecked on the star, "that a man has to con-duct hisself right; so's kids and the such will have somebody outside the home to look up to. I'm stayin'."

"Well, now, ain't that a right flowery speech," Burtell said with a grin. He jerked a thumb toward De Graff. "I agree with whatever the hell it was he said. I'm stayin' put."

I felt close to them ol' boys right at that moment. Like we was all part of a family. But I had to admit that it wasn't a right bright thing on our part, us stickin' around. Countin' the regular hands of the Rockinghorse and the Circle L, we was gonna be outnumbered about twenty-five to one when it came down to the nut-cuttin'. And them odds ain't good no matter how you look at them.

"Don't expect no hand-clappin' or medals to be hung on you when it's over," I warned them. "Those of us who are alive, that is. When all the shootin' is done, and the smoke all blowed away, folks is gonna start lookin' at us strange-like."

They nodded their heads. They knew what I was sayin' was true. After a town was all cleaned up, and it was safe for the ladies to stroll around unescorted, them that done the cleanin'-up usually didn't stick around long. 'Cause folks didn't have no more use for you. Human nature, I reckon, but it never did seem fair to me.

Maybe in this case, with Rusty and Burtell and De Graff

bein' known by most, it might be some different, but I doubted it.

I had me an idea that'd been roamin' around in my noggin for a few days. It was gonna be a chancy thing on my part, but with all these gunslicks comin' into the valley, I felt it was something that I had to do.

So, the next mornin', leavin' Rusty in charge, I just, by God, done it!

The boys, they didn't like it none, and they wasn't hesitant a bit about tellin' me their feelings on the matter. But I been known to be right stubborn at times, so before first light, I was saddled up and movin' out.

I wasn't long outside of town when I seen what at least a few hands thought of them signs me and the boys tacked up.

Every sign I come to had been shot all to pieces. And a couple of them had been used in place of paper and cobs. That didn't set too well with me.

I headed north for the first job of the day, cuttin' across Arrow range and then before long, I was on Rockinghorse land. The regular hands, they'd had their breakfast before dawn and was out workin' cattle, gettin' ready for a gather. The smoke from brandin' fires could be smelled wherever I rode.

Mostly, the punchers would stop their work and stand and watch silent as I rode past, headin' for the big house of Matt Mills. Some of them spoke to me, and I returned the greetin', as pleasant as the morning. But I could feel the hate in the eyes of a whole bunch of them, too.

But I spoke to them, too, real pleasant-like. They didn't like it; I got a kick out of it.

The first gunslicks I met up with was Hank Hawthorne and Dick Avedon.

I reined up and greeted them.

They sat their horses and stared at me until Dick found his voice. "Cotton, you damned fool! You never did have no sense, but this mornin' just proves to me that you're gawd-damn crazy!"

"Why?" I acted like I didn't know what he was talkin' about. "I'm peaceful, Dick. Besides, I'm the sheriff of this county." More or less. "And I can ride wherever and when-ever I please to ride. Right now, I'm headin' for a palaver with Mister Matt Mills. You two wanna ride along with me?"

They looked at one another, and finally, both of them grinned. Hank said, "You got more gall than Colonel Custer, Cotton. But yeah, we'll tag along. Somebody's gonna have to tote you back to town when Young Hugh shoots you full of holes."

I grinned at them. "How's he gonna do that? Shoot me in the back?"

Dick, he shook his head. "Don't sell the kid short, Cotton. The boy is uncommon quick with a six-shooter."

"I ain't seen none of his graveyards, Dick. All I've heard so far is mouth."

They didn't reply to that. So we walked our horses, ridin' easy in the saddle, all of us enjoyin' the coolness of mornin' in the high-up country. I didn't ask what they'd been doin' out here so early, and neither of them volunteered any informa-tion on the subject.

"Fine spread," I observed. "All that any man could want, I reckon. All I'd want." I let that simmer silent for a minute or so, knowin' one of them would pick up on it. Another thing I'd learned about most gunhands is that they liked to brag some.

Hank, he looked at me and smiled. "Yes, but greed is sometimes the great motivator, my boy."

Hank, he had him a full eighth-grade education, and he

liked to talk big words; but I wasn't sure that all the time Hank knew just what all them words really meant.

Like a few of the other gunhawks now in the valley, Hank could be likeable . . . but he was a cold-blooded killer, and it was best to keep that out front at all times.

"Valley's fillin' with hardcases," I tossed that one to them.

"That scare you, Cotton?" Dick asked, a not-too-pleasant grin on his face.

"Just scares me half to death, Dick. Why, I cried myself to sleep last night just thinkin' about how scared I was of people who ain't done an honest day's work in ten years."

Hank, he looked insulted at that. "Ain't no need to get testy about it, Cotton. We're friendly this morning."

"All right." We rode along for a spell and then I said, "You boys is drawin' fightin' wages. Ain't neither one of you watched the ass-end of a cow in hears. You've fought in range wars; you've probably rode the hoot-owl trail a time or two. But you ain't never kilt no lawman—that I know of. Times is changin' some, boys. Slow-like, but a change is comin' on. The trains and the long wires, they're linkin' up lawmen all over the country. Now, as soon as one lawman is kilt in California or Montana, them sheriffs and deputies in Kansas and Louisiana know about it within a week or so. Places to run is gettin' harder and harder to find."

"Where is all this jabber takin' us to, Cotton?" Dick asked.

"Either of you ever seen the jail up in Helena, Montana?" They hadn't.

"Cost more'un ten thousand dollars to build."

"So?" Hank asked, but he knew what I was gettin' at. Folks was gettin' awful sick and tired of outlaws.

"Well, that jail's got a bunch of cells, an exercise yard, big kitchen, and sleep-in quarters for the guards. Damn near escape-proof. Boys, you know the citizens out here are gettin' tired of lawlessness and all that it brings with it. Jesse and

Frank got thousands of dollars of reward money on their heads. Clell Miller, Charly Pitts, Bill Chadwell and a whole host of others is rottin' in the ground, all shot to crap and back. The Youngers is in prison. Bill Longley was hanged down in Texas. Wes Hardin's in prison. Ya'll know what I'm talkin' about. Ain't neither one of you stupid."

They didn't say nothin' for a long while, and they didn't look at me neither. But I could practically hear their minds workin' hard.

Hank, he looked over at me and said softly, "Cotton, it's all we know."

"Yeah. But that don't make it right, boys. Lemme tell you both how this here thing is gonna go down. Me and my deputies might not come out of this alive. Some of us are probably gonna get killed. But not before we take a bunch of you with us. And you both know that crap writ in them dime novels is just that—crap! There ain't no gang, nowhere, no time, *ever* treed no western town. And it ain't never gonna happen neither. Now boys, them rules I writ up and tacked up around the county is gonna be enforced in Doubtful. If they're not, about a hundred or so townsfolks—all of 'em has fought Injuns and outlaws and been in the war—is gonna get their rifles and shotguns and blow you boys all to hell and gone."

They both was quiet, both of them knowin' the truth in what I just said. It was just a little hard for them to swaller and I knew it. I'd have felt the same way, I reckon.

I didn't know if my words was gonna have much leverage with 'em or not. But I knowed I had to try to convince some of these ol' boys to give it up and ride on out.

If they didn't ride on, well, then, at least when I had to kill some of them, I could do it with a clear conscience and the certain knowledge that I had done my dead level best.

"You damn shore of yourself, ain't you, Cotton?" Dick asked.

"Pretty sure, Dick." I kept my voice low and calm.

"All right. But what do we get if we was to just turn and ride on out?" Hank inquired.

"The knowledge that you won't be a part of any bloodbath, with innocent women and kids gettin' killed."

"That ain't enough. You can't win this one, Cotton. Not this time, no way. There's too many of us. We could take you and your boys out just anytime we wanted the job done—and you know that, too."

"Haufman could. He'd shoot me in the back. You boys might take me—and that's in some doubt, and *you* know that—but with ya'll, it'd be from the front, eyeball to eyeball. And I'd get lead in you, you both know that."

"Thanks for that much, anyway," Hank said. "But don't count on it. If we're paid to do a job of work with a gun, it'll get done the best and simplest way."

So there it was. He was tellin' me that if it had to be done, he'd shoot me in the back if it just had to be. Well, it was good to know. Sort of.

"We'll think on what you said." Dick looked at me. "For now, we'll ride on ahead, tell the others you're on your way in, and to let you come on in."

"I'll appreciate that, boys."

They was gone in a gallop, leavin' me alone for the next half hour or so. If I hadn't done nothin' else, I had at least planted a seed in their minds. There was another thing or two that I'd learned about the majority of gunfighters: they liked a sure thing.

It was a pretty ride to the mansion of Matt Mills. And for the last couple of miles, I stayed with the road. Mills kept it in damn good shape, scraped down and leveled out.

Pretty soon, I come up on the grand mansion of Matt Mills, and it was just as fancy as ol' A.J.'s palace. And looked just as out of place, even at this distance.

Any my, my, but there was a gang of them drawin' fightin' wages all gathered up around the house and the grounds, just sorta loungin' around, you might say. Tryin' not to look too obvious.

But it was so obvious it was almost funny. Howsomever, I kept a straight face. Laughin' at a situation like this was a good way to get plugged.

I guess it was good that I didn't have much goosiness in me, for if I had, I'd have turned around and got the hell out of there.

But I just rode right up and swung down, loopin' the reins around a hitchrail and then stared up at King Mills hisself, standin' on the big porch.

"Good mornin', Mister Mills," I said, just as nice as pie.

Matt, he grunted something. But his boy, Hugh, he stepped forward. "Let me handle this tin badge, Dad."

The father, he flung out his arm and stopped the son. "Just stand back, Hugh. The Sheriff is a guest—although uninvited—and he'll be afforded the courtesy of a guest." He looked at me. "What do you want, Sheriff?"

"Just to talk."

"Oh?" The man arched an eyebrow. "How interesting. Talk about what, Sheriff?"

"Puttin' an end to the trouble."

He smiled. "What trouble, Sheriff?"

I returned the smile. If that's the way he wanted to play it . . . "Well, sir, it's been so peaceful around the valley, and all, I thought I might see if we couldn't stir up some trouble just to liven things up a bit.

Dick Avedon, he laughed out loud at that.

"Well, Sheriff," Matt said. "You have a sense of humor about you. That's always good."

"I reckon I do, Mister Mills. But my sense of humor ends with nightriders and the hirin' of gunhands when there ain't no real good call for them. And the pushin' and shovin' of little people when you and A.J. Lawrence got enough land to do you."

"Well, I see now the reason for your riding out." He smiled . . . thinly. "Very well. Please come up on the porch, Sheriff. I'll have coffee sent out. Will it be necessary for the men to stay close?"

Before I could say anything, Matt he said, "Do you know the whole story, Sheriff?"

"I don't know whether I do or not. I'll be honest about that."

He nodded his head and I unbuckled and untied my gun belt, looping it over the saddle horn. But of course, it plumb slipped my mind to tell him about the two-shot derringer I had tucked down in my right boot. An oversight on my part.

"You men go on about your duties," Matt said, and the knot of gunhands began wanderin' off.

Duties, hell! They didn't have no duties. Half of 'em wouldn't saddle their own horse if there was somebody around to do it for them.

Young Hugh, he give me a dirty look and wandered away. I just didn't like that damned snooty young man. And I wasn't tellin' no lie about it, neither.

A Mex houseboy brought the coffeepot—some sort of fancy service, it was, all silver and some pretty little cups—and we sugared and sipped and sat for a minute or so. There was some sort of sissy-lookin' little cakes on another platter, but I left them alone. I wasn't about to eat nothin' that I don't know what it is, even though they did look pretty.

Matt busted the silence. "Land to do us. That's what you said, wasn't it, Sheriff?"

"Yes, sir, it is."

"Ummm. Well, Sheriff, let me say this: Long years ago, three young men came out west. Had we stayed back east, we would have inherited great wealth. But we were adventurous young men. Eager to break out of the calm east and strike west."

Lecture time agin.

"Admittedly," Matt said, "all of us had money in our trousers. None of us were destitute."

I thought I knew what that word meant.

"But I'll admit, that with our leavin', our families had warned that we were forever breakin' all ties with them. So we were takin' a chance. But, oh, we had such grand ideas. We were the first white men to actually settle in this area. The very first in this valley. It seems a lifetime, but really only twenty-odd years."

It was good coffee, and I'm a coffee-drinkin' man. So I just enjoyed the brew and kept my mouth shut, listenin'.

"Land to do us," he repeated. "Well, certainly you are correct in that assessment, Sheriff. But that isn't the point. The point is, all the land that the little ranchers and nesters have taken . . . is land that we fought for. A.J. Lawrence, Rolf Baker, and me."

And I knew what it was all about then. It wasn't no big mystery. It wasn't gold or oil or silver or nothin' like that. It was pride and greed, pure and simple.

But a lot of men have died for a hell of a lot less.

I reached for the coffeepot, but that houseboy, he was Johnny-on-the-spot. He beat me to it and poured my cup right full. I reckon a man could get used to such treatment; but I had a feelin' it might make a body uncommon lazy, not havin' to do nothin'.

Matt, he sighed. "But we weren't taking into consideration the Homestead Act, passed by Congress back in '62. As a matter of fact, none of us knew anything about it. News was very slow in reaching those of us who braved the elements and the savages out here. We didn't even know Lincoln had been shot until a year after it happened. You know what I'm talking about, Sheriff."

I did for a fact and said so. Many, many times, I had personal grabbed up a year-old newspaper from somewheres and read it slow, every page, even the ads, so hungry for news was I. But, hell, even year-old news beats no news at all. Most of the time.

I sipped my coffee and waited for Matt Mills to continue. He got him one of those little funny-lookin' cakes and et it right down. I still was dubious of them.

He swallered and said, "And then, Sheriff, all of a sudden, I looked up one day and there were squatters occupying land that me and my men had worked nigra-hard to clear. And yes, Sheriff Cotton, for many years I worked right alongside my men, just as Rolf and A.J. have done."

And I didn't doubt that none at all. You could look at these men and tell that they were still powerful strong men. Even if two of the three were kinda skally-waggy and mean, you had to respect them. You wouldn't be thinkin' right, if you didn't. Some might not agree with me, but them's the kind like them folks back east, in their law-and-order society, sittin' sippin' tea in their warm and secure homes. They just didn't have no idea what the west was like. Not no more they didn't. Now, their ancestors did, for they braved the New World. But for generations, them back east had had it fair comfortable. With police officers and constables to handle the riffraff and the rowdies.

Out here, man, you was alone. You had your wits and a good horse and gun that worked. And that was it, brother. And was gonna be that way for a few more years to come.

"I know what it's like to top a crest and look down at the Big Lonesome, Mister Mills. Knowin' there ain't another white person within a hundred miles, or more. I do know the feelin'."

"You're western-born, aren't you, Sheriff?"

"Yes, sir."

"And you're a straight-ahead, no-nonsense sort of man, aren't you?"

I had to think about that. "Well, yes sir, I reckon I am."

He smiled. "I will confess, that was a sight to see, you putting Junior in jail. He had no call to brace an officer of the law as he did."

Now, wait just a minute! Just hold the wagon. I seemed to recall Matt Mills was some put out about that whole affair, at the time. What the hell was goin' on?

"Seems to me, sir, that there ain't much respect for the law in this valley."

"Are you including me in that assessment, Sheriff Cotton?"

I took a chance. "Yes, sir. I am." I looked over at him. "You're hirin' gunslicks, ain't you?"

"You're not exactly unknown in that department yourself, Sheriff."

"That's true. But I never went on the prowl for no unarmed man; I never burnt nobody out and killed the livestock. I never done nothin' like this bunch you and A.J. has hired."

"You don't hold back, do you, Sheriff?"

"It ain't my way."

Matt, he give out a long sigh. "But I do have respect for the law. I suppose, in your eyes, it might not seem that I do. But I do. But," and his voice hardened, "what is mine, is mine, and I will fight to the death for it."

"Includin' killin' the law if they stand in your way?"

He didn't reply to that. Wouldn't even look at me. And I knew then that for all his big fancy talk, he wasn't no better than the men he'd hired to do his killin' for him.

I said, "Fight to the death? That means the land that you once claimed; the land that the nesters and the smaller ranchers now hold?"

"Precisely, Sheriff. It belongs to *me*, damnit!"

He got control of himself, but it was done with a powerful effort on his part. And I knowed then that this man had been puttin' on one whale of a good act for me. I let him calm down and then said, "I guess, sir, that I'm gonna have to read up on this homestead thing you mentioned. Whatever I do, I want it to be legal, tried and true."

"I'll save you the trouble, Sheriff." He looked at me and I could see this man, this western pioneer, and he had been that, was no softy. A bastard, yeah, but he was hard as flint. "Most have stayed the allotted time, and all have improved the land, as is decreed by law."

"So . . . they're legal on the land, is that what you're sayin'?"

"That is correct, Sheriff. They are legally on the land."

The man was exasperatin'. "But still, knowin' you're wrong in the eyes of the law, you're goin' to fight? You're goin' to be responsible for the deaths of men, more men, and maybe some women and kids, too?"

"Putting it that way, Sheriff, it seems terribly hard on my part, doesn't it?"

"Sure seems that way to me, 'specially when you consider that you and yourn ain't missin' no meals and ain't likely to do so."

Agin, he wore that tight little smile on his lips. I didn't know where his pushy, goofy-actin' son had gone off to, and I hadn't seen hide nor hair of his daughter, Wanda. Which suited me just fine. Matt Mills ought to take a good strong bar of lye soap and wash out her nasty-talkin' mouth.

Matt, he got up out of his chair and walked to the porch railing. He had built right, the porch affordin' him a grand view. Breathtakin', almost. Matt, he stood for a time, then turned around and looked at me.

"Nice view, isn't it, Sheriff?"

"It's real nice, sir. Be pretty out here in the mornin's, I bet. Be nice to have coffee out here and just sit and sip and admire it all."

"Yes. I do that when the weather is nice enough. You and I do think somewhat alike, Sheriff."

Damned if I was gonna respond to that. But then, I didn't really know his situation; I ain't never had nothin' noways.

But deep down, a part of me could understand his feelin's. To see years of backbreaking work just took away from you. That would be enough to tip a man over the line of reason. But I also knew that it didn't have to be that way. But I wasn't gonna remind him of that just yet. I'd see if he'd come around and mention it.

And that weather-bit, hell, I knowed what he was gettin' at 'fore he ever went any further in his talk. It was his. Ever'thing you could see from this porch, and beyond, was his. He and his men, and there was graveyards I'd seen ridin' in, places in the earth where men had been planted after dyin' for the brand. It was his. All of it. Maybe not legal-like, but in his heart, it was his. And no man, or woman, was gonna take it from him.

But then I had to think about Junior and Hugh, the sons of these men. The things they'd done, the killin' and the rapin'. And their daddies had covered it all over.

Whatever feelin's I had for these two men, they dimmed somewhat when I thought of that. Just too lowdown. With that in mind, I reminded him of the obvious. "You should have had your hands file on it."

"Yes," he acknowledged. "Not doing so was both stupid and arrogant on my part. I think you are, Sheriff, an honest man. You really are. And I think you're one of the few in this big valley who will tell it to me straight, and damn the consequences. Am I correct in that, Sheriff?"

"Yes, sir, I reckon you are." Now what was comin' at me?

"And you're not afraid of me, either, are you, Sheriff?"

"No, sir."

"Or of my . . . gunhands?"

"No, sir. I'm just as good or better than any you got ridin' for you."

"Yes. I do believe that. But you do understand my point of view?"

"In a way, yes, sir. I don't think it's right to take somebody's land. But you didn't file on it. Now, the land you filed on, or had your hands file on, or bought for ten cents an acre, that land ain't bein' squatted on, is it?"

"No," he admitted softly. "No, Sheriff, that land isn't being squatted on."

I leaned forward, the dainty little coffee cup in one big hand. Damn thing wasn't good for no more than about three swallers of coffee. Useless to a coffee-drinkin' man. "Mister Mills, it ain't none of my business, but how much land do you have, anyways? Two hundred thousand acres? More? I've rode your land some. You got good water, good graze, ever'thing a man could ever want for. You could settle back and live like a king for the rest of your life. There just don't have to be no war in this valley."

Mills, he spun around, turnin' his back to me for a time. When he turned to face me, his eyes were blazin' with fury. And I got the thought that this man just might not be carryin' no full load upstairs.

"But the land is *ours,* Sheriff! Mine and A.J.'s and Rolf's. This entire valley is *ours!* The three of us fought the battles, cleared the streams, muscled out the boulders and logs and other of nature's blockades. In more than twenty years, I've personally helped bury more than twenty-five men, good men, on this land. I gave, outright, my foreman, Kilby Jones, ten percent of my wealth, simply because he stood by me during the hard times and never complained. It's legal—had Stokes draw up the papers. Sheriff, I'm not a bad man."

Matter of opinion, I thought, but had better sense than to say it out loud. It ain't wise to poke the bear in his own cave.

"But Rolf Baker ain't joinin' with you and A.J. in this fight to control the valley," I reminded him.

Agin, Mills calmed hisself, doin' it with some visible effort. "No. No, he isn't. But that didn't surprise me when he refused to join with A.J. and me. You see, Sheriff, of the three of us, Rolf, well, he was the thinker in the group, the planner. Oh, now, I'm not putting him down, don't misunderstand me. Rolf will fight if pushed, but it takes a lot of pushing. And, I suppose, with Rolf, well, he's content. Change doesn't bother him. I guess that contentment is the key word with Rolf."

I didn't think that at all. But I didn't say it aloud. No, I just thought that Rolf Baker wasn't no greedy man, wasn't no blackhearted man.

But Mills, he read the words in my eyes.

With a long sign, he said, "Sheriff, it's been nice talking to you this morning. I have found you to be a much more intelligent man than I first thought." He shook his head. "I wish . . ."

But I never did learn just what he wished. He put his back to me agin and stared out over the seemingly peaceful valley. It was like he knew that things was comin' to an end. Like all things do. But not bein' no deep thinker, I wasn't gonna point that out to the man.

Hell, maybe he thought he'd live forever. Some folks do. I've seen men like that before; seen 'em that even when death reached out with a bony hand to touch them, they wouldn't believe it.

Well, I'd been dismissed before, and knowed one when I seen it. So I stood up and tugged on my new hat. Mills, he turned around to look at me.

"Ain't no point in shakin' hands, is there, Mister Mills?"

That smile come to him agin. "No, Sheriff. I guess there is no point at all."

"I'm right sorry about that, sir."

"So am I, Sheriff. I have never wanted to be an enemy to the law."

"You don't have to be now, sir."

"Sometimes, Sheriff, a man runs out of choices. Now is one of those times."

Noddin' my head at him, I stepped off the porch and down to the hitchrail. I buckled up and tied down and mounted. I looked at Matt Mills, still standin' on the porch, watchin' me.

"Were you planning on seeing A.J. today, Sheriff?"

"I had thought on it."

"Take my advice and don't! You're a brave man, Sheriff, but no fool. I think you know that if you show up, alone, on Circle L land, you're a dead man."

For once in my life, I didn't argue with advice. I just took it.

Chapter Ten

I stopped a clodhopper on his way to town, ridin' a mule, and asked him to stop by the office and tell whoever was in there that I would be in late—I might not even be back in town before the next morning.

He said he'd be glad to do it and we shook hands and went our own way. With me headin' cross-country for the Quartermoon spread.

I had Miss Pepper on my mind, and that was a right weighty thought, but a very pleasant one, as I rode.

Skirting the Rockinghorse spread I touched on the range of Miss Maggie and Miss Jean, then began to relax a tad once I got onto the Quartermoon range. It'd been a while since I'd give Critter his head, and Critter, he was a horse that liked to eat up the miles. So I'd run him awhile, then walk him, lettin' him blow, then we'd have at it agin. Both of us havin' fun, like a couple of kids.

I'd sorta had this trip in mind all the time, so I'd packed me a clean shirt and britches and drawers in my saddlebags 'fore I left out. And I always carried a little poke of food and a small coffeepot with me.

It was beautiful country, most especially this time of the

year, with ol' Mother Nature beginnin' her renewal of the cycle of things. There was wildflowers by the millions, it seemed to me, of all colors, just winkin' and wavin' in the little breeze that blowed through the big valley off the high-up mountains.

This was the Big Lonesome, and it wasn't suited for ever'-body. But I enjoyed it. I enjoyed seein' a graceful hawk on the wing, all them things, and the clean fresh way the land smelled. Hell, I can't explain it. It ain't no damned poet!

I was just ridin' along, gawkin' at things, thinkin' of Miss Pepper, like some love-struck kid, when my eyes caught the reflection of sunlight off metal, off to my right, up in a stand of timber, lodgepole pine it looked to me. I left that saddle just as the rifle boomed. Critter, he squalled and I knew he'd been hit, and brother, that made me madder'un hell. I can't stand to see an animal abused.

Only long stretch I ever done behind bars was the time I come up with this white-trash fellow beatin' his little dog with a club. I took that club away from that man and goddamn near killed him with it.

Spent a month in jail for that, 'cause I didn't have the money to bond out. But not before I took that little dog to a dog doc and had him patched up and the doc to promise me he'd find him a good home.

Just pissed me off.

Man that would abuse an animal, 'specially a pet, his or somebody's else's, ought not to be allowed to live. And a couple of men that done that in front of me didn't. I like animals just a whole hell of a lot more than I do some people.

I hadn't let loose of the reins as I come out of the saddle, and I'd trained Critter to get on his side on command. As I jumped, Critter he come down with me, with me rollin' to avoid gettin' crushed. His eyes was all walled back in his head and I could tell he was just as pissed as me. I could see where the bullet had tore a small chunk of meat out of his right shoulder, but it didn't look to be that bad.

I whispered in Critter's ear and he looked at me like he understood what I was sayin' to him. Hell, I think he did. For an animal that ain't got a brain no bigger than a horse has, they're plenty smart. So Critter, he come up and stood over me, the reins trailin', while I lay on the ground as still as a church-mouse. I wanted that ol' boy up in the timber to think me dead.

Then I got to worryin' that maybe he'd shoot Critter. But no more shots came.

Oh, it was the back-shooter, Haufman. I couldn't prove it, of course, but it was him. And right there and then, I made up my mind that one of us was gonna be planted, or leave the valley . . . if ever agin we come face to face.

I laid real still for several minutes. Then, real faint, I heard the sounds of hooves, leavin' the area. I moved my head just a mite and seen horse and rider toppin' the crest and headin' out.

Mumblin' a few words that I didn't learn in Sunday school, I got to my feet, found my hat, and then led Critter over to a little creek. With my bandana, I bathed the bullet wound and packed it with moss, then covered that and secured it best I could with my bandana and a piece of twine from my saddlebags.

I had some horse liniment with me, most cowboys carry that, for use on themselves as well as the horse, but you just try pourin' some of that into a raw wound, and you'll get your butt kicked clear into the next county—quick.

I ground reined Critter and took me a hike up to that stand of lodgepole pine, right to the spot where I'd seen the sun come off that gun barrel. Took me some scoutin' around, but I found where he'd laid and then I found the brass he'd ejected from his rifle. And it was just as I'd figured.

It was a .44-.40, and the only person I'd seen with one of them was that bastard Haufman. I put the brass in my pocket and walked back to Critter.

I figured I was still some miles from the main house on the Quartermoon, and since I didn't see no hansom cabs around, that didn't leave me many options. So, leadin' Critter, I struck out.

Damn, but I hate to walk!

My feet was killin' me. Me and Critter had hiked and limped along for several miles before comin' up on a brandin' site. This was a Quartermoon line shack, with a brush corral and a small remuda. The cowboys watched as I walked up, leadin' Critter.

Then they got right upset when I told them what had happened.

"If you want a posse, Sheriff," one puncher said. "You got one ready-made."

I shook my head. "No point. He's clear back to town or to home base by now. I'm more worried about my horse."

These was cowboys, and horse-lovers, and they could understand that. Every cowhand has his favorite horse, and you get attached to them, and them to you. And while any cowboy will cuss his horse from time to time, you just let someone do a hurt to that animal. Brother, you best get ready to swing or grab iron.

One of them hands knew a right smart about horse-doctorin'. He said he'd tend to Critter and bring him in later if I wanted to drop a loop on one in their loose remuda.

Hidin' a smile, I agreed to do just that. They was good boys, and they'd do whatever they could to help me, but I could damn well rope and saddle my own horse. Out here, a man figures if you're big enough to tote iron around, you're big enough to break your own horses, much less saddle one.

I liked the looks of one of the biggest buckskins I'd ever laid eyes on. He looked like he could run all day and still have bottom left in him. But he had him a mean look in his eyes, and he was lookin' straight at me.

"That one," I said, takin' the rope from my saddle.

"Uh, Sheriff," a cowboy said. "That's Pronto. We call him Pronto 'cause just as soon as you get in the saddle, you get out of it pronto!, if you know what I mean."

I knew. I'd figured him for a horse that was gonna let you know who's boss. Well, I was fixin' to show him who was boss.

"I'll ride him."

The boys, they started wagerin'. Obviously, I had picked me a ring-dang-doo.

I built me a loop and caught Pronto on the first throw. A couple of hands held him while I got my saddle on him . . . after strippin' off all the unnecessary gear. As soon as I settled into the saddle, I knew this horse was gonna be a son of a gun!

I give out with a yell that would have woke the dead, and Pronto, he commenced to jumpin' and buckin'. Ever' time he'd go up and then come down, my teeth would rattle. But I'd been breakin' horses since I was no bigger than a popcorn fart, and he wasn't about to buck me off.

Them Quartermoon boys was hollerin' and yellin' and whoopin', enjoyin' the show. Pronto, he give one more sideways jump and then stopped, swingin' his big head around and glarin' at me, as if wonderin' what in the hell I was doin' still on his back and grinnin' at him.

He give me out one long breath and I could feel him relax under me.

"Whoo, boy!" a Quartermoon rider yelled. "Here she comes, Sheriff."

And the bettin' got heavier.

Now when a buckin' horse does what Pronto just done, one of two things is about to happen. Either they've give it up and gonna allow you to gentle them, or they're fixin' to carry you where angels wouldn't go.

Pronto looked at me lookin' at him. I patted his neck and grinned at him.

He showed me his teeth and then bucked me off and tried to stomp on me.

Scramblin' out of the way and catchin' him on a buckdown, I grabbed hold of the saddle horn and swung back onto that hurricane deck. Rakin' him with my spurs, he got mad and really cut loose. This was one buckskin that had rode straight up out of hell.

He twisted and turned and went up and come down. It was a damn good thing that I wasn't tryin' to ride him inside some stout-built corral, 'cause sure as shootin', he'd have tried to scrape me off, and I've seen cowboys get busted legs when a horse decided to do that.

There was still fight left in him and he showed me that he wasn't about ready to give up the battle. Pronto, he threw back his head and screamed just like a puma.

It took some time, but I finally beat him. Pronto, he decided to give up the ghost. I was plumb tuckered out when he got it through his head he'd met a rider he couldn't throw off. I didn't want to hurt Pronto's feelin's none, so I didn't tell him that I'd made a lot of money bettin' that buckin' horses couldn't toss me off. I'd tell him about that later, after we got to know each other some better.

I stripped the saddle off him and rubbed him down good with dry grass. He seemed to like that. He only tried to bite me twice and kick me once.

"Your horse is gonna be out of commission for quite a while, Sheriff," the cowboy lookin' after Critter said. "But that's one hell of a hoss you just rode." He looked at me friendly-like. "Nobody else has ever rode Pronto." Then he paid me the best compliment one cowboy could give another. "You're a top hand."

"Then why do you keep Pronto around?" I knew the answer before I asked.

He grinned. "Pronto goes where he wants to go, and he's

sired some fine colts. 'Sides, we like to set strangers on him for some fun."

I returned his grin, and we become friends.

Critter didn't even look around when I rode out; he'd spotted him a right pretty little mare and was makin' goo-goo eyes at her, and she was swishin' around him, actin' a fool; females bein' what they are.

Kinda hurt my feelin's. But I guess Critter was payin' me back for spendin' so much time with Pepper and ignorin' him.

I never thought I'd see a horse as good as Critter—and I sure wouldn't want Critter to know—but Pronto was one hell of a horse. Even after all that jumpin', screamin', and buckin' he'd done just a few minutes past, he didn't appear to be none tuckered out at all.

A Quartermoon hand, he seen me ridin' in and hightailed it to the main house, probably to kid Miss Pepper about her beau comin' in and to tell Mister Baker that I was ridin' in on Pronto.

But Rolf Baker, he was pure western man, he knowed something was wrong, bad wrong, just by lookin' at me.

"What happened, Cotton?"

Steppin' out of the saddle, I give the reins to a cowhand. The cowboy didn't look none too thrilled about the prospect of handlin' Pronto.

I looked Pronto square in the eyes. "Now, you let him take the saddle off you and rub you down good. You behave, now, you hear?"

Pronto butted me in the chest with his head and tried to step on my foot. Just his way of sayin' he liked me.

As he was bein' led away, he busted the air with a good one and that sent us all scramblin' for the porch. Pronto, he must have stuck his muzzle into the camp's bean pot.

Sittin' on the porch of the house, a cup of coffee in my hand, I told Rolf all what had gone down, startin' out with the details of my talk with Matt Mills and endin' with my horse bein' shot.

"And your horse?" Rolf asked. He could see that I was OK.

"He'll be all right. But if it's OK with you. I'll borrow Pronto for a time. Me and him get along."

"Of course. I'll give him to you, have the bill of sale ready whenever you choose to leave. But you are spending the night, aren't you?"

"Oh, please do!" Pepper said, taking my big rough hand in hers. "We really need to talk some, Cotton. About . . . important things."

I began to feel a little trapped, but hell, it was a trap I'd set for myself.

Her dad give her sort of a queer smile when she said that. Her mother's smile was more open.

"Well, sure," I said. "That'd be real be nice."

In the barn, I could hear Pronto kickin' the slats out of his stall. The cowboy come out of the barn at a dead run, cussin' and hollerin'.

Rolf looked at me. "Pronto sets his own rules, Cotton."

"Yes, sir. I sorta already figured that out."

My stomach drawed up some when Pepper said she was gonna do the supper cookin'. I thought at first that was the reason her brother, Jeff, was out with a gatherin' and brandin' crew. But Martha said he'd be back in time for supper.

I didn't have much time to ruminate on it much. Big Mike Romain come ridin' up just about that time.

His face darkened with anger when he spotted me sittin' in the porch swing, Pepper close beside me . . . real close beside me. When she sat down beside me, the temperature on that porch went up about ten degrees. And it wasn't just her neither.

I had been told by Rolf that A.J. had done the same as Matt . . . givin' Mike ten percent of his spread for his loyalty; so both men had more than a passin' interest in what happened in the valley.

I greeted Big Mike cheerful-like, and by doin' that, forced him to be civil to me. He done so, but man, he looked like he'd rather bite the head off of a live rattler than speak polite to the likes of me.

In a way, I could understand how come it was he hated me. He'd been courtin' Pepper for no tellin' how long, and gettin' nowheres, and here I come in, and we was cozy in no time.

"What brings you out this way, *Mister* Romain?" Pepper asked, stickin' the needle to him. Hell, she knew perfectly well why he was here.

I'll give Mike credit for courage. He looked at Rolf and said, "I would like to speak to you, Mister Baker."

"Now?"

"Yes, sir. And in private."

"Is something wrong, Mike?"

"No, sir. I would like to speak to you on matters concerning affairs of the heart."

Pepper, she hissed like a snake when he said that. Lookin' at her, her eyes narrowed down and her face turned pale. I could feel the tension buildin' deep inside her, pushin' aside the steam that had already built up.

Rolf stood up. "Very well, Mike. If you think it's necessary."

"I certainly don't think it is!" Pepper said, considerable heat in her voice.

"Now, Pepper," Big Mike tried to soorthe her. "You know you need a strong hand to steady you at times."

"I sure as hell don't need yours!"

"Pepper!" Her mother said. "Please remember that you're a lady."

"She's got her a strong hand," I said. "And it belongs to me."

"Oh, Cotton!" Pepper put her arms around my neck.

Rolf looked amused at the whole thing.

Mike was just plain mad.

"Now, you see here!" Mike raised his voice at me.

Me? Hell, I just opened my mouth and jumped right in. "And furthermore, Miss Pepper is spoke for—by me! I come out here to ask for her hand in marriage."

"Yes!" Pepper hollered, and I spilled coffee all down my britches-leg.

Damn stuff burned, too.

"Well, bless Pat!" Rolf said.

Martha pulled out a little hanky from somewheres and started blubberin'.

Mike, he glared at me. And I knew at that instant I had made me a powerful, hateful, and deadly enemy. Mike cut his eyes to Pepper. She was practically up in my lap and I was gettin' plumb flustered about the whole thing.

When Mike spoke his voice was charged with emotion. "I thought, Pepper, that you and I had reached an understanding."

"I never thought that at all," Pepper told him. "I have told you that while we might be friends, that was as far as it was going . . . ever!"

Mike's face was mottled with anger and hate. "I see. Well, it looks as though I have been laboring under a false impression. Quite a long ride for nothing, I suppose."

"Not for nothing, Mike," Martha had stopped blubbering. "Everyone now knows where the other stands, right?"

"Yes." Mike struggled to contain his anger. "Yes, of course. And that is always good . . . I suppose."

"Why don't you stay for dinner, Mike?" Rolf asked, the gentleman in him coming to the fore.

"Well . . . ?" Mike tried a smile.

"Yes," Pepper said sweetly . . . .very sweetly, and I braced myself for whatever. "I'm preparing supper . . . fried chicken."

Mike lost his smile. From the look on his face, he'd attempted to gnaw on her bird before, and love or lust or whatever on his part, damned if he was gonna try any more of it. "Oh, well, in that case . . ." Then he caught himself. "I'd better get started back if I'm to make the ranch before dark."

"Yes," Pepper agreed, "I think perhaps that would be best."

"You be careful, Mike," I told him. "My horse was shot out from under me a couple hours ago. There's a back-shooter out there."

He gave me a sharp look. "I suppose a man in your position would tend to make a lot of enemies, Sheriff."

"That might be true. Oh, something else. I had me a nice long talk with Matt Mills this mornin'. He sure is a nice feller—we reached an understandin' about things."

That shook Mike. He took a step forward, putting one boot up on the steps. "That's . . . very interesting, Sheriff. What did you two find to talk about?"

"Official business," I said mysteriously, and wouldn't say no more.

He stared at me. Hell with him. Let him stew awhile. Do him good. If I could work up a little suspicion between the Rockinghorse and the Circle L, that'd be fine with me.

"Ladies, Rolf, I'll take my leave now." He spoke around his hate and anger.

Him not speakin' to me didn't hurt my feelin's none a bit. But I wanted to needle him just a tad more.

"Oh, Mike!" The big man turned around. "Do me a favor, huh?"

"What is it?"

"Tell Haufman the next time I see him, I'm gonna run him out of the valley, or kill him. The choice is his to make. I thank you in advance."

"Why would I see Haufman? He doesn't ride for us. We picked names out of a hat and he . . ."

He shut his mouth, realizin' too late that he'd let the cat out of the bag.

With a low oath, he whirled around, mounted up, and galloped out of the yard. I felt sorry for Mike's horse, 'cause until he calmed down, Mike was gonna take his anger out on the animal.

Pepper grabbed both my hands and held on. Good thing I'd put the coffee cup on the porch floor. "Oh, Cotton! I'm so happy for the both of us. Aren't you?"

It was only then that I really realized that I was engaged to be married! Lord, have mercy! I swallered hard and mumbled something. I disremember exactly what.

Pepper give me a wet kiss right on the mouth and I got all flushed-up.

Damn, but I was warm. It was gettin' kinda late in the season for longhandles. I was gonna have to get me some of them regular drawers.

Rolf, he pried me a-loose from Pepper and shook my hand. Martha, she give me a little peck on the cheek.

A puncher come runnin' up. "What's all the hollerin' about, boss?"

"Pepper just got engaged, Buck!"

"You don't say!" Then he had to come up on the porch and pump my arm like he was fillin' up a bucket. "We'll have us a regular shivaree here pretty quick then, Sheriff. I'm happy for you."

Then he ran off to the bunkhouse to tell ever'body he could find.

"Oh, Pepper!" Martha took my place in the swing. "We have so much to talk about. Just the two of us."

"Yes, mother."

"We'll plan the wedding for the fall. It'll be so lovely that time of year."

"Fall, hell!" Pepper hollered. "Damned if I'm waitin' until fall."

"Now, you listen to me, young lady!" Martha raised her voice. "This wedding is going to be done in a proper manner. Just like it would be back in New Hampshire."

"Damn New Hampshire!" Pepper met her mother's tone. "This is Wyoming Territory."

Me and Rolf beat a hasty retreat off that porch, leavin' mother and daughter a clear battleground. The feathers and the hair was about to start flyin'. Pepper, she wanted to make it legal as quick as possible. Inside, she was hotter than a pot of Mexican chili.

And don't ask me now I know that. It wouldn't be gentlemanlike for me to reply.

Chapter 11

Jeff Baker rode in during the late afternoon and had time for a bath and a change of clothes 'fore supper—dinner, they called it—was spread out on the long and fancy table in the dining room. First time I ever et under a chandelier. With that many candles, I kept frettin' about the drippin's fallin' into the soup. Course, I didn't say that out loud. I'm dumb, but I ain't stupid.

And my, I never seen so much food in my life.

I picked at my food until I could get me several good looks at how the others was handlin' all the knives and forks and spoons. I never knowed how the gentry eat before. Looked kinda awkward to me, but I following right along and tried to pick up the hang of it.

There was a fork for this plate and a spoon for that bowl and two or three more instruments for something else. I never knowed eatin' could involve so much work.

Finally, I give it up and looked at Rolf. "Y'all just gonna have to excuse my ignorance, folks. I just don't know which thing to use with what."

"Don't let it worry you, Sheriff," Jeff said. "Personally, I never saw that it made much difference." He smiled at his mother. "But mother was and is a stickler for table manners. She grew up in New Hampshire."

I suppose that New Hampshire bit was supposed to be impressive to me. It wasn't.

"It's easy, Cotton," Pepper said. "You just start from the outside and work in with each course of food that's served."

"Oh! Well, I'll just be da . . . durned. So that's how it's done, huh."

Made me feel kinda dumb 'cause I hadn't figured it out myself.

"What's this we're eatin'?" I asked Rolf.

Rolf looked at me and smiled. "Lamb. Rather tasty, isn't it?"

It sure was. I'd never et no sheep before. I complimented Pepper on a good supper. Dinner. To Rolf, "I bet you'd get some dark looks from A.J. and Matt if they knowed you served up sheep for a meal, hey?"

"I'm going to start raising sheep, Cotton. It's really a very profitable venture." When I didn't say nothin', I guess he figured I was agin' that. He was wrong. "Does that offend you?"

"No, sir. I get along right well with sheep and them that raise them . . . providin' it's done right."

"Oh, I plan to do it correctly. That's the only way sheep and cattle can get along together. I have about thirty thousand acres that will be just perfect for sheep."

I wondered if he knowed just how much trouble he was gonna stir up by sheep-raisin'. He was settin' himself solid agin' the big cattle spreads.

As if readin' my thoughts, the elder Baker said, "Yes, Cotton, I know."

I nodded my head, then decided to change the subject. "Any of y'all plannin' on comin' into town tomorrow?"

"Why . . . no," Rolf replied. "Why do you ask, Cotton?"

"Don't," my voice was flat. "I'm gonna brace that back-shooter, Haufman tomorrow. If he's in town, that is, and I figure he will be. I'm either gonna run him out of the county or kill him."

Everybody stopped chowin' down with that statement. "We're going to have to discuss your future, Cotton." Martha said, in her soft way.

"When all this is over, ma'am, I'm gonna start ranchin'. But for now, it's pretty well lined out for me. I aim to either stop this buildin'-up war in the valley, or stand right in the middle of it shootin'. I took an oath to do that. And I ain't never broke my word in my life. I don't intend to do that now."

She inspected me with her eyes. "No, I don't imagine you have, Cotton. But you now have Pepper to think of."

"I do that mite near all the time anyways, ma'am." I could see that pleased them all, 'specially Pepper. I could practical see the steam comin' out of her ears. Kinda made me woozy in the pit of my stomach. And produced some other sensations in other areas of me, too. I was right glad nobody asked me to stand up just about then.

"Cotton," Rolf said, "I would like you to give me your thoughts on the upcoming war. No, wait! Cotton, what is your last name? Don't you think we have a right to know, especially now that you're about to become a member of the family?"

I give out a long sigh. I knowed I had it to do. "Well, I reckon so. But please don't laugh. I'm sorta sensitive about it."

So I told them.

Jeff, he had to leave the table, and I silently thanked him for showin' me that much respect before he busted right out laughin'. I would have hated to have punched out my future brother-in-law.

Rolf, he blinked a couple of times, then covered his mouth with a big table napkin. He took a sip of wine, then shook his head and damned if he didn't swaller the whole glassful.

"I think it's a lovely name," Martha said, with only a little smile. But her eyes sure was twinklin'.

"I think it's *grand!*" Pepper said. "Just think, I'll be Mrs. Pepper . . ."

"Don't say it aloud!" I blurted. "I'm thinkin' of changin' it, anyways."

"You'll do no such thing!" Rolf told me, considerable heat in his voice. "A man's last name is very important. To retain it means to perpetuate the lineage forever."

Now it was my turn to blink. I sure didn't have no idea what it was that Rolf Baker had just told me.

Jeff, he come back in and took his seat at the table. His face was all flushed and he looked like he'd just swallered a ladybug.

Martha cleared her throat. "Do you have any brothers or sisters, Cotton?"

"Yes'um. A whole passel of 'em. But I haven't seen none of 'em in years. Not since we was separated after our folks passed. Don't reckon I ever will see none of them. I don't have no idea what happened to any of them."

"How sad," Martha sniffed a couple of times. Looked like she was gonna bust out cryin'.

There'd been enough blubberin' for one day. "It ain't nothin' to get all worked up about. The little ones got cared for proper and us older ones made it all right, I reckon. The only one I ever really think about, is my brother, Jack."

Pepper glanced at me. "Something special about him, Cotton?"

"Oh, yeah, I looked up to Jack. Even though he had him a mean streak a yard wide. But he was always good to me. He pulled out 'fore the folks passed. But even as a boy, he was uncommon fast with a short gun. Why, once I recall seein' him . . ."

Then it hit me. Was it possible? Jack. Jack Crow! Could it be? God, I hoped not. But there was always that chance.

"You have a very pensive look, Cotton," Martha said.

I thought I knew what that meant, but I wasn't really sure. So I just nodded my head. "Yes, ma'am. I guess so."

Jack Crow! Was it possible?

The more I thought on it, the more I thought it just might be true. Although part of me desperately wanted it not to be. Then I remembered that pet crow Jack had one time. Somebody had told him that you could make a crow talk; but try as he did, he never could get no more than a squawk out of that bird. But Jack, he give it his best try.

A neighbor boy come over one afternoon, and for no good reason that anybody could figure out, he killed Jack's pet crow. Man, I never seen nobody go into such a rage as Jack done that day. A cold, killin' mad. And the boy who killed the bird? Well, that boy was found shot to death about two weeks later, killed with a single bullet wound to the chest.

The law? Hell, what law? There wasn't no law in that part of the country where we was raised up. I was . . . oh, about ten years old when that happened, and that was a long time 'fore any kind of real law and order come to that part of the wilderness.

"You're very deep in thought, Cotton." Pepper was starin' at me acrost the table. "What in the world are you thinking about?"

I was so deep in thought, her words just barely reached me.

I shook my head and laid knife and fork down on my plate, all my appetite suddenly gone. "I was thinkin' of a gunfighter name of Jack Crow . . . but I don't think that's his real name. He never liked his last name neither."

"I've heard of him," Jeff said. "He is reputed to be the fastest gun in the west. Other than Smoke Jensen, that is. But Smoke has hung up his guns, married, and settled down. Over in Idaho, I believe it is."

"He's married and settled down, but he ain't near'bouts hung up his guns yet."

"Why is this gunfighter, this Jack Crow, weighing so heavily on your mind, Cotton?" Martha asked.

I give out a long sigh. Everything was beginning to fit like a completed puzzle. Jack always did favor black clothing. Told me back when I was just a little shaver that someday he'd have a name for hisself and then he'd have all the black outfits he wanted.

I was conscious that everyone had stopped eatin' and was just sittin', lookin' straight at me, waiting for some sort of answer.

"Why?" I met their eyes. "'Cause I think he's my brother."

I didn't sleep too good that night. Done a lot of tossin' and turnin', with my head filled with boyhood memories about me and Jack and our ma and pa and all the other younguns. I wondered what had become of them. Were they doin' all right? Had they married and settled down? Did they have families and all that went with that?

I'd sleep a while and then wake up and start to thinkin' again. And all my thoughts had Pepper all mixed up in them.

I pulled out before dawn, after Pepper fixed me breakfast—she really could cook—and then give me a promise-of-things-to-come kiss right on the mouth. I rode Pronto into the darkness, headin' for town.

The night past, we'd all gathered up in the fancy sittin' room and I'd told them all about my childhood, and all that I could remember about brother Jack.

"Forgive me for saying this, Cotton," Rolf said. "But this Jack appears to be the carrier of the bad seed in your family."

He was sure right. I couldn't deny that.

"Ain't nothin' to forgive when a person is right, Mister Baker. And you're sure right. Now that I'm a man grown, and lookin' back, I an see where a lot of the things Jack done was just lowdown dirty mean."

All that was on my mind as I rode into the spreading silver

dawnin' of the day. But I wasn't dwellin' just on that. A good part of me was on the high alert for any trouble that might be hidin' in the shadows.

But all my attention to danger was for naught, and when I rode into town, the streets and boardwalks of Doubtful was quiet and empty of anything except for a few dogs and cats. I rode slowly to the stable and put up Pronto. I told him to stay calm and don't kick no slats out of his stall.

Pronto, he shoved me back up against the stall and tried to bite me.

The gimp-legged man had just opened his cafe as I walked up the boardwalk. Noddin' my good mornin's, I took me a table by a window and ordered coffee and breakfast.

Pretty soon, Rusty come walkin' up the way, his spurs jinglin'. He spotted me and joined me at the table.

Rusty, he ordered breakfast and coffee, and over coffee, I asked, "Anything interestin' happen while I was gone, Rusty?"

"You might say that." He sugared and creamed his coffee and stirred. "Buck Hargon, Doc Martin, and that Canadian gunfighter, Sangamon, rode in. They're over to the hotel."

"Least it's slowed down to a trickle. Hell, Rusty, there can't be that many more gunslingers that's out there out of work."

"Yeah." His reply was glum. "And for a fact, Jack Crow is comin' in. He was spotted a few days ago near the Salt River Range."

"Then he'll be in any day now."

"Yeah. Sheriff, do you realize they's more than fifty known gunhands now in the valley?"

"I know."

The cafe man brung us our food and for a time, we concentrated on eatin'. Then, pushin' our plates away, we poured more coffee and I brung Rusty up to date . . . but I didn't say nothin' about my gettin' engaged. That was up to Pepper and her ma to make that announcement.

"Your horse gonna be all right?"

"Oh, yeah."

"You sure it was Haufman?"

"It was his horse for a fact." I dug in my vest pocket and laid the .44-.40 brass on the table. "And I found this."

I'd found something odd about that brass, but I didn't say nothin' about it. I'd confront Haufman with it . . . after I beat hell out of them. Or killed him.

"Haufman come in early this mornin', Sheriff. I got up 'bout four and seen him ride in."

"I didn't see his horse when I stabled mine."

"Rode in on a shaggy mountain pony. Never seen the brand before."

"I seen that one in the corral. You got any idea where he is now?"

"Havin' breakfast at the hotel. Was when I walked past. And he don't look like he's packin' no iron."

"Yeah, that figures. That's one of his trademarks. Usually after a kill, he'll show up in town, unarmed."

I didn't want to kill Haufman. I just wanted to beat hell out of him.

I said as much to Rusty.

"He's a bull, Sheriff. I hear he used to wrestle 'fore he come out west."

"He did. And box, too. I seen him fight a couple of times. He's good." I met Rusty's eyes and smiled. "But I think I'm some better."

"I always knowed you didn't have no sense," Rusty said sorrowfully.

Back at the office, I dug in my war bag and come up with a pair of tight-fittin' leather gloves. That China-feller who taught me some tricky ways of fightin', he had them gloves made for me as a gift. He said, and he was right, that a man can hit harder wearin' gloves. And you don't do near'bouts the damage to your hands, neither.

I tucked the gloves in my hip pocket and looked over the mail; the stage had run while I was gone. There was a passel of wanted dodgers and not much else. I left the mail on my desk and took off my spurs, not wantin' to get all tangled up in them when I tangled up with Haufman. Then I stepped out on the boardwalk.

Takin' my time, I prowled the streets, not locatin' the German. Spottin' a little boy, I asked, "You seen a big, stocky-lookin' feller out this mornin', son?"

"Looks like a nester?"

"That's him."

"He's over yonder at the Wolf's Den." The boy pointed.

I thanked him and crossed the street. Steppin' up on the boardwalk, I pushed open the batwings and stepped inside.

Miss Mary was behind the bar with the bartender countin' out money. The swamper was cleanin' up the place, and Haufman was sittin' at a table, his back to a wall, playin' solitaire with a geasy deck of pasteboards.

Haufman would have heard the news that I was still alive, probably from a hardcase once Big Mike got back to the spread, so he didn't show no surprise on his face when I walked in. But his face was right and his eyes bright with tension, wary as a wolf.

Walkin' to the bar, I deliberately turned my back to him. "You missed, Haufman."

"I don't know vhat you're talking about, Sheriff Cotton."

"You're a goddamn liar!"

He began huffin' and puffin' like a steam engine.

"You missed me and shot my good horse, you son of a bitch. Now you get your shaggy horse and get your butt out of this county. Don't you never come back here."

I slipped on the leather gloves. They felt good on my hands. I turned to face him. His face was red with anger.

"I demand that you take back that slur against my mother, Sheriff!"

"You go to hell, Haufman! And ride your ugly horse there. I'm warnin' you, Haufman. You get out of town right now—ride!"

"You talk tough to an armed man, Sheriff."

"Well, now, I'm glad to hear that, Haufman. 'Cause in that case, I'm gonna kick your fat butt a time or two before I run you out of this town."

He laughed hoarsely. "You're a fool, cowboy. I have never lost a fight. I was a professional back east."

I unbuckled and untied, layin' my gunbelt on the bar.

I laughed at him. I wanted to make him so mad he'd lose all control. "A professional? A professional what, whore-master? A pimp, maybe. What'd you do, Haufman, pimp for your sister?"

That done it. With a roar of rage, he overturned the table, sending the cards flyin'. He charged me like an angry bull, knockin' tables and chairs ever' which-a-way as he come screamin' acrost the room.

I knowed one thing for certain: I couldn't never let him get his big hands on me, for the German was strong as a go-riller. And he hadn't been jokin' none when he said he'd never lost a fight. And he might have been a world-class champion if he hadn't killed a little fellow outside the ring.

I sidestepped and he crashed into the bar like a rampagin' elephant. I clubbed him on the side of the head, right on his ear. It stung him, I could see that, but it didn't even slow him down none at all.

He cussed me in German, and I didn't have to speak the language to know that he'd called me some terrible names.

I laughed at him. "Come on, you fat pig. So far, you ain't showed me nothin' but mouth."

Then the sucker hit me in the mouth with one of the fastest left hands I'd ever seen. It hurt me. But it was not a solid blow and I could dance back.

Howlin' his rage, he lumbered towards me. I snapped out a quick left and caught him on the mouth. The blood popped out from his thick wet lips and his head snapped back. I done a little dancin' like that China-feller taught me and a different light came into Haufman's eyes. He knowed then that he wasn't fightin' no cherry when it come to boxin'.

"I will destroy you at your own game, you stupid fool!" he hissed at me. Then he drew hisself up straight and raised his hands in the classic boxer's stance.

My reply was to kick him in the kneecap.

He give out a yell of pain, his guard droppin' for just a second. That was all I needed to give him a combination left and right to the mouth and to the jaw. Then I stopped in close and busted him right on his nose.

He staggered backwards and once more give me a good cussin'.

I didn't waste my breath returnin' the cussin'. I turned and he threw a right that missed. Steppin' under the blow, I once more popped him on the nose. The nose busted this time, and the blood went flyin'. Haufman, he shook his head to clear it, faked me, and then knocked the pure-dee piss out of me. He hit me so hard I thought the fight was gonna be over 'fore it even got goin' good.

I backed up, keepin' my guard up, and ducked around several tables until the fog lifted outta my head and the little birdies stopped chirpin' and I got back whatever sense I had. Haufman, he grinned through his bloody face and stalked me around the room, his big fists held up high. He swung a loopin' right hand, but I just ducked and didn't try no counterpunch; I knowed what he was tryin' to do: sucker punch me.

I danced around some and that seemed to make the bigger man mad as hell. "Vight, you coward!" he yelled at me.

"What's the matter, lard-butt? You gettin' tired already? I thought you was a professional somethin' or the other."

He squalled something in his native tongue and then damned if he didn't charge me. I didn't have time to get out of his way. When he run into me, he knocked me sprawlin' on the sawdust floor. But he'd been movin' so fast he couldn't check his forward speed. He stepped on me and I grabbed hold of one ankle and jerked hard.

He stumbled and then crashed into the back wall and just kept goin', right straight through the thin-cut pine. I heard him flounderin' around the storeroom, trippin' over boxes and barrels and cussin' in two languages. Jumpin' up, I ran into the dark room, runnin' full speed.

Damned if I didn't run into Haufman.

The force of my charge knocked the big man into the back door and the door went with him into the alley, crashin' out into the mud and stale beer, with me right behind the German.

Just as he was gettin' to his knees, I hit him four times, left and right, to the jaw, both sides. He went down in a bubble of spit and blood. I kicked him in the belly and he hollered and rolled until he come up on his feet.

I slipped in the beer and stumbled, almost fallin' down.

Then we went at it, standin' toe to toe and sluggin' it out. But I could taste the sweetness of victory just by lookin' into Haufman's eyes; they were beginnin' to glaze over. One of his ears was hangin' by a piece of skin, his lips was busted and bleedin', and his nose was smashed flat. His face was a mask of blood.

But Haufman wasn't through, not quite yet.

He sucker punched me and I went down on my back, rollin' away just in time to miss being crushed as he tried to drop both knees on me. Scramblin', I come up and kicked him right square in his big butt with the toe of my boot.

He hollered and spun around in the mud, just like a big ugly bug, his feet kickin' out, knockin' my legs out from under me. He was on top of me in a flash, his fingers diggin' at my eyes.

I managed to grab hold of one thumb and bend it back until it busted with a sickening sound. Haufman screamed in pain and I kicked him off me. This time I didn't let up until his face was damn near beyond recognition, it was so swollen and bloody. Finally, after I rared back and busted him square on the side of his jaw, Haufman just toppled over like a dead tree and lay still in the churned-up mud of the alley.

I hadn't been conscious of it, but a big crowd had gathered at both ends of the alley, standin' and watchin'. Strippin' off my gloves, I walked over to a water barrel and doused my face good with the cold water and then soaked my hands for a minute or two.

The photo-grapher, he come runnin' up the alleyway, totin' all his equipment, with Pritcher right with him. Langford begun poppin' pictures of Haufman, all bloody and muddy and still out of it.

"What happened here, Sheriff?" Pritcher asked.

"He tried to kill me yesterday; missed, shot my horse from ambush. I cornered him in the Wolf's Den and ordered him out of town. He didn't want to leave so I convinced him it would be best if he did."

Pritcher, he was scribblin' in a little notepad.

"Somebody get a rope and hang the bastard!" a man spoke out of the crowd.

"Be no un-legal hangin' in this town!" I told the crowd, and the man, he didn't have nothin' else to say about it. "We're not gonna lower ourselves to the level of the Circle L and the Rockinghorse, folks."

"Good, Sheriff. Very good. I'm proud of you," Pritcher said. "We must keep law and order to the forefront."

I was flexin' my hands, movin' my fingers open and shut. I didn't want them to stiffen up on me and not be able to hold a gun.

Truby, he come runnin' up the alleyway. He seemed right disappointed that Haufman wasn't dead. But he checked him twice just to be sure.

Burtell, Rusty, and De Graff had come up. "Get a bucket of water," I told Burtell, "and dump it on Haufman; get him on his feet. Rusty, get his horse from the stable and bring it around here. But keep his rifle. I want it for evidence." I hadn't told nobody, but when I closer inspected that brass from Haufman's .44-40. I seen where the firin' pin had wore some and was strikin' just off to the right.

Burtell, he dumped a bucket of water on Haufman and the German was sittin' in the beery mud, moanin' and cussin' and holdin' his head.

Rusty handed me the rifle and I waved the crowd back, firin' one round into the dirt. Ejectin' the brass, I inspected it; they matched up perfect, the pin strikin' just to the right a tad, but enough on the mark to fire the round.

I looked at Haufman. "You got a choice, Haufman. You can ride on out, or I'll hold you and try you for attempted murder. Make up your mind."

"I shall represent this poor unfortunate man!" Lawyer Stokes busted through the crowd, all full of hisself.

"You shut your mouth," I warned him. "And keep it shut." He shut up.

"I vill ride," Haufman glared at me through his swollen, piggy eyes. "But I shall not forget."

"You don't have to leave!" Stokes hollered. "The sheriff cannot order you out of town."

I eyeballed Stokes. "You wanna ride out with him, bigmouth?"

"You wouldn't dare!" the lawyer stuck out his chest and his chin.

"You wanna bet?"

Stokes just didn't have it in him to crowd me no more. He stood his ground for a few more seconds and then dropped his eyes.

Langford took a picture of me and Stokes, standin' nose to nose.

Pritcher was writin' fast in the little notebook.

"I'll keep your rifle, Haufman."

He cussed me in German.

Grinnin' at him, I told Rusty, "Escort him to the county line. South!"

Chapter 12

It was quiet in the valley for several days; or at least as far as I knew it was all quiet. If anything violent or underhanded went down, it wasn't reported to the sheriff's office. Then, on the morning of the fourth day after I'd whipped Haufman and ordered him to ride, A.J. and Matt come ridin' into town, accompanied by a gang of gunslicks. Big Mike and Kilby Jones were with them. They didn't even look my way as they rode past the office.

They rode straight to Lawyer Stokes's office and stayed all huddled up in there for half an hour or so, then they all went to see George Waller.

After a time, they all come troopin' out, not lookin' too happy about things. They met with half a dozen other people, all members of the town council. I had me a pretty good idea what was happenin'.

Rusty and Burtell was out in the country, just keepin' an eye on things, and me and De Graff sat in front of the office and watched the street. I figured George would be down to see me shortly, and sure enough, it wasn't no time 'fore he come hustlin' down the boardwalk, his face all shiny with sweat. Looked like he had him a powerful load on his mind.

"What's up, George?"

"Pressure, Sheriff, and plenty of it. But by God, the town council stood firm. I'm plenty proud of them all."

"Lawrence and Mills want you all to fire me, George?"

"Precisely, Sheriff."

I nodded my head. "And if you don't, they'll stop tradin' in town, right, George?"

He eyeball me suspicious-like. "Was you listenin' at a knothole, Sheriff?"

"Nope. But I was just wonderin' when they'd pull something like this. Now that you've all refused, what's their next move?"

George pulled out a bandana and mopped his face dry. "Well, it's like this, Sheriff. . . . They didn't come right out and say they wasn't gonna trade in town no more. But they sure come right up to the line before backin' off away from it."

I thought they were bluffin'. But I didn't tell George that. The next town, by wagon, was a full day's ride . . . maybe longer. And when the women at those ranches wanted something, like a dress or a sack of flour, they wouldn't put up very long with no two or three days, 'fore they got it. "And . . . ?"

"Leo Silverman told Matt Mills to go right straight to hell. Alex White, man who owns the Dirty Dog, he told A.J. where to stick his suggestions. And Belle puffed right up and said some words I didn't even think she knew! We're all behind you, Sheriff. All of us."

Maybe. Maybe for now. But I wondered about that. Talk is easy, but what if it wasn't no bluff? When the money stopped comin' in, would they all still feel the same way? I pondered on that some. Yes, I thought they would stick.

I sure hoped so.

"The small ranchers and the nesters gonna be enough to keep you all goin', George?"

"Yes." He smiled slowly. "Sheriff, this is something that we all have discussed at length, many times before. I mean, the businessmen of Doubtful. Personally, I think it's a bluff. But if it isn't, well, it'll hurt some, sure, but I think we'll all survive it. All they'll be doing, in the long run, is hurting themselves."

I nodded my head, for I was only payin' half attention to his words, my eyes not leaving the little man who was standing under the awning of the Wolf's Den saloon. Little Jack Bagwell. He sure seemed interested in something that was goin' on in the alleyway that housed Juan's Cantina.

I mentioned it to De Graff and told him to amble down thataway and see what was goin' on, if anything at all.

George, he stopped talkin' and looked. "What's wrong, Sheriff?"

"I don't know, George. But Little Jack is a cold-blooded killer. He likes to kill. And he ain't standin' out in the sun to get hisself no early summer's tan."

We watched in silence as De Graff come out of the alley and walked across the street to talk with Little Jack. De Graff, he come walkin' back toward the office, walkin' kinda quick for a cowboy. Cowboys, most of 'em ain't real taken with footwalkin'.

"What's up, De Graff?"

"Damn farmer over in Juan's. He says Jack claims he insulted him yesterday. He admitted he said some things to him. Little Jack told him to pack iron and they'd have at it in town today. They're gonna meet at noon."

"Well, damn!" I said. I sighed, 'cause there wasn't a damn thing I could do about it. Settlin' personal grudges with guns was the way it was, it was legal, for if a man packed iron, that meant he was ready and willin' to use it. Either that, or back down. I looked up at George. He knew it, too.

"Who's the farmer?" George asked.

"Some young feller name of Sonny Hickman. I don't know him."

"I do." George shook his head. "I kinda been expectin' something like this. Sonny is a young hothead who thinks he's a tough one. Come out here about three years ago from Indiana."

"Married?" I asked.

"Yes. Nice lady, too. I think they have two kids. Maybe more, now."

Another widder woman. 'Cause if this clodhopper stood up to Little Jack, he was shore gonna get killed. "What kind of iron is he packin', De Graff?"

"Converted .44, looks like."

Meaning that it had been changed to fire metallic cartridges. Gettin' to my feet, I asked. "What time is it, George?"

George clicked open his timepiece. I still hadn't bought me no watch. "Eleven-thirty, Sheriff."

"Let's clear the streets, De Graff. I'm gonna try to talk to Little Jack, but sure as hell, he was ordered out on the prod."

"I'll take my block, Sheriff," George volunteered. "Perhaps you can stop it."

"Don't count on that."

I took one side and De Graff handled the other. It took us about ten minutes. Folks cleared right off the boardwalk, but they didn't go far. They all lined up in the stores, movin' real quick to get a good place to view the fight. Then they'd all talk about how terrible it was. But they wouldn't none of them miss it for nothin'.

Finished, I looked up the street and damned if Pepper and her ma wasn't pullin' up in a buggy to the hitchrail to the dress shop—spelt Shoppee—still didn't look right to me. I quick hustled over there and took 'em by the arms and led 'em inside.

I was plumb shook to my boots when the screamin' began. A young lady, amply endowed—and dressed only in her scanties—started whoopin' and hollerin'. Like to have scared me half to death. I turned around and run smack into Martha. Pepper. She was laughin' so hard she couldn't hardly see, and even her ma was havin' a hard time keepin' a straight face.

My face? Hell, it was red!

I was back on the boardwalk faster than a cat can move. But it had been a right interestin' sight to behold. Pretty young lady. Hell, it wasn't my fault. She shouldn't a been paradin' around almost in her altogethers. 'Course, I reckon I should have knocked, it bein' a dress shop. With two p's and two e's.

But for now, I had more important things to worry about . . . mainly tryin' to figure out how to keep a clodhopper from gettin' killed.

I wasn't worried none about Little Jack.

I walked to where Little Jack was standin', leanin' up against the outer wall of the saloon.

He give me a disgusted look. "I reckon you're gonna stick your nose in this, Sheriff." It was not a question.

"Nope. But I would like to know what brung all this on."

Little Jack cut his eyes at me. "That damn nester tole me to get my ugly horse off of his potato field."

"Called your horse ugly, did he?"

"Damn shore did. And I ain't gonna take that from nobody, sure as hell not from no damn tater and hog farmer."

Well, people have been killed for a lot less than that, and I knew it was true.

"Little Jack, you mind terrible tellin' me what the hell you and your horse was doin' in the man's potato patch?"

"I ride wherever I damn well please to ride, Cotton."

"No, you don't neither. Not in this county. Now you want me to buy into his hand, Jack, you just get up in my face with your smart mouth."

I hid a smile. It was kinda amusin'. For if Little Jack Bagwell was to get up in my face, he'd have to find him a chair to stand on.

"Now, look here, Cotton. I got a right to defend my honor!"

"That you do, I ain't denyin' that. But it wasn't *your* honor, it was your horse's!"

"That don't make no difference."

"I don't need nobody to fight my battles for me!" the voice come from our left. Me and Jack both turned around and looked.

It was a hayseed, all right. From his clodhopper shoes to his overalls to his beat-up, floppy-brimmed hat.

But that gun in that raggedy holster on his hip made him equal to any man. And he had picked up the challenge, so it was his fight.

But I had to say it. "Back off, mister. Go on back home to your wife and kids. You ain't gonna lose no face by not fightin' Little Jack. Not in the eyes of them that matter, least-ways."

He shook his head. "No."

"You said your piece, Sheriff," Little Jack told me. "Now leave us be."

I didn't wanna put no hex on the farmer, so I didn't ask what he wanted on his marker. I just stepped back and pushed through the batwings of the Wolf's Den. Big Mike and Kilby and A.J. and Matt was all sittin' at a window table. I stood in the batwings and looked at them.

"You going to stop them, Sheriff?" Matt asked me.

"No, sir. It's a fair fight . . . at least the way it's writ now it is. Course, we all know it ain't. But that ain't up to me."

Matt stared at me. When he agin spoke, his voice was low-pitched. "You're a strange man, Sheriff. I'm having a difficult time understanding your motives."

"There ain't that much to figure, Mister Mills. I just be-lieve in doin' what I think is right, that's all. Right, bein' what the majority believes. Ain't that what this country is all about?"

The man give out with a long sigh. I was havin' some difficulty in figurin' him out, too. Ever'time I'd get an opinion fixed in my mind about him, I'd have to change it. He acted like that deep in his heart, he wanted to do right. But I didn't have no such trouble with A.J. He was just a plain ol' revolvin' son of a bitch. That meant that no matter which-a-way he decided to turn, he was still a son of a bitch!

I give all my attention to the two men now in the center of the street, about forty feet apart. Little Jack was maybe five feet, three inches tall, and that might be pushin' it, but he was snake-fast with a short gun. I knowed how it was he come to be a gunfighter, and it wasn't no pretty story. But then, neither was it all his fault.

Him bein' so little and all, he took some terrible beatin's and some awful ribbin' as a youngster. It was said that he went a little nuts from it, and I don't doubt it none. Folks can be uncommon cruel, and they don't really have to try that hard neither. Finally, so the story goes, one day Little Jack just took all of it that he could stand and killed a young man with a gun. After that, he had to flee from his Arkansas home. But he might have turned out bad anyways. For after that, he took to killin' like a beaver takes to buildin' a dam. He stepped over the line and got to where he liked to kill.

"I must offer my congratulations on your engagement, Sheriff," Matt spoke up.

He was a strange one, that Matt Mills. Without takin' my eyes from the life-and-death play out in the dusty, hot street, I said, "Thank you, sir. I consider myself to be a lucky man."

"You ain't married yet," Big Mike said, a sour note in his voice.

I cut my eyes to look at him. "And what the hell is that supposed to mean?" My own tone was harsher than I intended it to be. I just flat didn't like this big ox.

But he wouldn't reply. Just smiled kinda ugly-like at me.

Cuttin' my eyes back to the street, I knew the draw was only seconds away. Little Jack was laughin' at the Indiana man, and callin' him some right ugly names, too.

"I sure am glad the wind's right," Little Jack called out. "'Cause you stink as bad as them goddamn hogs you raise. What the hell do you, sleep with 'em?"

Little Jack was deliberately makin' the farmer mad, and the farmer was playin' right into his game. I could see the farmer's hands was tremblin' and his face was shiny with sweat.

"Hog-turd eatin', chicken-pickin', two-bit nester bastard!" Little Jack told him.

I never could figure that. Man will go into a cafe and order him bacon and eggs for breakfast, but make fun of the people who raise the chickens and the hogs. Don't make no sense.

"Are you gonna fight, you damn yellow nester?" Little Jack hollered, "Or run home and hide behind your wife's petticoats?"

The farmer's hand dropped to the butt of his pistol. He never had a chance. Little Jack laughed at him and then drilled him twice before the farmer could clear leather. The Indiana man stumbled, and then fell forward, on his face, dyin' in the dusty street.

I pushed open the batwings and stepped outside. "That's it, Jack. Get your horse and clear out of town. And I mean do it right now. I don't want no more trouble."

"And if I don't?" Little Jack turned to face me. There was a peculiar light shinin' in his eyes, a killin' light from within a man who enjoyed killin' people.

"Then make your play, Little Jack."

But Little Jack knew that even if he beat me to the draw— and I didn't think he could do that—I'd still get lead in him. He smiled and the light faded from his eyes. I seen him slowly relax. The Indiana man jerked once, and then was still, blood stainin' the dirt under and around him. "All right, Sheriff. I'm gone."

He got his horse from the stable and was ridin' out in a

couple of minutes. Come to think of it, anybody who knew a flip about horseflesh wouldn't never call that pretty little paint pony ugly.

I rode out to the Hickman place, gettin' there about two o'clock that afternoon. It wasn't much of a place. Sod-roof shanty and without even goin' inside, I knew it had a dirt floor that the Missus would sweep two or three times a day. It was a two-bit operation all the way around. I had me a hunch that the Indiana man was on his way out even before Little Jack showed up in his tater patch.

The place was rundown and just plain crummy lookin'.

There was already a bunch of wagons and a few horses and mules around the place. And the looks I received from the men wasn't all that friendly. I swung down off Pronto and tied him secure to the fence. One good jerk and Pronto could tear the fence down. It was a rawhide outfit all the way around. I turned to face the farmers, bein' careful to avoid gettin' kicked by Pronto. I knowed he liked me, but he had to show some independence every now and then.

"We thought you was on our side, Sheriff," a clodhopper called out from the knot of men.

I'd seen him around, but couldn't hang a name right on him. "I'm on the side of the law, mister. And there ain't no law agin' two men facin' each other with guns."

"But Hickman wasn't no gunfighter!"

"But even knowin' that, which he damn shore ought to have known, he still strapped on a short gun. I ain't sayin' it was right, 'cause it ain't, but in the eyes of the law, there wasn't nothin' I could do about it. That's something y'all gonna have to understand, damnit!"

I shut my mouth before I lost what little temper I still had left me.

Don't get me wrong—I did feel sorry for these men and their families. But when you ride through Indian country, you best ride like an Indian does, and the same applies for damn near any other situation. That's something these men had yet to learn.

I took a deep breath and said, "Now you all just settle down."

They didn't like it; they done a lot of mumblin', but I could tell they was just lookin' for some easy place to direct their anger, and they found it, to a degree, with me. But they also found out quick-like not to push me too much.

Most of these men had been out here only a few years, comin' from Ohio and Pennsylvania and such far-off places as that. Places where most people didn't tote guns and your neighbor was just a hoot and a holler away, maybe even right next door, all cramped up like a pigeon roost. Not like out here. They come from places where if a body got into a jam, you called the organized law and they'd settle it for you. Not like out here.

Inside, I could hear the Reverend Sam Dolittle prayin' and comfortin' the Widder Hickman. I looked at the men.

Maybe half of these men would make it out here—if that many. A lot of them would give it up and head on back east, some would head for a town of some size and clerk in a store for the rest of our lives, so they could have neighbors all around them. Not like out here.

I tried to understand their feelings, and I did, sort of. It was the sheer vastness of it all, the emptiness of it all. There is a damn good reason why it's called the Big Lonesome, 'cause it is. And man, out here, most of the time, you are on your own.

"All right, men, tell me what you know about this Hickman feller."

Well, they got to talkin', tellin' me what a fine feller he had been, and when they wound down, I thought they'd been talking about Jesus.

Now, I wasn't takin' up for what Little Jack had done; I pretty well knew he'd been sent out on the prowl. But I told these very same men, personal told them, that to stand alone was a dumb thing to do. That they had to band together and fight.

Reverend Dolittle, he was gettin' all heated up inside that dirt-floor shanty, his voice boomin' out. And he was givin' A.J. and Matt what-for.

When I didn't say nothing, just stared back at them, the men, they took to shufflin' their feet and lookin' at the ground and starin' at ever'thing but me. Things got real quiet, except for Dolittle's voice . . . he kept on harpin' on A.J. and Matt. Seemed like he should have been comfortin' the widder more than he was.

"Now tell me the truth," I told the group.

One man, he spoke up. "Sonny had a bad temper. And he thought hisself to be tough and good with a pistol. He said he didn't need no help to handle some ignorant cowboy. He said that if just one of us would stand up for our rights and kill one of these so-called gunhands, the rest of them would skedaddle out."

"And you all believed that crap?"

Their silence told me they had believed it, all right. Talk about dumb. "Boys, you're farmers, and probably good ones. But you're not gunslicks . . . more important, you're not western men. You don't understand the west and the people who live here . . ."

"Now you see here, Sheriff!" One farmer said, raisin' his voice. "What are you tryin' to say? That we're cowards?"

I wanted to reach out and grab him by his scruffy neck and slap him a time or two. But I held my temper in check. "No, I'm not sayin' that at all. I ain't knockin' none of you, courage-wise.

I'm sure you're all brave men. Hell, you come out here, didn't you? You can probably take your squirrel rifles and knock a squirrel out of a tree at two hundred yards. But you're not fast guns. Don't you see what I'm gettin' at?"

Some of them nodded. They got my drift. But a lot of them didn't. Those would be the ones who wouldn't make it out here. And it wasn't because they wasn't good solid men. It was just that they was fightin' what they didn't understand and wasn't makin' no effort to understand it. Wilderness, desert, swamp . . . if you understand it, you got a chance of survivin' in it. You get crossways of it, and you won't make it.

They stood and stared at him. The Reverend Dolittle had calmed down somewhat, but he was still givin' A.J. and Matt a bad time of it—and they deserved it, I reckon.

I left the grim-faced, angry bunch of farmers and walked towards the shanty to pay my respects to the Widder Hickman. Seems like there was gettin' to be a whole bunch of widder women in the valley all of a sudden. And I had me a deep-down in my guts feelin' that there was gonna be a lot more before it was all over and done with.

I didn't like to think that Pepper might become a widder before she even got hitched.

If that was possible.

Chapter 13

I got back into town just in time to see a cowhand from a small spread, the Crooked T, walkin' towards the Wolf's Den, and he was walkin' and had that look about him that he was trouble-huntin'.

I cut him off before he reached the boardwalk, me and Pronto between him and the saloon. "What's the matter here?"

"Git outta my way, Sheriff." He shoved Pronto on the rump and Pronto like to have took his hand off. The cowboy got out of the way just in the nick of time.

The cowboy, he started cussin'.

"Whoa, partner!" I told him. "You don't give me no orders. Now you just settle down and back off a mite."

De Graff picked that time to step out of the office and see us in the middle of the street. He come runnin' our way in that funny-lookin', bowlegged way all us have who've spent the biggest part of our life on the back of a horse.

"Rick!" De Graff shouted. "You back your butt off, now. Damnit, Rick, you hear me?"

"What the hell y'all gangin' up on me for?" the cowboy demanded. "I ain't done nothin' wrong—yet," he added.

"That's right, Rick. So 'fore you do something, like that 'yet' bit, let's us just step over to the other side of the street and we'll talk about who put the burr under your blanket."

He didn't like it none, but he finally turned around and walked across the street.

De Graff got all up in his face. "Now, what the hell was you goin' to do in the Wolf's Den? You know that's Circle L and Rockinghorse territory."

"Free country," Rick mumbled. "All right. It's that damn Mex gunslinger, Sanchez."

"What about Sanchez?"

Rick, he looked down at the dirt. "He insulted my boss lady."

"Pearle Druggan?" De Graff asked.

"Yeah."

"How?"

I was lettin' De Graff handle it; he knowed most of the people in the valley. I guessed that Rusty and Burtell was still out in the county.

"He's been sayin' things about her."

"What sort of things? Damnit, Rick, gettin' anything out of you is worser than pullin' a tooth from a bear!"

Rick shuffled his feet. "It ain't a fitten thing to say aloud."

"Then whisper it."

He whispered it. I was plumb taken aback. A body just don't say them sorts of things about no lady, especially no good married woman.

I finally spoke up. "Ain't this something for Mister Druggan to handle?"

"Yeah, Rick," De Graff said. "What about that?"

"He cain't. A rattler spooked his horse last week and he got throwed. Busted his leg. We drew cards to see who was gonna handle Sanchez. I won, boys!"

"You didn't win nothin'," I told him flatly. "Sanchez is pure poison with a six-gun." I started to tell him to back off and ride out of town, but then I realized I didn't have the right to do that. Damnit, this should be handled legal-like; I was beginnin' to see with a wider loop than I'd seen before. A man shouldn't be able to bad-mouth no decent person and get away with it without the law bein' able to take part. It just wasn't right.

I finally had to say it. "I can't stop you, Rick. You can go into any business in this town . . . but if I was you I'd stay out of that dress shop-pee. But I feel obliged to tell you to think about what you're doin' some more."

"What about the dress shop-pee?" De Graff asked.

"They's nekkid women runnin' around in there."

"Have mercy! You reckon they're still there?"

"'Nuff talkin'!" Rick said. "I done thought on it plenty. Missus Druggan is a good woman, so it's something I got to do."

Me and De Graff stepped aside and let the cowboy walk on acrost the street.

"It ain't right, Sheriff," De Graff said it quietly. "What's happenin' in this valley. I never thought I'd hear myself say that, but it ain't right. Rick ain't no gunhawk."

"Yeah . . . but he's got his pride." I spoke that with a taste of bitterness on my tongue. Pride had gotten a lot of men killed down through the years, all the way back to the cave people.

"I reckon, Sheriff."

We looked up and down the boardwalk. This time, we wouldn't have to clear the streets. The word had already been spread up and down the town. The street was empty.

Rick, he positioned hisself outside the saloon, the hitchrail to his right. I smiled grimly at that, for when Sanchez stepped out, he'd have the sun in his eyes . . . if he stepped out far enough.

"Rick ever dragged much iron, De Graff?"

"Not in Sanchez's class."

Well, that pretty much said it all. Now it was in the hands of God.

We waited, and I knew that Sanchez was doin' that deliberate; let the younger, inexperienced man sweat for a time.

"He's workin' on Rick's nerves," De Graff pegged it right.

"Yeah."

The batwings pushed open, and the Sonora gunfighter stepped out, a big wide grin on his dark face. I seen Rick stiffen just a tad.

"Ah, so," Sanchez said. "The little boy has come to defend the older woman's honor. How very noble! Are you certain you have no Spanish blood in you, Cowboy?"

Rick backed up, trying to pull Sanchez off the boardwalk and into the sun. But the Sonora gunhawk was an old hand at this. He knew if he stood where he was, the awning would keep the sun out of his eyes and cause Rick to sweat.

"Tell me something, young warrior," Sanchez smiled with the words, his very white teeth flashing. "Was the older woman's charms so great they are worth dying for?"

"What the hell are you tryin' to say, you son of a bitch?" Rick shouted.

Sanchez just laughed at him, not takin' no offense at the slur.

But then, I reckon it's hard to insult somebody by simply tellin' the truth.

Then Rick spoke his last. "Draw, you damned greasy bastard!"

Sanchez drew, and brother, was he quick. His first shot hit Rick in the right shoulder, knockin' the gun out of his hand. Then Sanchez stepped off the boardwalk and began puttin' lead in Rick. His second shot hit the cowboy in the left elbow, shattering it. Then Sanchez shot him in both legs.

The Sonora gunfighter then stood calmly over the badly wounded puncher and shucked out his empties, slowly reloading. He finally turned his back on the unconscious young man and walked back toward the batwings.

Just like Little Jack Bagwell, vicious and rotten to the core.

Sanchez was just pushin' open the batwings when the rifle shot hit him right between the shoulder blades, knocking him forward, dead as he fell into the Wolf's Den.

And I knowed right then and there that the valley war was on, and it was gonna go down in western history as one of the bloodiest. Right at that time, I wished I knew where to get in touch with Smoke Jensen . . . I could sure use the fastest gun in the west right about now.

Punchers and gunslicks began pourin' out of the saloon. "Hold it!" I shouted, running to the street. "Get back inside the saloon. First one who drags iron, I kill! This is Sheriff's Department business, not none of yours. Move, goddamnit, right now!"

They moved back inside, slowly and with much cussin' and grousin'. But they did vacate the boardwalk.

I didn't have no idea where the rifle shot had come from, but I wouldn't have put it past A.J. or Matt, or Big Mike, to have one of their own backshot just to blow the lid off the pot. I sent De Graff off to check the upstairs off the buildin' across the street. But I had serious doubts of ever findin' out who pulled the trigger on the rifle that killed the Sonora gunfighter.

And I knowed he was dead. He hadn't even twitched since the slug hit him.

Doc Harrison, he come runnin' up with Truby and his helper right behind him. The Doc ordered Rick to be taken to his little four-bed clinic located behind his office. He looked at Sanchez and then looked at me.

"Dead, Sheriff. I should imagine the bullet severed the spinal cord and then struck the heart. He died almost instantly."

"Good. In a way."

"What do you mean, Sheriff?"

"Sanchez's got brothers and uncles and cousins and the like that'll come up quick when they hear the news about his dyin'. Lobo, just to mention one of his kin."

We was standin' by the batwings of the Wolf's Den. The gunhawks that was gathered around smiled when I said Lobo's name.

The Doc, he paled. "Lobo!"

"Yeah. The crazy one."

"My God. How many more are there?"

"Hell, they's a whole passel of 'em. But the ones who ride together the most, so I've heard and read on dodgers, is Lobo, Pedro, Salvador, and Fergus."

Doc Harrison blinked. *"Fergus?"*

"Yeah, Fergus. He's sort of a half-brother to Sanchez. And he's crazy as a lizard—and just about as ugly."

Doc Harrison sighed. "You really haven't brightened up my day very much, Sheriff Cotton."

"Yeah? Well, I ain't done a whole lot for my day, either!"

"Fergus?" Jeff Baker asked me.

Late afternoon on the Quartermoon. Pepper and her ma was fixin' supper . . . dinner . . . and me, Jeff and Rolf was sittin' on the porch havin' tea. That's right—tea. Goddamnest-tastin' stuff I ever tried to drink in all my life. Didn't taste like nothin'. Weak as all get-out. But gentlemen was supposed to drink tea. I think I'd rather stay an ungentleman.

Rolf asked, "Any clues on who killed Sanchez, Cotton?"

"Not nary a one. De Graff found the brass, .44 round. But it ended right there."

"But you suspect? . . ."

"I don't have no suspects, Mr. Baker. Hell, it could have been anybody in the county. Big row now is where to plant him. Dolittle is raisin' Holy hell about him bein' buried—or plannin' to be planted—in the main burial grounds. Says he won't tolerate it. So I reckon Sanchez will go to boot hill. That Dolittle is a strange one."

Jeff nodded his head and sipped his tea. I wished they'd both turn their heads so's I could dump my cup out. "How did someone of Spanish ancestry get to be named Fergus?"

"Fergus ain't Spanish. I don't know what the hell he is. And neither does he. He ain't no kin at all to the Sanchez family." I put that tea cup down; I just couldn't abide no more of it. "Fergus was taken by the 'Paches when he was just a baby; raised up by 'em. Until the Injuns threw him out of the camp. They couldn't abide him either. And you know that when an Apache can't abide a person, that person's got to be rotten through and through."

"And then the Sanchez family found him and took him in to raise?" Rolf asked, takin' a sip of tea.

"Not really. They was gonna stake him out on an anthill for rapin' their sister. So the story goes that I heard. Caught 'em both buck-assed nekkid in the barn."

Rolf spilled tea down the front of his shirt at that. I'd rather spill it down my shirt than drink the stuff.

Both men sat and stared at me.

"Come to find out, so the story goes. Fergus didn't rape the sister at all. It was a, well, mutual understandin' between the both of them. She didn't have no sense either."

"I beg your pardon?" Rolf inquired politely.

"She up and married Fergus. All this was years ago. They had two kids. They grown men by now. Outlaws—Tyrone and Udell. I imagine they'll be comin' along with the rest of the family. And they're crazy, too."

There was a look of total disbelief on Rolf's face. He shook his head and sighed. "What happened to the sister . . . ah, the lady Fergus married?"

"She ain't no lady. You can bet your boots on that."

"Would you please elucidate?" Rolf said.

I looked at him. "Huh?"

"Go into greater detail, please."

"Oh. Well, the Apaches took her durin' a raid. But they brung her back in about a week. Told Fergus they was sorry they ever took her and would he please take her back? They said they'd give him ten horses if he'd take her off their hands. Fergus held out for twenty horses and they settled on fifteen."

Mister Baker, he stroked his chin for a moment. "Incredible story."

"You ought to see her one time. That woman invented ugly and mean."

"Will she be coming along with the others?" Jeff asked.

"God, I hope not!"

The *Doubtful Informer* ran big headlines on the shootin's.

TWO VICIOUS KILLINGS IN ONE DAY!

The Streets of Doubtful Run Red With Blood.

Then Pritcher ranted and raved for a whole page on the influx of gunfighters in the county.

I showed the paper to De Graff and the others. "Do any of you know what influx means?"

"I think it's something like the croup," Burtell said.

"You mean they brung in a disease?" Rusty asked.

"I reckon."

"I'll ask Pepper. She'll know. How's Rick doin'?"

"Bad," Rusty said.

Rick died from complications on the same day Hickman was gettin' planted. Truby was gettin' rich in the valley, and the worst was yet to come. The Crooked T boys come ridin' into town just as the funeral parade was movin' slow toward the graveyard on the hill. Those professional mourners was shoutin' and swayin' and earnin' their money, the women squallin' and the men moanin' low.

It was a right nice sight.

The Crooked T wasn't a real big spread, when held up to the likes of the Circle L or the Rockinghorse, but they had ten hands, and all ten come to town. And they was huntin' any trouble they could find.

I rounded up the boys. "That's it," I told them. "We just can't allow this town to be turned into no shootin' gallery. We've got to stop this right now."

We checked our guns and filled up our belt loops with .44 rounds, stuffin' our pockets with shotgun shells. Then the four of us walked right down the center of the big main street, all of us carryin' Greeners. There was a handful of Rockinghorse and Circle L punchers in the Salty Dog; for once, no gunhawks in town. Rusty and Burtell faced the batwings of the saloon, me and De Graff facin' the Crooked T boys.

"You boys want a drink of whiskey or a beer," I told the grim-faced riders, "that's fine. Have your refreshments at the Cantina or at the Dirty Dog. But you stay the hell away from this saloon. First one of you starts trouble, I put your butt in the pokey. Now does ever'body understand that?"

"What about them in yonder?" I was asked, with a jerk of his thumb toward the Wolf's Den.

"They're gonna leave town right shortly. I am personal gonna escort them to the town boundary. After that, they're on their own. What you boys do outside of the town limits is your own affair. You got all that?"

The riders inside the saloon was all lookin' out, not likin' none of it.

A faint smile touched the lips of the Crooked T spokesman. He looked to be the foreman—a cowboy can usually tell who's the boss without bein' told. "We'll have our drinks at the Salty Dog, Sheriff Cotton. Then we'll be leavin' out— peaceful. Unless we're pushed into something. If that happens, I can't guarantee nothin'."

"I appreciate that, boys."

When they had swung their horses and crossed the street, Rusty said, "You settin' them punchers in yonder up for a killin', Sheriff?"

"No, Rusty, you and Burtell wait until the Crooked T bunch gets inside the saloon. Then you escort the riders in yonder out the back door and to the stable, then out of town. You tell them boys to ride and keep ridin'. Maybe we can pull this thing off."

"I hope so," Burtell said. "I'm sure tired of moppin' up blood in this town."

We lounged around for a few minutes, then Rusty and Burtell stepped casual-like into the Salty Dog and done what I told 'em.

Out of the corner of my eye, I could see the punchers slippin' toward the stable and mountin' up.

It worked fine, only I wasn't figurin' on the Crooked T bunch havin' a spy watchin' us. But they did, and he seen Rusty and Burtell leadin' the punchers out of town, usin' the back alleys. No sooner than the outnumbered punchers left the rear of the Salty Dog, the Crooked T boys was runnin' out of the saloon acrost the street and in the saddle, hot after them.

I caught up with all three brands just in time to witness the shootin'.

One Rockinghorse rider was knocked off his horse by the gunfire, head-shot and dyin' as he slipped from the saddle to the ground. A Crooked T puncher was gut-shot, just barely hangin' on to the saddle, by the horn.

"Get the Doc!" I yelled over my shoulder to De Graff. "And Truby, too."

As I galloped past the graveyard on the hill, the Reverend Dolittle had been warmin' up his vocal cords for his service on the Mound.

I sure hoped he could keep his voice from leavin' him, for I had me a hunch it was gonna be a record-breakin' summer for plantin' folks in the valley.

And there wasn't nothin' I could do to stop the firefight between the brands. Not unless I wanted to ride smack up into the middle of it and probably get myself killed. And I didn't have no intention of doin' anything that stupid.

It was over and done with in about two minutes; but them two minutes seemed like a week and a half. All the Rockinghorse and Circle L riders was down . . . dead, dyin', or bad wounded. Four of the Crooked T boys had been blowed out of the saddle. I could see right off that two of them were dead.

The warm early summer's air, with no breeze to speak of, was filled with gunsmoke and the smell of sweat and fear and panicked horses. I walked Pronto up into the middle of the now quiet but bloody battleground and sat my saddle, glarin' at the foreman of the Crooked T. He had took one in the arm and another slug had grazed his hard head.

"Well, mister, you done it now, and I reckon you know it."

He wound a handkerchief around the flesh wound in his arm and didn't say nothin' to me until he'd finished with it. Wipin' the blood from his face, he lifted his eyes and met my stare with a hard one of his own.

"Had to be, Sheriff. And you know that well as me. Rockinghorse and Circle L has got to be cut down to size. These punchers," he waved his hand at the dead, them dying, and the wounded, "they're just as bad as the gunhands. The folks in the valley have had a gut-full of it. So if there's gonna be a war, let's do it and get it over with."

He was right, and I knowed it. But I didn't have to like it. "It ain't gonna be that easy, partner." Out of the corner of my eyes, I could see a lone rider, walkin' his horse easy-like towards us, comin' from the south. Behind us, I could hear Doc Harrison's buggy comin' fast. And in the distance, the voice of them on the hillside singin' a sad song. A mourner cut loose with a long slow wail. Dolittle must have run out of steam.

A puncher from the Circle L had rode up, sittin' his horse close to me, listenin' and eyeballin' things.

Doc whoaed his team and jumped out, his black bag in his hand, and begun tendin' to the wounded. Truby's meat-wagon—not the fancy one—was comin' up fast, in a cloud of dust. And I could see that lone rider was mounted on a black horse, and the rider was dressed up all in black.

My guts churned just a bit, for I had me a sinkin' feelin' who it was.

The rider come close and reined up. We sat our horses and stared at one another. Finally, he pushed back his hat and grinned at me.

"Well, well," says he. "Bless my soul. If it ain't Cotton Pickens!"

That Circle L rider thought it was funny. Most folks do. He started laughin'. He stopping thinkin' it was so funny when I leaned over and knocked him clean out of the saddle.

I'm right touchy about my name.

BOOK TWO

I begin to smell a rat.
—Cervantes

BOOK TWO

Chapter One

"How you doin', Brother Jack?"

"Tolerable well. You're lookin' fair yourself, Brother Cotton. Howsomever, that badge you're wearin' does take something away. I never thought I'd see no kin of mine ever totin' no goddamned badge around."

"I never thought I'd see the day when no brother of mine would turn out to be a cold-blooded killer, neither."

The Circle L rider was on the ground, holdin' his mouth where I'd popped him. And no one else had laughed, neither.

Jack, he smiled, but it was a cold smile, totally empty of any humor. And his eyes was like that of a dead man. Maybe inside, he was dead.

"We'll have to get together for a drink, Brother Cotton. We can talk about our boyhood and such."

"We'll sure do that, Jack. But we'll have to do it quick."

"Oh?"

"Yeah. You ain't gonna be in town for very long, Brother Jack."

That cold, death's-head smile touched his mouth agin. But not his eyes. "No warrants out on me, Cotton. None at all. And it's still a free country. There was a war fought to decide that, remember?"

"You start trouble in this county, Jack, and I'll come after you. And that's a pure-dee promise from me."

"I hope you don't, brother. I wouldn't want to draw down on my own blood kin."

"But don't think I won't, Jack."

He nodded his head, a wariness touching those cold eyes. "Is there a hotel in town, Cotton?"

"Doubtful Lodging."

He cocked his head to one side. "Are you funnin' me, brother?"

"Nope."

"Weird town, Cotton."

"In more ways than one, Brother Jack. And gonna get weirder."

Jack, he touched his hat brim and said, "See you around, Brother." He rode on, without lookin' back.

"Is he really your brother, Sheriff?" Burtell asked.

"Yep."

"He somebody we ought to know?" De Graff asked.

"I reckon. Boys, you just met Jack Crow."

Nobody even smiled at that.

That Circle L rider, he climbed back in the saddle and said, "I'll get you for sucker punchin' me, Sheriff."

"You better shut that trap 'fore I decide to shoot you."

He rode out after that, still holdin' his bloody mouth.

"We got more problems, Sheriff," De Graff called. "Look yonder."

I looked. A whole passel of clodhoppers, in buckboards and wagons and ridin' horses and mules, was comin' at us. And settin' back a-ways, another bunch of men and women. I recognized them as small ranchers and their wives.

"Now, what the hell . . . ?" I muttered. I never have been a man who liked surprises very much.

"Whatever it is," Rusty said, "it ain't no good."

I silently agreed with that.

"Somebody get me another wagon!" Truby hollered. "I can't carry all the dead."

"Hell with the dead!" Doc Harrison yelled. "I've got to have more wagons to carry the still living, man!"

I looked at a bystander, his mouth hangin' open. "Ride into town and send more wagons out here. Have some of them lined with hay."

Lee Jones, one of the small ranchers I'd met on my prowlin' around the county, was the first to reach us. His eyes took in the bloody scene. I began to put things together then. I hadn't noticed it before, but the family resemblance between the men was real strong.

Kilby, the foreman at the Rockinghorse, was some kin to Lee. Brother, I'd guess.

Looked like to me there was gonna be more than one set of brothers at odds with each other in this valley war.

"What's goin' on here, Sheriff?" Lee asked.

"Couple of brands got all crossed up with each other. What are you folks up to? You're a tad late for the funeral."

"Hear there's gonna be a big weddin' in the valley right soon," Lee replied, shiftin' around my original question.

"Pretty soon, I reckon. You wanna tell me what's goin' on with you people, Lee?"

He didn't look none too happy about my askin'. "We're gonna have us a big county meetin' at the a-rena, Sheriff." His reply was sullen.

The arena, I had discovered soon after gettin' to be made sheriff, was one of them things like folks such as the Greeks and the Romans had—accordin' to Pepper—but they built theirs, this one was formed up by nature. It was located on the other side of town, and sometimes, so I was told, when a travelin' show would come through, that's where they'd play. Course there wasn't no tables or chairs, but the ground had been picked clean of little rocks, and it was right comfortable. Lots of big flat rocks to sit on or have picnics. And there was a big flat ledge on the base of the hill to use as a stage.

Pepper wanted us, weather permittin', to get hitched up there. I thought that idea was a tad showboatish for my tastes.

But more than likely, that idea was her ma's—put on a spectacle for the folks to see.

"First I've heard of it, Lee. What's the meetin' all about?"

"Well, Sheriff, you be there at five o'clock and you'll sure find out."

I didn't like the smart-aleck way he said that. "I'll sure be there, Lee."

We was still moppin' up the blood and totin' off the bodies, livin' and dead, when Matt Mills and his kids and all their hands come ridin' past. It made quite a show. Matt, he reined up and looked at me.

"I don't appreciate not being told about this county meeting, Sheriff."

"I just heard of it myself a few minutes back. I ain't got no more idea what it's about than you do."

"Ummp!" he said, and rode on.

"Uppity bastard!" De Graff growled.

Then, from the other direction, here come A.J. and all his brood and hands and gunslingers. Gettin' to be a regular circus.

And then, with a sigh, I looked up the road and here they come, more trouble, Al Long's brothers, Cledus, Stan, and Luther. They was all narrow-faced, lean-lookin' men. And they wasn't known for their friendliness and for overflowin' with the milk of human kindness.

"When this place blows," Burtell said, "it's gonna go up like a fireworks show."

"Yeah," I agreed. I looked up at the Long brothers. "Howdy, boys!"

"Pickens," Cledus returned the greetin'. They all reined up close together. "I heard a right distressin' thing the other day, Pickens. It was told to us that you kilt our brother, Al. Is that right?"

"Yep."

"Why?"

"'Cause he was wanted by the law. When I asked him to turn hisself in proper-like, he refused and drew down on me."

"You shouldn't oughtta done that, Pickens."

"But I done it. And you boys best not cause no trouble in this county."

"You know why we're here, Pickens, so get ready for it."

"Yeah, I got a pretty fair idea, Cledus."

"We heard yesterday that Sanchez was back-shot," Stan managed to speak around the big chaw in his mouth.

"That's right. News travels pretty fast, I reckon."

"Well, we hurried on when we learned that. We wanted to be the ones to put lead in you 'fore the Mex's kith and kin got here and done it." He grinned, exposing stained and broken teeth. For a fact, he wasn't no thing of beauty. Be a close call between him and a pile of road apples.

This day had been plumb tryin'. And I had me a gut-full of smart-mouthed people. "I wish you'd shut your mouth, Stan," I told him. "Somebody's liable to come along and mistake it for a empty privy hole."

He squalled like a stuck hog and grabbed for his gun; but I was ready for that. Sidestepping, I jerked off my hat and hit his horse smack in the face with it. That horse reared up and Stan took him a backwards tumble right out of the saddle. Without lookin' back to see who was doin' it, I heard the sounds of hammers bein' eared back and seen Cledus and Luther stiffen in the saddle.

Stan was just gettin' to his feet when I reached him. Drawin' back, I knocked him flat on his butt on the ground. He hit hard and swallered his chew. Man, you never heard such hackin' and coughin' and spittin' and cussin' in all your life. He wound down with, "You gawddam two-bit, tinhorn, no-good badge-totin', piss-ant!" Then he got to his feet once more.

I slugged him again, smack on the side of his long jaw. His eyes was rollin' back in his head as he was fallin' bassackwards. He was out cold when he finally hit the ground.

"Arrest him, Burtell. Tie him acrost his saddle and chunk him in the bucket."

"On what charge?" Cledus squalled.

"Threatenin' the life of a peace officer. You wanna join him in the pokey?"

"You bastard!" Cledus yelled. "By Gawd, Pickens, we'll git you."

I reached up and jerked him out of the saddle, tossin' his bony butt to the ground.

"Arrest him, too," I told Burtell. "Stick 'em both in the bucket."

"With pleasure, Sheriff." Burtell reached down and jerked Cledus' guns out of leather.

"Has you gone slap-dab crazy with that there badge?" Luther hollered. "You keep on and I ain't gonna have nobody to drink with!"

"You would if you'd take a bath ever' now and then. Howsomever, I could stick you in the pokey with your brothers. How about that, Luther?"

"You post the bond, Pickens, and I'll come bail 'em out." He spurred his horse and was gone at a gallop, headin' for the nearest saloon.

Stan and Cledus on the way to the lockup, the dead toted off, and the wounded in the clinic, I asked Pritcher. "What's this county meetin' all about anyways?"

"I am sorry to say that I just became aware of it, Sheriff. But I am certain the ramifications of it will be awesome. Don't you agree?"

I blinked. "Yeah. Took the words right out of my mouth."

There must have been at least five or six hundred people livin' in the county, and from the looks of things, all of them was in town for the meetin'.

I had time for a bath behind Wong's place and a change of clothes. Pepper had left word that she would meet me at the office at four-thirty; we'd walk to the arena together. I had just straightened my kerchief and plopped my hat on my head when she walked into the office.

She come straight to me and put her arms around my waist. "I'm scared, Cotton."

And she wasn't kiddin' none. I could feel her tremblin' as she pushed close to me. "What's the matter, Pepper?"

She pulled back and looked up at me, her blues all misty with little-bitty tears. "You really don't know what this county meeting is all about, do you, Cotton?"

"I ain't got a clue."

She walked around the office for a few seconds. "Well, Lee Jones and the others are meeting to map out plans to start a company of irregulars to police the valley."

"Irr-what?"

"It's an army, Cotton."

"An *army!*"

"Yes. It's a military-type group of men, with a couple of officers and sergeants and stuff like that. Just like a regular company of cavalry. Jeff overheard some men talking the other day and told us about it. Father thought they were only pipe-dreaming; that's why he didn't send someone in right away to inform you of it. Dad only found out the validity of it this morning."

I understood most of what she said. Enough to know I didn't like none of it. Things like these here irregulars might look good on paper, but put into practice, they don't hardly ever work out. What it boils down to is that they ain't nothin' but vigilantes, and oftentimes they get to the point—if they didn't start out thataway—where they ain't no better than the people they're fightin'.

I said as much and then waited for Pepper's reaction.

She smiled at me. She was lovely, with the sunlight pourin' in through the window, sparklin' in her honey-blond hair. "That's exactly what Father said you would say."

"You got any idea who's gonna be headin' up this bunch of irregulars?"

"A most unlikely candidate, at first glance," Rolf Baker said, steppin' into the office. "I'm sorry, I was not eavesdropping intentionally. The door was open and I could not help overhearing your conversation."

"That's all right, Mister Baker. What do you mean, a most unlikely candidate?"

"The Reverend Sam Dolittle."

"Say . . . *what?*"

"Believe it or not, but it's true, the preacher was a Union cavalry officer during the war between the states. Don't sell him short on bravery, Cotton. But the problem is, the man is a fanatic."

Then I recalled his words out at the shanty. It began to fit. "What's that fanatic-thing mean?"

"That the Reverend Dolittle is not a reasonable man on certain issues."

"Oh! All right. You mean he might go off the deep end and do something real stupid?"

"Precisely, Cotton. Fanatics, on either side of an issue, can be quite cruel and savage. That's something I would not like to see in this valley."

"Yeah, me neither." As if I didn't have enough to worry about, now this. But I had to say, "In a way, I don't blame the people for formin' up like this. But I don't like it at all."

We started towards the rock arena, walkin' slow. Since near'bouts the whole town was gonna be there, I had assigned the deputies to keep watch on the town.

We walked, me and Rolf in the front, Pepper and her ma behind us. Rolf said, "Cotton, what are your feelings on Matt Mills?"

Jeff had joined us. "I don't know, Mister Baker. Sometimes I get the feelin' that he don't want all this trouble. Then at other times, I'm thinkin' that he's a greedy, uppity man who wants to be king of the whole valley—and ever'body in it to be his slaves and bow down to him. A.J., well, he's just a bastard. Excuse me, ladies."

Pepper laughed and her mother shook her head. "We came out here together, you know," Rolf spoke softly. "Years ago. Three adventurous young men. We all left substantial wealth behind us. And our families virtually disowned us all. There were no white people in this valley when we came here."

"Yes, sir. I know."

"I hate to say this, Cotton. The three of us having been through so much together . . . but I don't believe Matt is sane. A.J. is, or has changed into, a vain, greedy, and ruthless man. But Matt . . ." He give out a long sigh. "Matt is . . . well, disturbed."

"Nuts, you mean."

Rolf, he smiled sort of thin-like. "Well, I suppose you could phrase it like that."

I seen Brother Jack loungin' in front of the hotel. Haltin' the parade up the boardwalk, I said, "Y'all want to meet my brother, Jack Crow?"

"Are you serious?" Martha asked, lookin' all around her.

"Yes'um." I waved to Jack, signaling him to come on and join us.

He walked slow toward us. I got to admit, he struck a handsome figure. But his walk was pure gunfighter. More of a stalk than a walk.

"Nice-looking chap," Rolf observed.

"Yes," his wife agreed. "And there is a strong family resemblance there, Cotton."

"And it ends right there, ma'am. Jack is as crazy as a bessie-bug."

Pepper stepped up and touched me on the arm. "Why is he here, Cotton? Your brother, I mean."

"To kill me."

She gasped and her pa said, "By the Lord, Cotton! You can't mean that! The man is your brother, after all."

"That don't mean nothin' to Jack. I told you, he's plumb loco. When he gets closer, look in his eyes. That'll tell the whole story."

By then, he was up to us. I introduced ever'body all around, endin' with, "Brother Jack, this is my fee-ancy, Miss Pepper."

Jack, he eyeballed Pepper, an odd look in his cold, snakey eyes. Then he looked at me. "You done yourself proud, Brother Cotton. Pepper Pickens. Kind of a nice ring to it. I sure do hope the weddin' comes off without no hitches."

"What do you mean, Jack?"

That cold smile from him. "Well, Brother, you're in a dangerous sort of job. Anythin' might happen up or down the line. Now, if you was to quit totin' that star around and take up ranchin' or farmin', well, that might change matters just a whole lot." Without changin' expression, he added, "If you get my drift."

I met him look for look. "Oh, I get it all right, Jack. But you know me . . . when I start a job of work, I tend to see it right through to the end. Remember?"

"Yeah. Yeah, I do. Pa could always count on you to do your

chores like a good little boy. Well, I was in hopes you'd grown out of that. That don't make my job a bit easier. And I think you know it. Ladies." He tipped his hat.

"Mister Crow," they said in unison.

"Gentlemen," Jack said to us, and then he walked away. He sure had him a fine-lookin' set of matched .45s. Fancy, pearl-handled guns.

"What was he trying to say to you, Cotton?" Pepper asked, her hands on her hips.

I sighed. "Well, I reckon you could say he was tellin' me to quit sheriffin' or he was gonna have to kill me. That's the way I took it."

"Surely, *surely,*" Rolf said, "you have to be mistaken."

"I don't think so, sir."

"His eyes are frightening," Martha said, her voice low.

"Yes'um."

"Snake eyes," Jeff spoke up. "It's like looking into the eyes of a rattler."

"Yeah," I agreed. "Just before he strikes."

Chapter Two

"The situation in the valley has become intolerable," the Reverend Sam Dolittle thundered, his voice booming and bouncing all around the natural amphitheater, touching all there. "If civilized behavior is ever to come to this little paradise on earth, we—the citizens—are going to have to take a stand against the forces of darkness. Those evil men who lurk about us, tails and horns hidden from mortal eyes, those men who wish to enslave us with their greed and ruthlessness and heathenistic behavior."

Sermon time agin.

"I am but a simple peaceful man," Dolittle lowered his head dramatically, "but even peaceful men sometimes reach a point where they must step out of the white robes of friendship and compassion and lay aside the plow for the sword."

Buckle on and tie down and drag iron, I reckon he meant.

"Yes!" he thundered. "They must gird their loins for confrontation."

I didn't have no idea what he just said, but it sounded plumb uncomfortable to me.

I looked around when the preacher paused to take him a long gulp of water and pull in some breath. I met the eyes of

Johnny Bull, standin' across the pit from me. He smiled and touched the brim of his hat. I done the same. Like me, Johnny, he knowed the time for talk was just about up. From now on, it was down to the nut-cuttin'.

The Rev, he droned on and on, gettin' present-day troubles in the valley all mixed up with biblical quotations . . . and gettin' a good many folks all stirred up, too. Now, in the valley and in the arena, there was some folks who had formed up a different type of church than what most believed in. These folks claimed to sometimes get in the spirit so deep that they get to talkin' in tongues and communicatin' with the higher-up spirits . . . up yonder, in the sky. De Graff, he said his sister joined one of them churches and was a different person afterwards. And I figured that if the Reverend Dolittle got them folks stirred up, that would be a sight to behold. Right unforgettable.

And Lordy, Lordy, but there was some gunslicks ever'-where you was to look. I touched glances with Waldo Stamps and Tanner Smith. Then I met the eyes and the ugliness of Injun Tom Johnson. And right over there was Nimrod, standin' with Ike Burdette and Tulsa Jack. Not ten feet away from them was Miss Maggie and Miss Jean, with their hands with them. Little Jack Bagwell, he had climbed up on a flat rock so's he could see what was goin' on. Big Mike was there, with his eyes hardly ever leavin' Pepper.

"Wahooo!" someone shouted, and I like to have jumped out of my boots. "Praise the Lord and load up the guns, brothers and sisters!"

I figured right off the bat that he was about to get in the spirit.

The woman with him, she raised her arms up over her head and shouted, "I feel it! I feel it! It's touching me! Praise the Lord!"

I craned my neck to see just who was feelin' her. But I couldn't spot nothin'. Made me kinda eerie feelin'.

"We must band together and *fight!*" Dolittle hollered. "We must rise up and slay the dragon of evil and raise the banner of decency and righteousness. We must kill the many-headed dragon before his evil numbers drag us all down into the pits. And if in doing so the valley runs red with blood, then so be it!"

"Wahoo!" a woman screamed. "Ughum booum washin' clock-bock!"

"What the hell did she say?" I whispered to Pepper.

"Hush, Cotton!" she shushed me.

When I looked agin, that woman had passed out and was layin' on the ground, her man just a fannin' her with his hat to beat sixty.

"I have prayed mightily, friends. And I have fasted long. In my mind I have walked through the shadows of the valley of death, with evil all around me . . . and I have spoken with the Lord. He has instructed me to pick up the sword and smite my enemies, smite them both hip and thigh."

Now, as for me, I had to draw the line at smitin' somebody on the hip and thigh. I never saw no sense in doin' that. I always found it best to just shoot them and be done with it. Damn a bunch of hip-smitin' and thigh-smackin'.

And right then, in the middle of a bunch of men and women gettin' in the spirit and shoutin' in tongues, the Reverend Sam Dolittle, he lit the fuse on the keg of powder.

He pointed a long finger straight at A.J. and Matt. "There is the evil," he squalled. "There they stand, with all their smugness and conceit and plans for endless human suffering. Right there stand Satan's cohorts—the destroyers!"

Lawyer Stokes got to jumping' up and down and flappin' his arms. "On behalf of Misters Mills and Lawrence, I'll sue you for slander, Preacher!"

"Then sue and be damned!" Dolittle roared. "And damn your black heart to the burning, smoking pits of hell, you

Godless heathen! You consort of the wicked, you cohort of the Prince of Darkness, you purveyor of wickedness and debaser of morals and truth and light. *Damn* you!"

Man, I was lovin' it! I stood there just grinnin' like a fool. Damn, but this was gettin' better and better. I always did like a good hellfire and brimstone and hand-clappin', singin', shoutin' service. I looked over at Johnny Bull. He was grinnin' just as big as me and I seen him wink and laugh.

One kinda large lady, she all of a sudden got the spirit flung on her and she commenced to speakin' in tongues, doin' a pretty good buck-and-wing and two-step as she was shoutin'.

"Frickin' and frackin' and jukin' at the jim-jam!" she hollered.

That wasn't exactly what she said, but that's about as close as I can come to repeatin' any of it.

"Sister Lorene is in the spirit!" a man hollered. "Hallelujah, sister."

My early churchgoin' got the better of me. "Yeah, sister, hallelujah!" I was clappin' my hands and pattin' my feet until Pepper gave me a good poke in the ribs and a dark look. I straightened right up and acted sheriffly again.

The Reverend Dolittle and A.J. Lawrence was still hollerin' and yellin' at each other, over the din of tongues and hand-clappin'.

"You can't say those kinds of things about me!" A.J. hollered. He waved his cigar in the air. "I'll see you in a court of law, preacher!"

"You cigar-suckin' sinner!" Dolittle fired back. "There is a stink in this place this evening; the smell of evil. And it is emanating from *you!*" He pointed.

I didn't know what emanatin' meant, but it sounded nasty to me.

Another lady got all up in the spirit and began dancin' and

prancin' around, speakin' in strange tongues. "Froggie in the cloggin' bottom sittin' in the mud!"

Or something close to that.

Then she just passed plumb out, falling backwards and landin' on her ampleness, her dress all hiked up.

"Sister Abigail!" another lady admonished her. "Cover yourself!"

"Her drawers is showin'," a man yelled.

'Bout fifty people, mostly men, went rushin' over there. But they was too late for any sightseein'. Sister Abigail had done jerked her dresstail down. But her eyes was still all walled back in her head and she was stiff as a board.

Now, I got a little suspicious of that. If the good lady was all caught up in the spirit, seems like to me that it wouldn't make no difference what was showin' if she was passed out.

But I reckon that ain't for me to say.

'Bout a dozen sodbusters, they formed up a line and set to singin' and shoutin' and praisin' the Lord in song.

Dolittle was still rantin' and ravin'. "The good people of this valley shall form an army of the Lord and drive the evil to the brink, like lemmings to the sea."

"To hell with you!" A.J. shouted.

Ol' Matt shouted, "Form your goddamned army." He shook his fist at the preacher.

The voices overpowered him. "Bringing in the sheaves, bringing in the sheaves . . ."

"Any of you bastards set foot on Rockinghorse land and I'll . . ."

". . . we shall come rejoicing, bringing in the . . ."

". . . see your butts hangin' from the nearest . . ."

". . . sheaves."

". . . tree limb, you god . . ."

". . . Bringing in the . . ."

". . . damned nester trash!"

". . . sheaves!"

Fistfights broke out, with men flailin' away at each other. With a sigh, I jerked iron and put two shots in the air. The arena went as silent as a grave. "That's it!" I shouted. "This meetin' is hereby con-cluded and over and done with, too. I ain't gonna have no killin' this afternoon." I pointed a finger first at Johnny Bull, who rode for the Circle L, and than at Fox Breckenridge, who rode for the Rockinghorse. "By the authority I got as sheriff of this county, I hereby say that both of you are deputies and you will help me clear this mess out of here."

"A deputy sheriff!" Fox squalled. "Cotton, you can't do this to me. I got my reputation to think of!"

"Stokes!" I hollered. "Give me a rulin' on what I just done."

"He can do it," the lawyer said, but it looked like it hurt his mouth to say it.

Johnny Bull, he thought it was funny.

"All right!" I yelled. "Break it up and clear on out of here, and I mean do it right damn now—move!"

The crowd, they didn't like it, but they commenced to move, anyways.

"Christian soldiers!" Dolittle hollered from the rock stage. "All of you to the House of God." He glared at me. "And you have no jurisdiction in a church, Sheriff."

"He's right on that," Stokes said.

The crowd slowed down and turned around at that, mumblin' amongst themselves. I raised my voice to be heard. "I don't care where you go. But you bunch up and start any trouble, talkin' about hangin' and shootin' and killin' each other, and I'll put your butts in the pokey. And if any of you think I won't do it, you just, by God, try me."

"Just who in the hell do you think you are, anyways?" a man hollered from out of the crowd, probably standin' behind his wife.

"The sheriff of this county. And I was swore to uphold the laws and that's what I'm doin'. I don't give a damn what brand you ride for, or what piece of ground you might plow. . . . I'm gonna keep the peace. Now clear on out of here!"

"Oh, doesn't his voice just fairly ring with firm authority," Boardin' House Belle piped up. "I just love a strong man!" She looked at me. "I'm fearful of the mood of this crowd, Sheriff. Would you escort me home?"

"I'll have one of my deputies do it, ma'am." I grinned at Fox. He called me a terrible name!

It was full dark in the town and the Reverend Dolittle was still raisin' sand and holy hell at his church. The church was jam-packed full with a whole bunch more out on the lawn. I had closed down all the saloons and warned them not to reopen until the next day. They didn't like it, but they done it.

At least for this night, I had kept the lid on the boilin' pot.

Fox Breckenridge had just galloped by, headin' for the Rockinghorse. His hat was on backwards and he was barefoot, his shirttail hangin' out. "You son of a bitch!" he hollered at me. "I'll get you for this."

Looked like Belle had found her a new man.

Probably wouldn't be seein' much of Fox in town no more. Which was all right with me.

Johnny Bull had ridden out right after we got the arena cleared out. Being a deputy wasn't nothin' new to Johnny. He'd been a damn good deputy some years back.

Burtell, he had taken him a stroll down to the church and had returned, takin' a seat with me and the others in front of the office.

"They got their army, all right, Sheriff," Burtell reported. "And the Reverend Dolittle has been named a colonel of it. There's a hundred men, all told. Pete Taylor, the rancher owns the Diamond T, he's been named as a major. Two farmers,

Bob Caldwell and Bill Noland, they been named captains. Sheriff, ain't it agin' the law to form up a private army?"

"Durned if I know. I don't think so. But Judge Barbeau will have to give us a rulin' on that, I reckon."

From the church and the grounds around it, a couple of hundred voices was raised in song. "Onward Christian Soldiers."

I didn't blame the people for gettin' together and formin' an army. But De Graff summed it all up for us.

"There's a bunch of people fixin' to get killed in this valley," he said gruffly. "Don't them folks know all they're doin' is playin' right into the hands of Lawrence and Mills? This is what they want. They'll kill off a bunch and get the land for a song."

"No, they don't know that," I spoke up. "Them folks think God is on their side in this. And maybe He is, I don't know. What I do know is that if there was three times their numbers, when they go up against all these seasoned gunhands, just a whole lot of 'em won't be comin' back to their wives and families."

"And there ain't nothin' we can do about it?" Rusty asked. "I mean, legal-like?"

"Not a damn thing. Just follow along behind 'em and help tote off the dead." I looked towards the east, as a growin' glow on the horizon caught my eyes. I pointed it out to the boys.

De Graff, he grunted. "Somebody's house and barn is on fire. Ass-kickin' time in the valley, boys."

At first light, me and Rusty was in the saddle, ridin' toward where we'd seen the fire flames in the night.

Within seconds of our spotting the fire, the church had emptied and folks had lit out of town, ridin' lickety-split toward the fire, all of them knowin' it would be burned down to the ground by the time any of them reached the scene.

But fortunately for all concerned, especially the law, none of the Rockinghorse hands, Circle L hands, or gunfighters had remained in town—the saloons closed—so there hadn't been any trouble.

It was a farmer's house and barn, naturally, and the smell of coal oil was still strong in the air when me and Rusty arrived, hours after the fire had burnt itself out.

When we reined up, there was about forty-some-odd men gathered. Hog farmers, nesters, small ranchers, and the like. And they was all wearin' the same colored blue shirt and dark britches; each one of them had a yellow bandana tied around their neck.

Dolittle's Irregulars.

They was irregular, all right. It was the damndest-lookin' bunch of men I'd ever seen. But they sure thought they was something, though.

The Reverend Dolittle rode over to us, his big horse just a-prancin'. Colonel Dolittle was all dressed up in his Union Army uniform—minus the U.S. brass—and he was full of hisself. He was wearin' two pistols in the army flap holsters. Looked like Remington .44s. The 1858 model. His men was all carryin' different types of weapons. From shotguns to Sharps.

"Sheriff!" Dolittle spoke, his voice hard and loud and damned irritatin'. "What do you intend to do about this outrage—if anything?" he added, and that made me plumb hot under the collar.

"Well, sir . . . *Colonel* sir . . . first off, I want you and your so-called army to get the hell out of here and go back to tendin' your own business. Let me and Rusty prowl around some and try to pick up some tracks."

"I personally found tracks, *Sheriff*. Also the cans containing the combustible fluids used to ignite the fire. The tracks lead east, toward the Circle L range. I have already dispatched several men in that direction."

"Have you now? Well, mayhaps you'd tell me on what authority you done that and what you intend to do if your dispatchers find the men."

"My authority is commanding officer of the Army of the Lord. And when we find the men responsible for this nightriding, we shall hang them, since it is quite obvious to me that you are incapable of enforcing the law in this valley."

First time in my life I ever hit a preacher. But I sure popped this one. I leaned over and knocked him slap out of the saddle. He landed on his butt and started hollerin'.

He was stunned. He just didn't believe anything like this was actually happenin' to him. His mouth opened and closed about a half dozen times before anything come out that even resembled understandable words.

"I'll . . . I'll have your badge for this!" he finally yelled.

"Fine, preacher. You just do that. And then after you've done it, try to find someone who'll take the job and operate within the limits of the law. Think about that, you overbearin' loudmouth."

I didn't have no way of knowin' it at the time, but I was only a few hours away from turnin' in my badge, voluntarily.

Dolittle's so-called Army of the Lord had not moved. They could have easy taken me and Rusty out of action, but instead, they just stood still and watched as I knocked their Colonel out of the saddle and then stepped out of the saddle and jerked Dolittle to his feet and shoved him toward his big horse.

"Now you get up there and ride, preacher. And if I ever need your help in law business, I'll sure ask you." Turnin' to his army, I yelled, "Ride, damnit—right now!"

They rode. With their blue shirts and matchin' britches and yellow bandanas, they rode out. I didn't know where they was goin', and didn't much care, as long as it was away from me.

"Let's start trackin', Rusty. Maybe we can catch up with those men Dolittle sent out before anything bad happens to them."

We found the men Dolittle had dispatched, as he put it. Found them on the ground, mostly shot all to hell and gone. One Circle L puncher was on the ground, a big bloody hole in his chest. He was dead as a cold hammer. It looked to me like they had been waitin' for the law to arrive.

"Any of you boys wounded?" I asked.

They shook their heads no.

I pointed to a puncher. "You . . . ride into town for Truby. No need to get the Doc. Ride, cowboy, ride."

He took off and we dismounted. I inspected the bodies of the men. Lookin' around, I asked what had happened.

A puncher shoved his hat back on his head. "We was movin' cattle to the lower graze." He pointed. "Right there they is. These men come ridin' up like they was God Almighty and said we was under arrest for nightridin'. Told us they was the En-forcers . . . something like that. I told that one," he pointed, "to go right straight to hell. That's when that one," again, he pointed, "shot Jimmy out of the saddle with a shotgun; blowed him clean out of the saddle. We finished the fight and you can see how it come out. That's it, Sheriff."

I believed him. These men were not gunfighters; they wasn't tied down in no quick-draw rig. They was just workin' cowboys—but they was tough. They'd fight for the brand if somebody come along and pushed them enough.

'Bout that time, Big Mike and Junior come ridin' up. I could tell they was cocked back and lookin' for a fight.

But I wasn't gonna give it to them, not just yet. So I pulled their fuses quick. "Just sit easy, boys. The fight's over and I intend, by God, to see that it stays over . . . least for now."

Big Mike stuck his chin out at me. I got to admit, it was a temptin' target. "You plannin' on takin' my crew to jail?"

"Nope. These men," I waved at the Enforcers, "had no business on your range. And they opened the dance. No charges agin' your hands, the way I see it."

Big Mike, he stepped back and stared at me. Oh, he knew that I knew—without bein' able to prove it—that some gunhands from his payroll had fired the man's house and barn. But it wasn't this bunch of cowboys who'd done it. And I wasn't puttin' no innocent man in jail just 'cause he rode for a couple of bastards.

He stared at me for a time, then stepped up real close, pushin' his face up to mine. "What the hell does it take to rile you, Pickens?"

"Sometimes, not much, Mike. But on the other hand, I'm usually pretty easygoin'. Most of the time, that is."

"Is that right?"

"Yeah." I raised my voice so's all could hear. "You see, Mike, I figure there's enough folks in the valley ridin' around all primed and cocked for trouble, without you or me addin' to it. Don't you agree?"

I smiled at him. He knew I had deliberately put him in a bind agin, right in front of his own men. There wasn't nothin' he could do except agree with me. But man, I could see the hate shinin' at me through his hot eyes.

When he spoke, his words was low, meant only for me. "We'll tangle, you and me. Sometime, somewhere. I'm lookin' forward to breaking every bone in your body, you jerk!"

I stepped back and grinned, clasping him on the shoulder. "Why . . . Mike . . . thank you! That's the nicest thing you ever said to me."

His men was all lookin', wonderin' what it was he'd just said. They couldn't hear, so they had to guess at it. And Mike? Lord, but he was some kind of mad.

Mike choked back a curse and slipped away from my

friendly hand on his shoulder. His face was red as a beet as he swung back into the saddle. Without lookin' back, him and Junior galloped off.

I looked at the Circle L punchers. "You boys give me your names, and you can get back to shovin' cows around."

Me and Rusty rode back to town with Truby and the bodies of Dolittle's Irregular Enforcers. 'Bout twenty of Dolittle's Army of the Lord was meetin' with him at the church. Dolittle and his bunch come runnin' out and makin' all sorts of noises about what they was gonna do to them that killed the men.

"You!" I pointed to Dolittle. "You ain't gonna do nothin' about it. I done warned you, preacher. Now don't push me no more."

He mumbled something under his breath and wheeled around, stalkin' off, his men followin' him, mutterin' dark things . . . just low enough so's I couldn't hear none of it.

Soon as I stabled Pronto and was walkin' up the boardwalk to the office, George Waller come rushin' up, all in a sweat. That was the sweatin'est fellow I ever did see.

"Where are the prisoners, Sheriff?"

"What prisoners? There ain't no prisoners—yet," I added. Then I told him what all had happened.

"Those damn fools!" he swore. "Out playing soldier boy when they ought to be home, gettin' in a crop and tending to their business."

I agreed.

George, he cussed some more, and walked around in a little circle on the boardwalk. Then he looked up at me. "I forgot to tell you. There is a United States Marshal waiting to see you in your office, Sheriff."

Me and the Marshal shook hands and then got right down

to business. He careful inspected the pictures Langsford had took of Al Long and then went over each and ever' item in Al's kit once I got it out of the safe. Al's brothers had been bonded out of the bucket and wasn't nowhere around, that I could see.

"Congratulations, Sheriff," he told me. "You sure bagged you a good one. Where do you want the re-ward money sent?"

I pondered on that for a time. "Where are you out of, Marshal?"

"Lander, for the time bein'. Tell you what, I can have the money deposited with Wells Fargo and give you a receipt for it. If you'd like to do it that way. It'd be the safe way."

"That sounds good to me." I signed for the money and then said, "Sit back and pour yourself another cup of coffee, Marshal. I got to bend your ear some."

Chapter Three

I took it from the top, from the shootin' at the saloon that first night I rode Critter into town, right up to the present moment.

That Marshal, he poured him yet another cup of coffee and leaned back in his chair. Rusty, Burtell, and De Graff had joined us in the office. There was a nice breeze blowin' in through the barred and curtainless widows, and it was a pleasant day.

The Marshal, he sighed and shook his head. "And you want my advice on the best way to handle it, right?"

"I'd sure appreciate it."

"Git the hell outta this valley!"

I give him my best dubious look.

"That ain't exactly what you wanted to hear, right?"

"That's it in a nutshell."

He sipped at his coffee and thought for a moment. Then he began to smile. "I think I got it!"

"What?" I leaned forward and listened to him explain his plan. The more he talked, the more antsy I got. When he finally wound down, I said, "Man . . . I got enough badges as it is. A deputy U.S. Marshal—me?"

"But it's perfect, Sheriff—don't you see? Right now, there ain't nothin' I can do. I got to ride clear down to Medicine Bow to settle a dispute. By the time I get back, you'll probably be dead or shot up real bad, and then I can issue federal warrants and me and other Marshals can make a move." He shook his head. "It's bad business to kill a U-nited States Marshal. We frown right hard on that."

If the thought the last look I give him was strange, this one should have curled his toenails. "Uh . . . now wait a minute, Marshal. You want to give me this badge so's I can get killed?"

"Or shot up. Look at it this way, Sheriff: think of the great service you'd be doin' the good people of this valley."

"Well, yeah . . . but what about *me?*"

"Well, hell, I never said the plan was perfect, did I?"

"You shore didn't! Look here, could I be a U-nited States Marshal and still be sheriff of this county?"

"Oh, sure. We do that all the time."

"What's it pay?"

"Not very damn much. But where you make your money is the six cents a mile they give you when you travel. And that's all the time. Plus, you get to keep all the re-ward money. And that can add up right smart."

"Six cents a mile could add up."

"Shore does."

"You stay put. I got to find George Waller."

George, he was leery at first, until I told him that as a U-nited States Marshal, I'd have a whole lot of authority and I would still be around to help out if he'd name Rusty the sheriff after I turned in my badge.

"Well, that ain't up to me. If you want Rusty as sheriff, all you got to do is appoint him to your position, and put it in writing. Then he serves out the remainder of your term."

And that's how Rusty got to be Sheriff of Puma County.

* * *

"Raise your hand, Cotton Pickens."

I raised my hand and was sworn in. It was a sight more fancier badge than the one I pinned on to Rusty's shirt. He sure was proud of it, though.

"What else?" I asked, polishin' the fancy badge with my shirtsleeve.

"A whole lot more," the Marshal said. "This was the easy part."

The Marshal, he took him a deep breath. "Now listen up, I got to re-cite you something, from memory. As a legal swore-in Deputy U-nited States Marshal for this here district of the Territory, this here is what you can and cain't do. First thing you got to remember is this: You got to bring 'em in, alive or dead. It don't make no difference. But you got to bring 'em in 'fore you can collect any re-ward money. And they don't stink so bad—most of the time—if they're alive. But bring 'em in.

"Now then, a Deputy U.S. Marshal can arrest a person with or without no warrant first issued, if you got knowledge that a crime has been committed, about to be committed, or somebody is thinkin' on committin' a crime. You can arrest for murder, manslaughter, assault, with intent to kill or maim, attempts to murder. Arson, robbery, rape, incest, burglary, larceny, adultery, horse-stealin', cattle-rustlin', changin' brands, someone gettin' all up in your face and bein' smart-mouthed, obstructin' justice, willfully and maliciously placin' obstructions on a railroad track, and just about anything else you can think of. You have the full power of the U-nited States government behind you, and you don't have to listen to no pissant district judge. You can do anything you wanna do with an Injun. You understand all that? Good. Now where's the outhouse? I gotta take a crap!"

The smile on Rolf Baker's face changed to a real frown when I rode up and he spotted the U.S. Marshal's badge pinned on my shirt. But the frown quickly disappeared and he was all smiles again as he shook my hand.

When I'd looked in the safe once more, back at the office, I'd found a packet of papers, rolled up tight and tied with string. I hadn't said nothin' to the boys, savin' the papers to read by myself later. And they all dealt with A.J., Matt, and Rolf. The sheriff who'd been killed last year had himself a suspicion that the Big Three wasn't exactly on the up and up, and he'd done some diggin'. He hadn't come up with much; just enough to make me have a little naggin' suspicion in the back of my mind that Rolf Baker wasn't on the clean side, as he would like me to believe. Lots of things just weren't addin' up in my head.

The sheriff had seemed to think that the Big Three had come here from New York City. Why he thought so, I didn't have no idea. But I was gonna find out the truth, if I could. Now, as I wasn't tied down in town no more, I could roam, and that's what I intended to do.

'Cause something about that U.S. Marshal's badge sure caused worry to jump into Rolf's eyes. And he wasn't by hisself, neither. The only one who didn't have worry in their eyes upon spottin' the badge was Pepper, and she fairly squealed with delight. But Martha and Jeff, they didn't like it at all.

It was just real odd. And it made me suspicious as all get-out.

On this trip, I had packed me a bedroll and several days worth of grub. I was gonna stay out in the valley, or beyond, just movin' around, lettin' people see me in my new capacity.

Pepper didn't see it, but some of the softness had been sliced off of her family's friendliness towards me. It was enough to put me on the alert, and I didn't like it at all. I had me a gnawin', sick feelin' in my belly that wasn't put there by none of Miss Pepper's fried chicken. It was there 'cause now I believed that Rolf and Jeff was all mixed up in something real bad.

What, I just didn't know. But the Federal badge on my chest meant that I was gonna have to be the one to find out—or Rusty would and then share it with me.

But any way it was cut, it might mean the end of me and Pepper . . . if I waited. So I decided to wade right in and take the plunge, so to speak.

Me and Pepper, we went for a stroll down by the little creek that ambled along not too far from the main house.

"Pepper, I got me a plan. Now you might not like it. If you don't, say so."

"Let me say something first, Cotton." Now she had a worried look in her eyes.

"All right."

"Something is wrong here at the ranch."

"What?"

"I . . . don't know for sure. I was riding yesterday, on the north range, high up. I crossed Jeff's tracks and decided to follow him, thinking maybe we could sit and talk like we used to do. Something we haven't done much of lately. Then I was giving my horse a rest when I spotted several riders heading my way. I pulled into a stand of timber and watched them. They reined up and waited."

"Was you close enough to them to recognize any of them?"

"Yes. They were gunfighters. I recognized that Stamps person and that Dundee man. There were two more that I'd seen in town."

Waldo Stamps and Clay Dundee.

"You're sure you were on Quartermoon range?"

"Oh, yes. Positive. But then . . . Jeff and my father rode up and dismounted. They talked with the men at length and father gave them something. Cotton, it was money!"

Well, there it was. The sheriff who'd been killed was right, and my own hunches had been correct. But I wished they wasn't. All I could do was give out with a long sigh.

"What does it all mean, Cotton?"

I was truthful with her. "I don't know yet, Pepper. But it can't be nothin' good. Does your father or brother know you spotted them?"

"Oh, no!"

"Your ma?"

"No. No one else. You're the first I've told about it."

"Keep it that way, honey. Don't let on to nobody. I think that's best for the time bein'."

"All right. Whatever you say. Now what was it you were going to tell me?"

"Pepper, I don't want no great big fancy weddin'. I just want a little simple one."

"So do I." She spoke soft, her words just audible over the burbling of the little crick. "But what is this leading toward?"

I took me a deep breath. "Pepper, let's e-lope. Tonight!"

That kiss she planted on me was answer enough.

There's some sort of sayin' about the best-laid plans of people. But I disremember exactly what it is. But it sure applied to me that comin' night. Me and Pepper had agreed to hightail it out of the county as soon as the house got dark with folks in bed. But when I got to Pepper's bedroom window, I could hear the sounds of cryin' from somewheres in the house and Rolf was sittin' in a chair by the window, and he was plumb unfriendly towards me.

"There is no need to sneak about in the night, Cotton," he said, a hardness to his voice. "Pepper has changed her mind. Changed it about a lot of things."

"Yeah? Well, I didn't figure you was here to give away the bride."

"You will no longer be welcome at this house, Marshal Pickens. And there will be no wedding. Now, or ever. Is that perfectly clear to you?"

"Real clear. But I would like to hear it from Miss Pepper herself."

"My daughter is, at the moment, indisposed."

"What the hell does that mean?"

Rolf glared at me. I could almost feel the heat from his eyes. He was some hot. "Look, you ignorant saddle bum, ride out of here. Keep riding. If you have any sense at all—which I doubt—you'll ride clear out of the state. Now do you understand all that? Is that clear to you?"

Sure was. In a way. So I tipped my hat and tipped on out of there. But Rolf Baker was forgettin' one important item. As a sheriff, I had me some power; but as a U-nited States Marshal, I had me a hell of a lot more power. And now I had me a plan.

I didn't think it was Pepper who'd changed her mind; I felt her daddy had done that for her. And not allowin' her to speak to me had just made me mad as hell.

So, Mister Rolf Baker, let's just see what New York City has to say about you.

At dawn, I rolled out of my blankets and made me a pot of coffee for breakfast. Then I broke camp and kept on ridin' south. I'd had a few hours sleep after hours of hard ridin'. By noon, I would be a full county away from Doubtful.

The sun was right up over my head when I rode slow down the dusty main street of the town. I had stopped about two miles out of town and took me a bath in a little creek. Man, but that water was some cold!

I told the boy at the stable to leave Pronto alone; just give him all the corn he could eat and be careful doin' it. He bites. Although I doubted he would bite a young boy.

I got me a room at the hotel, shaved, and changed out of my dusty clothing. Then had me a cafe-fixed meal. At the telegraph office, I identified myself to the agent.

The Marshal who had swore me in had give me a whole batch of government scrip—to use in place of money—and I laid some of that wad down on the counter.

"Grease your tappin' finger, Mister Agent, 'cause you got a lot of messages to wire out of here."

I was in that town for the better part of three days before I got replies to most of my inquiries. And when I added them all up, it didn't make for no real pretty picture.

They had thought themselves to be mighty slick young men, Matt and A.J. and Rolf. But when you skimmed off the grease that rose to the top of the stew, all they turned out to be was swindlers, foot padders, con men, and murderers. I seen right there and then why they didn't want no telegraph wires runnin' out of their valley, and why they chose such an out-of-the-way place to settle down in.

And the wives of the Big Three? Well, I couldn't prove it, but after a whole batch of wires from California, it looked like, when you compared dates, that the three women was mail-order whores out of San Francisco.

The description of one of them filled Martha to a T. So she wasn't no hotsy-totsy fine lady from New Hampshire; she was a saloon girl from the Barbary Coast. Her real name was Cindy Meeker. And if it was true, and I suspected it was, she had her a shady past.

According to the wires I got, and there was a whole slew of them, the young men had been borned in what was known as the Old Brewery in New York City . . . in the old Five Points section. I didn't know what that meant; I was just readin' what was wrote down for me, and the telegraph agent was probably glad to see me go. I 'bout ruined his writin' hand. The U.S. Marshal's office in far-off New York City had give me a good batch of background on the Old Brewery.

Coulter's Brewery, as it was originally known, had been built back in 1792. Then, in 1837, the big place was turned into a tenement house, with more than a hundred rooms in it. The hallways was known as Murderer's Row. Lots of kids that was borned there didn't even see daylight until they was well into their teens. It must have been quite a place.

Hell-hole would probably be a better name for it.

Folks was killed there for no more than a penny, and that was proved by the police. Before the good women of the Ladies' Home Missionary Society moved in and bought the place back in '52, it was estimated that there was a murder a day for fifteen years. Over five thousand killin's. When the police finally moved in on the place, in force, they toted out more than a hundred sacks of human bones.

This, then, was what Matt and A.J. and Rolf had been borned into or moved into. A world of thugs and murderers and rapists and the whole scummy lot of such people. I couldn't even imagine what it must have been like, not in my wildest dreams—or nightmares, as the case would be.

They was the sons of whores and worse. And they had the

best teachers in the world for crime. And they all three learned their lessons right well.

They moved out of the Old Brewery, according to the wires I got back, when they was young men, and began to educate themselves. But their hearts remained black as sin. The three of them formed up a gang and killed for money . . . killed, among other things. Really, there wasn't nothin' the three of them wouldn't do for money. Nothin' at all.

They made them a small fortune and then the coppers got on their trail after a particularly savage rape, murder, and kidnappin'. The three young men headed out west.

The rest was history. They dropped out of sight and become cattlemen, gettin' rich and powerful doin' it.

I guess Rolf figured that I was the perfect patsy for his daughter. As Sheriff, married into his family, he figured I'd play along with whatever he done, and the Big Three had probably drew straws or high carded it or something to see who was gonna be the bad guys and who would be the nice one. That was just headthinkin' on my part. I didn't know for sure. But when I hung on the U.S. Marshal's badge, that changed the whole picture.

Seemed like the messages from back east and from California never would quit comin' in . . . all of them about Rolf and A.J. and Matt and their once-loose women. And them women had been rounders . . . bad through and through. There wasn't no tens of thousands of dollars of reward money on the men's heads, not like what was on the James Gang, say, but there was a right smart amount of money involved.

I didn't want no reward money for this. I couldn't never look at Pepper again if I took money for turnin' in her father. So, me? Hell, I didn't know exactly what to do.

I wired back to the U.S. Marshals' office in New York City and told them that maybe I had something on the men. . . . I'd let them know.

It just seemed to me that I'd lost Miss Pepper no matter which-a-way I turned or done or planned to do. One thing was for certain in my mind, however, and that was when I finally made up my mind what to do with the Big Three, when it was over, and if I was still alive, I wasn't gonna stay in the valley. Not without Pepper.

Well, I was in love, but I could get over it.

Least that's what I tried to convince myself.

Chapter Four

I took my time headin' back, just lookin' around. Really, I was checkin' out the country for a place to settle, and I found me a nice little valley about fifty miles south of Doubtful. The valley was all lush and green and pretty with wildflowers; had a little stream runnin' through it. I found me a place where a cabin would fit nice. It was all a wild and beautiful and lonely place.

And the quiet valley fit my present state of mind right well.

Now, I knowed I wasn't no thing of beauty, but I guess I was sort of wild and uncurried, and it looked like I was gonna stay lonely. I guess I was feelin' sorry for myself. And that ain't something I often do.

But damnit, a man needs a woman and vice versa. A man who don't never take a woman for wife grows old bitter-like, all dried up and sour-actin'. And I didn't want to turn into no withered old sour apple.

I picketed Pronto and climbed me a little hill, place I'd thought the cabin would fit, and hunkered down, lettin' the wind blow gentle on me, while I squatted amid the grass and sweet-smellin' wildflowers.

"Now, you just wait a minute, Cotton," I said aloud, speaking to the big empty—it really wasn't empty, of course, but it felt that way. "Pepper's pa told you she didn't want you around no more. But you never heard it from her. So until she speaks the words, just pull yourself together and straighten up some."

Pronto, he nickered low and lifted his head, lookin' at me, like he sorta understood what I'd just said. And then all of a sudden, his ears come up and he tensed.

When he done that, I come up and rolled, hittin' the ground just as I heard the boom of the rifle. The slug slammed into the ground right where I'd been, with another one right behind that. I rolled towards the slim protection of a little fallen log. Another round sent splinters flyin'. Rollin' again, I jerked out Pronto's picket pin and we went runnin' into a stand of timber. Jammin' the picket pin deep, I shucked out my rifle.

Whoever it was that'd been trailin' me was plenty good, and I had me an idea who it might be.

Haufman.

Takin' me a big swallow of water from my canteen, I looped the canteen straps back around the saddle horn and commenced to get my bearings.

It had to be Haufman. For I'd heard it said that once you done him a hurt, or humiliated him, he was on your trail forever; bastard didn't forget nothin'. And I sure hurt and humiliated him plenty good.

Pronto was protected from anything but a stray bullet, and I was in a good position in the thick timber. But I wasn't really sure just where the shots had come from.

Squattin' behind a tree, I studied the terrain above me, then pondered a while on where I'd been hunkered down when the slugs struck. I thought I knew just about where the German might be shootin' from.

With that in mind, I thought, all right . . . so now what? We could spend the whole rest of the day pot-shootin' at one another and never hit nothin' except air.

"Well, Cotton," I muttered, "let's us just take the fight to him."

I slipped out of the far end of the timber and then, with the woods to my right, began workin' my way up the hill, always stayin' low, behind plenty of good cover.

Then the timber abruptly came to a halt and, for a minute, I figured I wasn't no better than I had been. But then, lookin' around, I seen where I had a better view of his approximate location. I made up my mind to just sit tight for a time.

He fired a couple more times into the timber, just to keep me honest, I reckon. But his smoke gave me his exact location, and it was a good one, so I thought at first glance.

Just then the wind picked up right smart and I seen where Haufman—if it was him—had made his second mistake. His first mistake was takin' a shot at me and missin'.

The wind moved the bushes behind where he was; moved them enough so's I could see the rock wall behind his location. Grinnin', I eared back the hammer on my Henry. Ricochets are something terrible to hear, and they make ugly, rippin' wounds. So I just leveled that Henry and let it bang as fast as I could pull and lever.

Man, he went to cussin'. I could hear him as plain as if he was standin' right next to me. Shovin' fresh loads into my rifle by feel, not takin' my eyes off where I now knowed he was, I put another half dozen rounds off that rock wall.

He tried to return the fire, but the location he now had to fire from was not a very good one; it left him too exposed. I put some rock splinters into his face and that done it for the back-shooter.

He just couldn't take no more of it. He made him a run for it and I drilled him, dustin' him from side to side. He went up on his toes, stayed there for a few seconds and then fell forward on his face. He slowly slid down the hill a few feet and then was still. He was dead, or standin' so close to it he could feel the chill, for I'd seen my bullet pop dust when it entered and then splat blood as it come out the other side of him.

Makin' my way over to him, movin' slow, stoppin' often behind cover just in case he had taken him a partner. But he was as alone in death as he had always been in life.

Not that I was feelin' sorry for him, for I sure as hell wasn't.

It's all black and white. It's got to be that way. There are them that want to change that; to make a thug or criminal or whatever you want to call them that are bad something else. And someday they'll probably get their way, too. Even out there in the West times was changin'. But when the mood of the people changes to where they're feelin' sorry for the bad ones, something precious will be lost. Nobody ever locks the doors to their houses; the latch string is always open. That'll change fast when the laws start favorin' the criminal.

I shook off them thoughts, not wantin' to be around if and when something that dreadful ever occurs.

I located his rifle; another .44-.40, then found his horse and led him over and picketed him. Goin' through Haufman's pockets, I found a wad of money. More than five hundred in gold and paper.

I debated on what to do with the money, and had made up my mind to try to find some relative of his to send it to; that is, until I found the note in Haufman's purse.

As we talked of, Sheriff Cotton Pickens must be eliminated.
It was signed *R*.

Well, I just sat there and give out a sigh. For that pretty well blew the candles out on the cake, right there and then. R couldn't stand for nobody else other than Mister Rolf hisself. That, and the way the note was worded all fancy-like. And there was something else: I'd seen Baker's handwritin' several times before at his place. That kinda tied it all up with an ugly-colored bow. Right final.

So I stuck the money in my pocket. Right nice amount of cash to tote around. Made a body feel important. When I got back to town, I'd just, by God, buy the fanciest watch ol' George had in his store—compliments of Rolf Baker.

But first, I had me a job of work to do.

Gettin' the bedroll from behind the saddle of Haufman's horse, I rolled him up in the tarp and tied him snug. He was a load puttin' acrost the saddle—dead weight, you might say. But I tied him down good on that sudden skittish horse and walked down the hill to the timber where I'd left Pronto. Pronto didn't like the smell of that dead man either.

"Settle down, Pronto. I can testify that he didn't smell no better when he was alive."

Pronto tried to bite me, but I got out of the way in time.

It was kinda eerie that night, campin' with a dead man all rolled up. And that presented yet another problem: I didn't want him to stiffen out straight. Hell, I'd never get him bent over the saddle again. So before turnin' in, I horseshoed Haufman and staked him in that position, so when I waked up and he was stiff, he'd fit proper over the saddle.

I ain't totally ignorant.

I hit Quartermoon range just about noon the next day, and when a puncher seen me and that wrapped-up body, he lit out for the big house.

Me? Hell, I just rode right up onto the front yard as big as pie. Rolf and Jeff was waitin' on the porch, both of them wearin' short guns. No sign of Pepper or her ma. The hotsy-totsy former Cindy Meeker from Frisco, turned New England swell.

"I told you that you were not welcome at this ranch, Pickens," Rolf said. "Now what is the meaning of this intrusion?"

"I brung your man back to you, Baker."

"I don't have the foggiest idea what in the world you are

babbling about this time, Marshal. Get that disgusting burden off of my lawn."

I had gone over in my head a few lies I was gonna tell if it come to it—just to see what kind of reaction I'd get out of the Brewery Kid.

I jerked my thumb toward the horseshoed Haufman. "Haufman." Rolf paled and took a quick intake of breath, his eyes narrowin' down.

"Really? You don't say." He could recover quick. "Well, men who live by the gun usually die by the gun, don't they, Marshal?"

I sat my horse, just starin' at him. I had to admire the man's actin' ability. He'd sure missed his callin' by not goin' on the stage.

"Well, Marshal . . . why in the world would you think Haufman worked for me?"

I smiled at him. OK, if that's how he wanted to play it. "Well, Baker, you see, I found a note in Haufman's pocket. And he talked some 'fore he passed on to his Maker. I wrote it all down and left it and the note with the sheriff a couple of counties over. Insurance, you might say. Then I wired the U-nited States Marshal's office and told him what I'd done . . . without mentionin' no names, of course."

Rolf, he had to steady hisself agin' the porch railin'. Man looked like he was about to have him a stroke or two.

I could see that Jeff's hands were shaking. He wasn't in real good shape either. And I wondered how much about his ma and pa's background the young man knowed. If I had to guess, I'd say plenty.

"What . . . uh, what . . . uh, do you? . . ." Rolf stuttered. He cleared his throat. "What is your next move, Marshal?"

"A lot of that depends on you, Baker. If you get my drift and all."

"I . . . uh, certainly get part of it, Marshal." He cut his

eyes to the house and I knew that somebody was in ear range
of our words, and he didn't want them to hear none of it.

"I'll be usin' the sheriff's office in Doubtful 'til I can get
my own proper office that's fittin' a U-nited States Marshal
like me. Now, I'll be ridin' out to see Miss Pepper, since we
have some business of the heart to attend to. I'd take it un-
kindly if you was to try to stop that. I might take it so un-
kindly that I'd do something for pure hatefulness. Like
sendin' some telegraph wires to folks back east. New York
City would be one of the places."

Rolf slowly nodded his head. And right there and then, I
seen a man age before my very own eyes. He knew that I'd
done sent all them wires, and that I was holdin' the hole cards.
All of them aces, too. And he wasn't holdin' nothin'. My hand
was pat, his was busted. Rolf, he had been, up to that
moment, a right nice-lookin' man . . . handsome, even, I suppose. But now? Hell, he looked like a wore-out tramp on the
dole. The flesh on his face seemed to sag with age. Jeff had
sat down in a porch chair, his hat off, his face in his hands.
The little shit knowed it all. And he agreed to be a part of it.
Damn his black heart to hell!

Rolf had lowered his head. He lifted his eyes to mine. His
eyes were lifeless. "Well, Marshal." His voice was awful
shaky. "I think that . . . no, I'm sure that . . . well, we can work
our way of this terrible morass . . . this situation," he hastened
to explain, and I'm glad he did, 'cause I sure didn't have no
idea what more-ass meant. Well . . . I knowed what it *sounded*
like. "Yes, I certainly believe we can."

"That sounds good to me. I like a sweet pie."

Some of the life came back into Rolf's eyes. Jeff's head
come up and he stared at me. They both bit at it and took it,
swallerin' the bait and the hook. I always had liked that
sayin' about if you was to give a fellow enough rope, he'd
hang himself.

Stepping out of the saddle, I cut Haufman loose. The body hit the ground with a dull smack.

Inside the house, I heard a woman give out with a little gasp. That had to be Pepper. Cindy Meeker had seen more dead bodies than me. Workin' the Barbary Coast like she'd done, she'd helped murder and steal and shanghai men out to sea many, many times during her short but colorful career . . . most of it spent on her back.

And with Pepper there, and able to hear all the words, I didn't want to drag her into none of this slimy mess. I'd tell her I was settin' up her pa, the next time I see her. "I'm tired of totin' him around, Baker. You plant him."

"Oh, but of course, Marshal! Son," he said, with a sly smile. "I guess I'd better get used to callin' you son, hadn't I?"

"Yeah," I said wearily, suddenly tired of the whole stinkin' mess. "I reckon you had, at that . . . pa." Goddamn, that last word made my mouth ache to say it.

Rolf, he grinned like an egg-suckin' dog and Jeff grinned right along with him.

"Welcome to the family, Cotton!" Jeff blurted out. "Damn, but it's good to have you back home. Ain't it, Father. I mean, isn't it?"

"Yes. Don't overdo it, son. Time for celebrating will come later. After," he looked at me, "Cotton and I have a little chat. Right . . . son?"

"Right." I just couldn't call him pa. I just flat could not do it.

"I'll get some hands to help with the body, Father." Jeff left us.

"I'll personally see that he gets a good Christian burial, Cotton. That would be the Christian thing to do, wouldn't it?"

I swung back into the saddle. This rotten son of a bitch wouldn't know a Christian act if Jesus was to come up and shake his hand. "I want you to be sure to give him a . . . good Christian burial."

I rode out, deliberately putting my back to Rolf. But I'm gonna tell you what, the center of my back was some kind of itchy until I got out of rifle range.

Chapter Five

Back in town, I called the boys in and swore them all to silence. Then I told them all that I'd learned about the Big Three.

The three of them, they just sat real still for a long moment, looks of shock and disbelief on their faces. Finally, De Graff stood up and began pacin' around the room.

"It begins to figure, now that you've dug up the bones, Marshal. A.J. and Matt, they got greedy. And Rolf, he knew that too much attention might bring them all down, like a house built of cards. Then you come along and got yourself the sheriff's job. Rolf seen a way out and pushed you and Pepper towards each other, not knowin' that you two would really get sweet on each other. Then, when you took the Marshal's job, he seen it might all come apart, or he thought it would, and he jumped the gun, sendin' Haufman out to kill you. That about tie it all up?"

"Sounds good to me."

"Now what, Marshal?" Rusty asked. "Are we gonna go after the Big Three and try to nail them on the New York City charges?"

I'd been givin' that some serious thought. On some charges, so I'd read up on, there was a time period; after that, the charges wasn't so good. Wouldn't stick in a court of law.

On the murder charges against them? Well, all that happened more than twenty-five years ago, and two thousand miles away. And really, all any of them had to do was to claim they was born in some rural area back east, and their parents was dead. Meanin' that there wasn't no real way to prove Mills and Lawrence and Baker was guilty of anything.

I put all that into words and let the boys ruminate on it.

Burtell finally said, "Personal, I think it would be a waste of time, you ask me. I don't think nothin' could ever be proved agin' any of them. People change in twenty-five years; lots of witnesses, if there ever was any, would be dead. Others would be moved away and gone. All right, so them three ain't nothin' but blackhearted scoundrels, not fit for no human bein' to associate with . . . but you might be able to strike some sort of deal with them." He looked at me.

"Yeah. A way to end the valley war."

"Right," Rusty agreed. "If the Big Three would agree to pull back to their legal range lines, and let the nesters and smaller spreads alone, we just kinda put those old charges on the shelf and let them gather dust. It'd be worth a try, you ask me."

"If it ain't too late," De Graff's remark was sour-given.

"What do you mean?" I asked.

"You're all forgettin' Colonel Dolittle and his Irregulars. You can't tell nobody about the charges, and the odds of them believin' Mills and Lawrence is gonna be good boys from now on is slim to none."

He was right. That was something to think on.

I stood up. "Well, I'll just go over and have a talk with Dolittle. Sound him out on it."

"No!" Dolittle thundered. "Absolutely not. No way would I ever believe anything from the mouths of Mills or Lawrence."

"You wouldn't even give it a try, Preacher?"

"No! I have spoken with God, and God has ordered me to wage a Christian war against the evil that prevails in this valley."

I stared at him. "God . . . spoke to you, Preacher? He told you that?"

"In a manner of speaking, yes."

The preacher's jaw was still a little poked-out from when I'd popped him. All right, I'd tried a reasonable way, now I'd try something else. "Preacher, I'm a U-nited States Marshal, and I am orderin' you to disband this here army of yours. If you refuse, I will call in other Marshals and have warrants swore out agin you and ever' man in your Irregulars."

He swelled up and puffed out his chest. "You wouldn't dare do that to me. You don't have the authority to do anything like that!"

"You better not try me, Preacher. I'm gonna bring peace to this valley . . . one way or the other. Now, I've showed you a peaceful way. I suggest you take it."

"The Lord does not respond well to threats, young man."

"That's sure true, Preacher. But I ain't talkin' to the Lord; I'm jawin' with you. And you're a mortal man, just like me." But I had me a feelin' that the preacher had got hisself and the Lord all mixed up together.

Dolittle got to walkin' around his little office and wavin' his arms and shoutin'. "I'll pray for your lost soul, Marshal Pickens. For it is indeed obvious to me that you have shifted your allegiance from the path of the righteousness to the dark ways of sin and sinners."

Right then and there, I knowed what Preacher Dolittle really was: a big windbag. But there's one thing about windbags that the preacher didn't seem to realize. When he led his army of irregulars agin' a hundred or more gunfighters, he'd discover, probably too late, that a .44 slug can punch a mighty big hole in a windbag.

I stood up and stared at him. "I done all that a man could

do, Preacher. But I'll add this: you're fixin' to get a lot of pretty good men killed in this valley if you don't back off this stupid plan of yours and break up this so-called army."

"Nonsense! I shall lead my Christian army into the valley of death, and we shall emerge victorious, waving the banner of Christ."

More than likely, what they was gonna do was come out with their tails tucked between their legs . . . them that come out at all, that is.

But I didn't say no more. There just wasn't no point to it.

I walked out of the preacher's office and went straight to George Waller's store.

"Yes, Marshal?"

"Gimme that watch right there." I pointed to the fanciest watch in his showcase. "And wind it up and set it proper for me."

"Certainly. And how about a nice fob for it, too?"

"Yeah. That'll be right nice. And I want two hundred rounds of .44s while you're rootin' around back there."

He blinked. "Two hundred rounds?"

"Yeah. All hell is fixin' to bust loose in the valley, George. So you just best get ready for it."

With the watch tucked secure by a chain into my vest pocket, I walked over to Doc Harrison's office and caught him in and not busy. "Doc, how are you fixed for medical supplies?"

"Why . . . very well, thank you. I just this week received a shipment. What a strange question, Marshal. Why do you ask?"

"'Cause you fixin' to get real busy, Doc. Your wife's a nurse, ain't she?"

"Why, yes, she is. And a very good one, I might add."

"Anybody else in this town know anything about doctorin'?"

"Ah . . . there are a couple of good ladies who have some nursin' experience."

"You gonna be needin' 'em, Doc. You got a good supply of leeches?"

He smiled. "The medical profession stopped using them some years back, Marshal."

"Just checkin'."

I left him starin' at my back, a funny look on his face.

The next mornin', as I was saddlin' up, I noticed a whole bunch of horses in the corral, with brands that I didn't recognize. I asked the stable boy about them.

"They rode in last night, Marshal. Them six horses there," he pointed, "belongs to some men that look Mexican. Or at least half of them does. I don't know what them others does look like. They're kinda, well, funny-lookin'."

"Yeah, I know." Lobo, Pedro, Salvador, Fergus, and his goofy-actin' sons, Tyrone and Udell.

"Where are they?"

"Over to the hotel. It's plumb jammed up full, so I heard."

"Boy, when the shootin' starts, and it might pop at any time, you hunt you a hole and get in it, you understand me?"

"Yes, sir!"

Me and Pronto, we set out for the Quartermoon. Pepper was out for a ride and she galloped up to me, leanin' over and givin' me a wet smack right on the lips. I was gonna have to admonish her for bein' so brazen, I reckon.

She sat her sidesaddle and grinned at me. "Your ears are all red, Cotton."

"Are not!"

She laughed and we rode on. My ears did feel like they was burnin' some. But damned if I was gonna admit it.

"Cotton, what in the world is going on? The other night, my father ordered me into mother's room. I didn't want to go, and then he hit me, and forbade me to ever see you again." She turned her head and I could see a faint bruise on the side of her face. Pissed me off.

She said, "Now, all of a sudden, he says he made a terrible mistake and it's all right for us to go ahead and plan our wedding."

"Well, me and your pa had us a disagreement, Pepper. Man stuff." Damn, I didn't know what else to say. I just couldn't bring myself to tell her about her parents' past, as dark and checkered as it was.

"Uh-huh," she said, and I knowed she didn't believe a word I'd said.

I underestimated her intelligence; men have a bad habit of doin' that with women. Seems like we'd learn after awhile.

As we rode, she said, "Father is not as nice a person as he has led people to believe, is he, Cotton? And please don't try to lie to me. You can't. You get all flustered up when you try."

I thought on it some. "Ever' man has a dark trail behind him, Pepper," I finally said. "If he don't, then that man ain't lived very much. I been on the hoot-owl trail myself." I had been, yeah, but like I said, it was just to see how it was like.

Piss-poor, was what it was like.

"And my father's dark trail . . . ?"

"He . . . well, he got into some jams as a young man. A boy, really. Lots of boys do that."

Her smile was sort of sad to look at, and it hurt me way down deep. "Did he get into trouble back in New York City, Cotton?"

That shook me clear to my boots. Just how much did she know about her pa? "I really don't know where it happened, Pepper."

She glanced at me. "Your ears are as red as fire, Cotton."

"Are not!"

"Are too! Cotton, two years ago, a man came to the ranch to see my father. Said he was an old friend from New York City. My father was not very happy to see him."

I just bet he wasn't glad to see him. I waited for her to continue.

When she didn't, I said, "Well, what happened?"

"The man went riding with father. He was not a very good rider. Jeff tagged along despite father's requests that he not. The man had an accident; fell off his horse and his neck was broken. Not many months after that, the man who was sheriff of the county was mysteriously killed."

The man who had pointed out the right trail for me to take by leavin' them papers tucked 'way back in the safe.

"I became very interested in my family tree, Cotton. So unbeknownst to mother or father, I began some discreet inquiries. I had everything posted to Doctor Harrison's address in town. Cotton, my mother is not from New Hampshire. Everything came back a dead end."

I didn't say nothin'. Let her talk it all out in her own way.

"By that time, I had noticed that Jeff and my father were becoming very secretive. I still don't know what about. When I asked mother, she pretended that she didn't know what I was talking about, that I was making it all up."

She went on. "None of the New England Bakers that I could contact ever heard of any Rolf Baker. Finally, a doctor friend of Doctor Harrison interceded and wrote him. He advised him to tell me not to pursue the matter any further. I elected to heed the rather ominous missive."

I knew most of what she just said. But that interceded ominous missive bit went plumb over my head. Sounded like to me she was talkin' about cannonfire.

I made up my mind right there and then to start readin' more ever' day.

"My father, and probably A.J. and Matt as well, are wanted by the law back east, aren't they, Cotton? Probably back in the city."

"Pepper . . . don't make me say no more on it. I was you, I'd ask my daddy to tell you about it."

But she wasn't gonna be put off that easy. "What note were you and father talking about?"

So she'd heard it all. With a sigh, I reined up and handed her the note I'd taken off of Haufman's body.

"I reckon you'd better read this yourself."

She read it, then reread it, turnin' white as a ghost. She folded the note and give it back to me. Then she swung down and walked towards a little stand of willows by a crick. I got the feelin' she wanted to be let alone, so I loosened the cinches and let the horses blow some.

Pepper, she snorted and blubbered and finally wiped her eyes and blew her nose on a little hanky. Then she called out, "And you intend to do what about it, Cotton?"

Walkin' to her, I squatted down, careful not to stick myself in the butt with my spurs. "I'm gonna let the dead lie, Pepper. If your pa will help me put an end to the valley war, ain't gonna be no more said about what it was that happened when him and the others was young."

She sat for a time, her back to a tree. A pretty, fair, blond-haired young lady that was suddenly forced to look at her ma and pa in a much different light. "My parents have lied to me for years. You told me to ask them about it; I did. All they did then was heap more lies on top of the lies they'd already told me."

"Pepper, put yourself in their place—what would you have done?"

"I can't answer that. No one can. Now I want the truth, Cotton Pickens. If I'm to be Mrs. Pepper Pickens, I want to know every last bit of what you've found about my father and my mother and their past. All of it, Cotton!"

When a woman gets that tone of voice, a man best bare his soul, if he knows what's good for him. So, sittin' there by that bubblin' little crick, lookin' straight at the only woman I'd ever loved—the way a man is supposed to love a woman—I told her what I knowed about the Old Brewery.

I told her what a nightmare it must have been for them

forced to live within its confines. I told her about some incidents of people who tried to leave, and they was stoned to death or strangled by folks on the outside, fearful of them who lived in the big old place. I told her how the place was filled up by incest and rape and all sorts of other unmentionable stuff. And how them livin' in there didn't have no good or real chance to come out of it a good person. I told her that maybe, just maybe, her pa had come from a fine family; how many good boys who had fallen out with their daddies ended up in that awful place, and to try to understand what it must have been like for them livin' there.

"I can't believe that you are sitting there defending the man who ordered that Haufman person to kill you, Cotton."

"I ain't defendin' him, honey. But what is past is done with. What good would it do anybody to make it public?" And I told her about my settin' up her pa, and how he grabbed for the bait, him and Jeff.

"That isn't surprising." She turned her blues on me. "I shall leave the ranch with you, Cotton . . . this day. I'll stay with Doctor Harrison and his wife in town."

"As you wish, Pepper."

"And we'll be married whenever you say."

"That would pleasure me mightily."

After that, one thing led to another, and we sort of got carried away. Like I said, I was gonna have to speak to her about bein' so brazen. Someday.

We was both a mite rumpled when we got to the main house. A grass stain here and there. I was plumb tuckered out. Pepper, she looked fresh as a daisy. Women can sure bounce back in a hurry. Amazin'!

And her ma took one look at us and knew what had been goin' on. She should, she was an expert at it. On it. Whatever.

"I'm going to stay with Doctor Harrison and his family," Pepper announced. "I shall be gathering up some things in my room. Please excuse me all."

I wish she'd gather up something to give me some energy; felt like I'd been wrestlin' steers all morning.

"I thought you would be gentleman enough not to tell her, Marshal," Rolf said.

"I didn't tell her. Couple of years back, she began tryin' to trace her family tree. Had the letters come to her in town. Do I have to tell you the rest?"

The man, he aged some more. "I have been considering your offer, Marshal. I have decided to decline. I don't think you can prove a goddamned thing, to be blunt about it."

"That's the way I seen it, too. But it was a good try, weren't it?" I grinned at him.

"Yes. I suppose I shall have to reassess my opinion of you. You just look rather stupid."

If that was a compliment, I'd had better ones.

"Well just carry your prissy butt on out of here then!" Martha's squallin' reached us from the other room. "And damn you anyway!"

"Cindy's about to let the hammer down, ain't she?"

Rolf kind of pulled back in surprise. "You have been digging, haven't you, Marshal?"

'Fore I could reply, Martha hollered, "Your *father?* Hell, Rolf isn't your father. I don't know who is. Some goddamn sailor, I suppose."

Rolf smiled sadly. "I did buy a pig in a poke when I contracted for her, didn't I?"

I reckon that was one way of puttin' it. "I came out here to ask you to help me put an end to the valley war, Rolf. I suppose that's just smoke blowin' in the wind, now, isn't it?"

"To be sure, Marshal. To be sure."

"Think you and Matt and A.J. will win it, huh?"

"Yes, I believe we shall, Marshal. Were I you, I would stand back. For we are about to cut the hounds loose."

"Oh, hell!" Martha/Cindy ripped. "I know what you and that saddle bum been doing. You damned little slut!"

There was the sound of a blow, the sound of flesh being smacked, and smacked good. And I wondered who had hit who.

Martha/Cindy, she flung open the front door and stepped out, one side of her mouth all poked out. Despite himself, Rolf smiled. "I warned you about her temper, Martha."

She looked at him and said that word that women just don't never use. She said it several times.

Then she looked at me and cut loose. That woman traced my family tree all the way back to the caves and beyond. Rolf? He just sat down on the steps and rolled him a smoke. He offered the sack and papers to me and I took them. I rolled me a tight little smoke while Martha/Cindy continued to turn the air blue.

I tried to give back the tobacco and papers but Rolf waved them away. "Keep it. A man should enjoy one truly fine sack of tobacco before he dies. That tobacco is imported."

Pocketing the makin's, I said, "You gonna be the one to do the deed, Rolf?"

Martha, she had finally wound down and wandered off. I was glad to see her go.

"Oh, no, Cotton. I couldn't do that to Pepper. She isn't my flesh and blood, but I love her as if she were. No, but I understand some of the gunslingers are drawing straws to see who gets to brace you."

"Who won?"

"Two of them. Ford Childress and Black-Jack Keller. They'll be calling you out into the street late this afternoon."

He dropped his cigarette butt and ground it out under the heel of his boot. Looking up, he smiled at me. "Poor Pepper. Looks like all her dreams will be dying in the dirt in a few hours."

Chapter Six

I had seen Pepper safely to Doc Harrison's place and then had stabled Pronto. Back at the office, I checked and cleaned my guns while I told the boys about Rolf's comments that day.

"Ford and Black-Jack is in town, all right," Burtell said. "They're over to the Wolf's Den."

"Drinkin'?"

"No. Stayin' sober as a judge."

"We'll back you up, of course," Rusty said. "That goes without sayin'."

I shook my head. "No. This is my fight. Ain't no concern of yours."

They started to protest and I waved them silent. "I ain't no brave man nor no fool, boys. If they call me out, plannin' on double-teamin' me, I sure ain't gonna play it fair and square. Bet on that."

"Well, what are you gonna do, Marshal?" De Graff asked.

With a grim smile, I took down a Greener and loaded up both barrels. "Even up the odds and play dirty."

Burtell looked out the window. "Here they come, Marshal."

"The boardwalks empty?" I asked.

"Clean as a whistle."

I let them get close before I opened the door. Standin' in the door, I presented only my left side to the gunhawks, holdin' the double-barrel sawed-off in my right hand, barrel down, pressed close to my leg so's they couldn't see it.

Behind me, I heard De Graff chuckle. Never takin' my eyes off Black-Jack and Ford, I heard him say, "Personal, I never could see the sense in walkin' out into the street and gettin' killed."

Ford and Black-Jack had stopped in front of the office and turned to face me, still standin' in the door.

"We come to call you out, Cotton," Ford said.

"Say it plain, boys."

"What you mean?" Black-Jack asked.

"Tell me your intentions this day."

"Why, hell! To kill you!"

"That's all I needed to know." They thought I was gonna play it straight. Step off the boardwalk and face them in the street. That's the way them penny-dreadful books always have it. Personal, I liked the odds on my side.

"See you boys in hell," I said, turning in the door and liftin' the shotgun. I had the hammers eared back so I just let 'er roar and buck, both barrels.

Shore did make a mess in the street. Plumb disgustin'. That shotgun was loaded with nails and ballbearins and little-bitty pieces of scrap iron, and it tore them boys up some awful. The charge I put into Black-Jack lifted him right off his boots and flung him backwards. The other charge hit Ford smack in the face and took it all off. Wasn't no way anybody could tell who he was, or had been.

Tim Marks, that no-count, he come runnin' up the street, his face all flushed and his lips curled back like a snarlin' dog.

I handed the shotgun to Rusty and stepped out onto the boardwalk.

"Goddamn you!" Tim, he hollered. "You, yellow-bellied

dog. You ain't got the nerve to face nobody fair and square. Draw, damn your eyes!"

So I drew. I never wanted the handle of gunfighter. And never sought to play up the name even after it was hung on me. Like Smoke Jensen, I tried to shy away from it. But it stuck anyways.

Tim, he never even cleared his holster. My .44 slug caught him dead center in the chest and he staggered, somehow stayin' on his feet.

He tried to lift his Colt, but he didn't even have the strength to jack back the hammer. I seen his eyes begin to cloud over as life left him. He slowly sank to his knees, his .44 fallin' out of leather as his hand slipped from it.

I punched out the empty brass and reloaded, this time even puttin' one under the hammer, something I rarely did. Slippin' the hammer-thong off my left hand gun, I walked up the boardwalk towards the Wolf's Den.

I heard and seen Rusty, Burtell, and De Graff come out and spread out into the street, all of them carryin' Greeners. They paced me all the way to the saloon. I guess they figured that if a fight was to come, let's do it!

But the gunslingers that was still in town that day didn't want no more of it . . . not for that day. They'd watched as three of their own went down, knees in blood, and that was enough.

I pushed open the batwings of the saloon and stepped in, the boys right behind me. The batwings squeaked softly as they swung to and fro.

"Anybody else want to try their hand?" I tossed the challenge out to the quiet gatherin'.

No one did. Like I said, they wasn't afraid of me or the boys. But the luck was with me that day, and them ol' hardcases knew it.

"They got dealt bad hands, Cotton," Lydell Townsend spoke quiet-like. "But they'll be another day."

"Not in this town there won't be," Rusty said, his voice carryin' steel in it. "From this moment on, you boys is banned from Doubtful."

Some young gunslinger—or who imagined hisself to be—pushed his chair back and stood up, his hands over the butt of his tied down low .44. He must have been one of them who'd rode in the night before, for I didn't know him.

"To hell with you and your orders, Sheriff!" he called out.

The Greener's roar was deafenin' in the room. Rusty must have personal hand-loaded that charge with nitro. Not only did the charge damn near blow the kid in two, it flung him clear out a window and into the street. I mean, blowed him through the window, past the boardwalk, and into the dirt.

Them other hardcases didn't move. I mean, they didn't even breathe real deep.

Finally, Joe Coyle said, "We'll be takin' our leave now, Sheriff."

"Fine," Rusty said, and I knowed then that he was gonna make a fine sheriff. "Don't come back. Don't never show your faces in this town again. I'm placin' that warnin' clear. I'll kill the first one of you I see."

"That ain't gonna set well with our bosses," Lydell said.

"Tell your bosses I said to go right straight to hell!" Rusty told him.

"I'll shore deliver the message personal." Lydell stood up, but he was careful to keep his hands away from his guns.

"Ride!" Rusty barked.

They rode.

When I stepped out of the hotel the next mornin', I knew all the talkin'-time was done with. It was just a feelin' from deep inside my guts. The town of Doubtful was quiet . . . too quiet. I walked to the desk and looked that dandy-gent in the eyes.

"Hotel seems quiet this mornin'."

"Yes, sir, Marshal. Almost all of our guests have checked out."

"When?"

"Late last evening, sir." His Adam's apple was bobbin' up and down and his face was gray with fear.

He knew something. "You know something that I need to know?"

He shook his head, his slicked-back hair fallin' out of place.

I reached over the counter and grabbed me a handful of shirt and tie and shook him like a dog with a rabbit. "You better talk to me, sissy-pants."

"Lord have mercy! I don't wanna die, Marshal!"

"Who's threatened to kill you, boy?"

"All of 'em!" he fairly screamed it out. "I overheard them talking last evening."

"What was they talkin' about?"

"They've challenged Colonel Dolittle and his Irregulars to a battle. It's happenin' today, Marshal. North of town in the Big Piney area."

With a curse, I let him go and hustled over to the Sheriff's office. The boys was up and havin' coffee before headin' out for breakfast.

Quickly, I told them what the clerk had told me. "Burtell, you see if Dolittle's in town."

"What do I do if I find him?"

"Sit on him!"

But Dolittle was gone, and so was his horse. His wife told Burtell he had gone to fight the Lord's battle and would soon be returning, victorious and flush with victory.

"Well, shit!" says I.

"Maybe we can overtake them," De Graff suggested. "What do you think, Marshal?"

"No," my reply was slow-given. "No, I think that's what somebody would like for us to try."

"What do you mean?" Rusty asked.

"They wouldn't try to take the town," Burtell said. "There ain't nobody ever treed no western town that I know of. These shopkeepers and store-owners would get right hostile."

"Ambush," De Graff said. "They've figured to kill two birds with the same stone. Us, and Dolittle's army."

"That's the way I see it. Well, Dolittle and his men are full-growed. If they ain't got no better sense than what they've showed so far, I ain't gonna try to stop them. We'll just sit tight and see how flush with victory they are in a few hours."

It was a pitiful sight. Near'bouts a hundred men had ridden out. By late afternoon, they begun to straggle back in. And there wasn't no flush from victory on none of their faces.

"How many you counted so far?" De Graff asked me.

"Thirty-four sittin' their saddles. I don't know how many was in them wagons over to the Doc's office." I looked at the boys. "Y'all stay put and keep alert. I'm gonna amble down to the clinic and see what there is to see."

It was bad. Dolittle's Irregulars had rode right into an ambush. And if I'd ever seen a bunch of spirit-broken men, this was them.

But I couldn't find hide nor hair of Colonel Dolittle. I found Pepper, helpin' the Doc's wife with the nursin'.

"Any word on what happened to the preacher?"

"He turned tail and run away," a man spoke from his pallet on the floor. "Last I seen of him he was high-tailin' it back thisaway. He's probably hidin' under the bed at his house."

Some of the others who was able began talkin' to me. The ambush had worked to a T. The Irregulars had ridden right into the trap, not suspectin' nothin' of the sort. One man said he personal seen ten dead; they was blowed out of the saddle right at the first volley.

One man, he just laid on the floor, on his pallet, both his legs broke where his horse had fallen on him after being shot out from under him, cryin' soundlessly, the tears runnin' down his face.

Like I said, pitiful.

When I stepped back outside, the rest of Dolittle's army was gathered around the office and the clinic. One man, Bill Nolan, one of the appointed Captains, walked up to me.

"I reckon we was fools, Marshal."

"No. You had the right idea, but you just chose to follow the wrong man. And speakin' of the wrong man, where is he?"

"At his house. He's all tore up inside, Marshal. Don't be too hard on him. Basically, he's a good man."

"Basically, he's a puffed-up jackass. Preachers ought to preach and keep their noses out of everythin' else."

Nolan, he sighed. "I reckon so, Marshal."

"You got any accurate count on the dead yet?"

"For sure, thirty-eight."

Pitiful.

The final tally turned out to be forty-four dead.

It was noon of the next day when the Doc, all haggard-lookin', walked slow up the boardwalk and sat down beside me in front of the office.

"Have you spoken with the Reverend Dolittle yet, Marshal?"

"Nope. Don't have no plans to do so neither. The man's a damn fool. I don't like to associate with fools. Good way to get a man killed."

The Doc, he didn't say nothin', but I think he sort of agreed with me. "There will be a mass funeral tomorrow, ten o'clock."

"Good. This time of the year, a body don't keep for very long."

"Have you formulated any plan for dealing with the men who ambushed the Irregulars?"

"Nope."

Doc Harrison, he was some kind of surprised at that. "I beg your pardon, Marshal?"

"First of all, Doc, it ain't up to me. I'll help out the sheriff if and when some warrants is issued. But look at it this way: Dolittle and his Irregulars was an armed body of men, ridin' on private range, with intentions of committin' an act of armed aggression. Mayhaps you'd like to tell me who is right and who is wrong?"

"In other words? . . ."

"None of the Irregulars I've spoke to can tell me a single name of the men who ambushed them. Like a pure-dee damn fool that he is, Dolittle led his army into the Big Piney; a place that seems made for ambush. He didn't send out no scouts, he didn't break up his men; had 'em all bunched up. The fire came from both sides of that wooded draw. Nobody saw nothin'. They just died."

The Doc, he didn't have no more to say on the subject. He just got up slow and tired-like, looked at me, nodded his head, and walked slowly back down the boardwalk, toward his office. I felt sorry for the Doc. But even though I knowed it to be wrong, I just couldn't work up much pity for them that had got killed or hurt. It was just a damn fool thing they done.

It was one whale of a funeral; started at ten o'clock and at five that afternoon it was still goin' on. Dolittle was not handlin' the services. Two preachers from another town had been brought in for that. Nobody had seen hide nor hair of Dolittle. And despite my feelings toward the fool, I was gettin' sort of concerned about the windbag.

So, puttin' aside what I'd told Doc Harrison, and leavin' the sounds of the mourners and marchers behind me, I strolled down to Dolittle's house, some ways from the church house.

His wife was sittin' on the front porch, in a rockin' chair, doin' some needlework. She stared at me without no greetin'.

"I come to inquire about your husband, Ma'am."

"He isn't here, Marshal." Her voice was low and sort of eerie-soundin'.

"Where is he, Ma'am?"

"Rode out this morning."

A feelin' of despair struck me hard. I had a hunch what the preacher was doin', but I hoped I was wrong. "Rode out . . . where, Ma'am?"

"He rode east, Marshal."

"Was he armed, Ma'am?"

"Yes. Yes, he was. Heavily armed."

"He didn't tell you where he was goin', Ma'am?"

She stared at me. "He said only that he was going to vindicate himself."

Now, I wasn't real sure what vindicate meant. But I figured it was gonna turn out bad for the preacher. I thanked the lady and left out of there, headin' for the stable.

That Rolf Baker, he was a strange one; yesterday, he'd had my horse, Critter, brung back to me and stabled. Critter still was some hurt but healin' well. I patted him and saddled Pronto, ridin' back to the Sheriff's office.

De Graff was sittin' out front. Due to the many funerals, I had to ride through the alleys and walk around to get to the front of the office.

"What's vindicate mean?" I asked him.

"Damned if I know, Marshal."

I told him what Mrs. Dolittle had said.

"You gonna go lookin' for him, Marshal?"

"Thought I might."

"I'll go with you."

"You get your horse. I'll meet you back here in a few minutes." I had spotted Pepper across the street. Duckin' through the crowds, I got across the street without bein' run down.

"Pepper, what does vindicate mean?"

"It means to clear oneself from doubt, blame, guilt or suspicion."

That's what I thought it meant . . . sort of. I thanked her and ducked back across the street, avoidin' the professional mourners that was sobbin' and hollerin' and moanin'.

Me and De Graff rode out of town, headin' north towards Rockinghorse range.

"You think Dolittle's in trouble, Marshal?"

"Yeah. I think he's in bad trouble."

Chapter Seven

We found his big horse first. The big fine animal was dead. Somebody, or a whole bunch of somebodies, had shot it about a dozen times. Wasn't long 'fore we come upon Preacher Dolittle, and it was a humiliatin' sight. It was something that I never believed in.

The man had been stripped naked and then tarred and feathered. He was staggerin' along, babblin' out of his head.

"Somebody comin' up behind us," De Graff said.

It was Doc Harrison and Pritcher, from the *Doubtful Informer*, and they was in a wagon.

Doc's face turned white as a fresh-washed sheet when he spotted the Preacher.

And from the north, here come Matt Mills' boy, Hugh, with a couple of gunhands ridin' with him. As they come closer, I could see they had tar-spots all over their clothes.

Now, I didn't much care for the Preacher. He might have been a pompous windbag, but he wasn't no bad person. And he didn't deserve nothin' like what he'd just got.

"Preacher, can you understand me?" I had to ask it several times.

Finally, his eyes cleared some and he nodded his head.

"Who done this to you?"

He tried to answer, but no words would form.

"Was it young Hugh and his bunch?"

He nodded his head.

And Hugh and them gunhawks was grinnin' real smart-ass-like as they reined up. "What you got there, Marshal Pickens?" Hugh smirked. "Looks like a big ugly crow, don't it?"

I didn't say nothin' to him. I guess he was figurin' on anything but what I done. I just jerked him off that horse and dumped him on the ground. As I done that, De Graff dragged iron and eared the hammer back, catchin' them two gunslingers by surprise.

I give Young Hugh a right smart kick on the side of his head and he was still as a rock. Then I proceeded to strip him buck-assed nekid. I looked up at the gunhawks; their faces was gray. They had them a hunch what was comin'. But they was only half right.

"Get off them horses and peel down to the where-with-all," I told them. "Or I'll kill you right now!"

They believed me. They come out of them saddles faster than a bat can fly and commenced to takin' off their clothes.

And I'm gonna tell y'all, they wasn't none of them no joyful sight to behold standin' there in their birthday suits.

"Take the preacher back to town," I told the Doc and Pritcher. "And tell the folks in town I'll be comin' in right behind you. Have a welcomin' committee ready for this bunch."

The Doc, he smiled grimly. "It will be my pleasure, Marshal. I'll notify Langford and have him ready, too."

"I think that would be a real nice touch, Doc."

Young Hugh sure could fling words around. Buck-assed nekkid, barefooted, with his hands tied behind his back and a rope around his neck, he told me and De Graff what his daddy was gonna do to us. He swore on his grandmother's grave and on everything holy that he would see us horse-whipped, dragged, staked out on anthills, drawn and quartered, and all sorts of stuff.

Ever' now and then, I'd give a little tug on that rope and he'd go sprawlin' face-first in the dirt and then I'd drag him a few feet 'fore I'd let him get back up. After a while, he got it through his head that if he'd shut his mouth, I'd quit pullin' on the rope.

The gunhawks, they had more sense than Young Hugh; they din't say nothin', exceptin' an occasional "ouch," or "damn!" when they stepped on a burr or a sharp rock.

I halted the parade when we come to the hill that looked down on the town of Doubtful.

"My, my!" De Graff said, with a wicked glint in his eyes. "Would you just take a look at all them folks linin' the streets of town."

I looked back at the sorry trio. "You boys hold your heads up high, now. You 'bout to be the stars of a parade."

That set Young Hugh off again. Man, but he done some cussin'.

Johnny Bull, he picked that time to come ridin' up from the east. He sat in his saddle for a few seconds and then he got to laughin' so hard he had to step down and sit down in the dirt.

When he finally wiped his eyes and got back up, I asked, "Do you know these two-bit gunhands, Johnny?"

"Oh, yeah. That one who's short in the pecker department calls hisself Blackie. The other one is a punk from down Utah way. His name is Ray. They're tinhorns, both of 'em."

Blackie, he glared at Johnny. "Someday I'll kill you, Bull!"

That set Johnny off again. He wound down chucklin' and looked at me. "I done quit the Circle L, Cotton. You mind if I ride along with y'all?"

"Not at all, Johnny. You be lookin' for a job, then?"

"I might take one if it was right for me, for sure."

"Why don't you talk to Rusty. He could use another deputy."

Johnny, he smiled at me. "I just might do that, Cotton. Yep, I just might."

"Goddamn traitor!" Young Hugh yelled at Johnny.

Johnny laughed at him. "I really hope I never have to see you again like this. I'll have nightmares for a month as it is."

Hugh spat at him.

The whole town had turned out for this spectacle. Langford was there with his picture-takin' equipment, and he was pourin' the powder to it and poppin' away.

The crowds that lined both sides of the main street didn't act up none. Nobody tossed no rotten fruit or eggs at the men. They just laughed and laughed . . . and I think that hurt Young Hugh more than if they'd thrown things at him.

I looked back just in time to see a cloud of dust that looked like a prairie storm comin' our way. No one had to tell me who it was: Matt Mills and the whole Rockinghorse crew.

Rusty, he stepped off the boardwalk just as we reined in. "I'll take the prisoners, Marshal. Full responsibility for them." He winked at me, then turned to Young Hugh. "I imagine you're gonna want to see your daddy, son. So I'll just tie this end of your lead-rope to the hitchrail, then y'all can jaw all you want."

Young Hugh, he cussed and spat at Rusty. Rusty patted him on top of his head. "There, there, boy; you just settle down."

The Rockinghorse men all reined up in a long line, spread out, facin' me and the boys and Matt's ass-showin' son and gunslingers. And they was some pitiful-lookin'. All dusty and sweat-streaked, their feet cut up and stone-bruised. Young Hugh just couldn't take no more. He just busted out bawlin' and yelled, *"Daddy!"*

I caught the eye of Waldo Stamps. Now me and Waldo was

on opposite sides of the fence in this matter, but he had to take off his hat and cover his face with it, it tickled him so. I could see Hank Hawthorne and Joe Coyle and Pen Castell, and even some of the regular Rockinghorse crew felt the same way. It was funny to them.

But it wasn't funny to Matt nor to Kilby Jones.

I looked at Young Hugh. "That all you got to say to your pa, boy? Just 'Daddy'?"

Matt, he let me have it then. "This is the most uncalled-for act of barbarism I have ever witnessed, Marshal."

"Even worse than what went on at the Old Brewery, Matt?" I tossed it to him softly; not many others heard it.

Even though I'd guessed that Rolf had told him and A.J. both, it still shook him. He had to grab hold of the saddle horn to steady hisself.

When he finally found his voice, he said, "The sins of the father should not be held against the son, Marshal."

Just then, Doc Harrison pushed his way through the crowd. "Marshal, the Reverend Sam Dolittle just died."

I waited until the crowd had stopped buzzin' at that news, then I looked at Hugh and Blackie and Ray. "The charge is murder, boys. Lock 'em down hard, Rusty."

I reckon that before Matt had left the ranch that mornin', he sent a rider gallopin' off to the nearest telegraph office and sent Judge Barbeau a wire . . . or maybe it had been done days before, I didn't know. But the judge had just taken his summer's vacation, would be gone for six weeks, or more. And then maybe the judge had seen some bad times on the way and just decided on his own to hit the trail. Like I said, I don't know. But he didn't appoint nobody to hear his cases while he was gone, so that left Hugh and Blackie and Ray in the bucket, safe from a hangman's noose for six weeks, or more, or so I thought.

I got word from the U.S. Marshal's office to go look into some outlaws that was supposed to be holed up down on the Crazy Woman. That was gonna be three or four days there and at least that many days back.

When I got back, the valley had exploded.

Rusty had a bandage on his head, De Graff was favorin' one leg, and Burtell still had a mouse under one eye.

But what had first caught my eyes was that the front door of the jailhouse had been tore down.

"Break-out?" I asked.

"Lynchin'," Rusty said.

It had happened two days back. I had been to the Crazy Woman and didn't find hide nor hair of any outlaws. I was one day on my way back when, as Rusty put it, "Some gawd-damned men wearin' hoods over their heads come bustin' into the jail and conked me on the noggin with a club!"

De Graff picked it up. "I come up out of bed in my drawers and broke my big toe when I run into the damn bedpost. By that time, them hooded men was all over us, punchin' and kickin'. They didn't come in to kill us, 'cause nobody dragged iron until the cells was open."

Burtell said, "They hog-tied us and took the prisoners out in the country and strung 'em up. We found 'em about dawn. The last two days has been hell. Nesters' places burned down and the people shot as they ran outside. Men and women and kids alike."

"Can you ride?" I asked De Graff.

"Oh, yeah. The swellin's gone down near to normal. I just have to be careful pullin' my boots on, is all."

"You have any idea who it was busted in here?" I asked Rusty.

"Sure. But knowin' and provin' ain't the same. It was Gimpy over at the cafe, Leo Silverman, the pitcher-taker,

Langford, Alex White from the Dirty Dog. Hell, it was the whole town and lots of the farmers!"

"Which way did you come in?" De Graff asked.

"Through the pass."

"That's why you didn't see nobody, then," Burtell said. "Nobody comes in, nobody goes out of Doubtful. Somebody blowed the west pass so's the stage can't get through, it's runnin' south of us now 'til the road gets cleared."

"The Big Three have sealed off the town?"

"That's it," Rusty told me. "That crazy-actin' Sanchez bunch has signed on with the Rockinghorse. Al Long's brothers is with 'em. The Springer boys is with the Circle L. And Rolf Baker's brought in a few. And Buck Hargon, Doc Martin, and the Canadian gunslinger, Sangamon, they went with the Quartermoon."

"Miss Mary at the Wolf's Den?" De Graff said. "She pulled out day before yesterday. Just up and left."

I looked around, missin' somebody. "I thought you hired Johnny Bull."

"I did. He's out trying to talk some sense into some of the hardcases he knows right well. He's tryin' to convince them that doin' what they're doin' is gonna bring the Army and ever'body else in here after them. I don't think he's havin' much luck."

"Pepper?"

"She's all right. She and Doc have taken over the church house and are usin' it for a hospital."

"My brother?"

"He's still in town. Stayin' over at the hotel and stayin' out of trouble. I ain't got a clue as to who brung him in here."

"Maybe nobody did," I finally said, after thinkin' that over for a time. "I thought for awhile it was Rolf; but, now I'm not so sure. Well, I come in through the pass, I reckon I can go out the same way."

"No, you won't," Johnny Bull stepped into the office. "By now, they'll have it plugged up tight. I know," he added grimly. "I just been there; found your tracks. I met your brother headin' out. He's gone."

"Have any luck with the gunhawks?" De Graff asked him.

"Not a bit." His voice was filled with disgust. "I told them they all ought to be ashamed of themselves, killin' women and kids. They just laughed at me. They said that nits grow into lice, so what the hell difference does it make?"

He turned to face the window lookin' out on the now nearly empty street. "I reckon I've killed twenty men. Half of them while wearin' a badge down in Colorado and Arizona. The other ten," he shrugged, "range-wars, showdowns, stand-up-and-look-'em-in-the-eye fights. I had me a bad feelin' when I took this job of work. I almost didn't take it."

"I was some surprised to see you here," I told him. "Tell me, if you know, what have Lawrence, Baker, and Mills promised them drawin' fightin' wages? Has to be somethin' more than money."

"I figure it's land. Free and clear and in their names. You see, they know, like I know, and you know, Cotton, the day of the gunfighter is comin' to an end. I figure maybe five years, ten tops, and it's gonna be near'bout over. This is their chance to turn respectable . . . providin' they don't leave no witnesses."

It took a couple of seconds for the full impact of what he'd just said to hit me. "You mean . . . ?"

He looked me square in the eyes. "They're gonna have to kill every man, every woman, and every child in the valley. If their plan is to work, they can't afford to leave nobody alive!"

Chapter Eight

"You can't be serious!" Doc Harrison shouted. "My God, man, that's the most . . . I . . . the most monstrous thing I have ever heard of!"

"I believe that's what they intend to do," I stuck to my words. "And I been thinkin' on it some. We could try a bust-out, and maybe some of us would make it. But a lot of us wouldn't."

"And your plan of action, Marshal?" Pritcher asked.

I shook my head. "I can't help them that's still out in the valley proper. I hate to say it, but they're on their own. The Big Three, accordin' to what Johnny and Rusty have learned, has planned this out right clever. When the supply wagons come, they got hands ready with wagons to off-load the flour and salt and coffee and beans and such, tellin' the freighters they'll take the stuff into town. And they're payin' cash money for the bills of ladin' right there on the spot."

"Then they are planning on starving us out," George Waller said.

I shook my head. "No. Think about it, George. When was your supply wagons due in?"

"Why . . . yesterday, as a matter of fact."

"And they run . . . ?"

His face turned grim. "Once a month. They come in convoys for safety from highwaymen and Indians." His face tightened some. "We are completely cut off."

"Those men have to give me my medical supplies!" the Doc blurted. "I've got sick people, hurt people that might die without them. I'll just go talk to the men."

"No you won't!" I shoved him back. "You'll do no such thing. They'll kill you, Doc. And we need you right here in town."

Pepper spoke up. "Then what is your plan, Cotton?"

I smiled at her. "Why, Miss Pepper, we are goin' to have a party. It's gonna go on 'round the clock. They's gonna be drinkin' and dancin' and singin' and shoutin'."

"Have you lost your mind, Marshal?" George asked.

"Nope. I just feel in the mood for a party, that's all."

It must have been quite a sight and show for them I knew was on the ridges above the town watchin' and spyin'. We filled up all the empty whiskey bottles we could find with colored water and sodee pop. Then we had us a street dance. Several people "passed out" and had to be toted away, lookin' like to them watchin' that they was passed out from too much whiskey.

We took turns, so none of us would be all tuckered out and unable to fight when the other side made their move on the town. I figured two days, and I was right on the money.

The women in the town, includin' the soiled doves, they had them a high old time, really kickin' up their heels and whoopin' it up, and it went on day and night.

At night we'd string lanterns and put up torches to give the party light. And it was durin' that first night, that the men began gettin' in position all around the town. They carried all the food and water and ammo they could stagger with and got into where I assigned them and stayed there, quiet, not movin'.

Boardin' House Belle, she had her a hell of a time, dancin' with ever' man in sight. She grabbed me for a reel three times and damn near crippled me, stompin' all over my feet. De Graff was the only man in town she didn't dance with, he begged off 'cause of his bad toe. Even Wong got trapped into doin' a reel with her, and if that wasn't a sight to see. Wong, he was a-jibber-jabberin' in China talk—I knowed he was cussin' her—and Belle just grinnin', lovin' ever minute of it.

And it was at night that we stashed weapons all around the town: behind water troughs, under the boardwalk, in places that was easy for us but hidden from them when they come ridin' in.

And the kids, they had a big time, a drinkin' that make-believe whiskey and whoopin' and hollerin' and dancin'.

"Aren't they cute?" Pepper said.

But I got suspicious and grabbed one of them bottles. The little buggers had got into the real stuff while we wasn't lookin'. They wasn't actin'. Hell, they was all *drunk!*

Their mommies put them to bed and the party rolled on.

Dawn of the second day give the watchers a different sight. The boardwalks was littered with passed-out people, men and women, the women with their dresses hiked up damn near to their never-see-it. I was sprawled out in front of the Salty Dog, on my belly, as was nearly ever'body else; that was the only thing that might give the plan away, but that couldn't be helped. 'Cause we had shotguns under us.

All the hidden marksmen was in position and we waited, motionless as the sun broke free and it was full dawn. Then I heard the sounds of hooves.

"Nobody move," I called out. "If they touch you, you're all passed out. Don't nobody screw it up now."

About a half dozen rowdies was the first in town. And I got to give it to the women. Them gunslicks got them some quick feels of places where they shouldn't have felt. But the ladies, bless their hearts, they didn't move.

More riders come in, and finally I heard one shout, "Come on in. Hell, they're all drunk and passed out. Dumbest goddamn thing I ever heard of anybody doin'. There's Johnny Bull. Somebody kick that son of a bitch."

I heard the boot hit Johnny, and it must have hurt something awful. But Johnny, he didn't move.

Openin' one eye, I could see the street, from one end to the other, was filled with gunhands. As we had planned, I lifted my hand just slightly and let it fall to the boardwalk, and that opened the real dance.

Two dozen shotguns on the roofs of the buildings roared and bucked as the passed-out people come to life, with pistols and rifles and shotguns.

It was carnage.

I put both barrels of my Greener into Ugly Injun Tom Johnson, the blast completely liftin' him out of the saddle and flingin' him, several different pieces of him, into the dirt.

Grabbin' up another shotgun, I fired both barrels into a knot of Rockinghorse riders, punchers, but they was drawin' fightin' wages, so that made them fair game.

I cleared three saddles with that blast.

Droppin' the Greener, I hauled out both pistols and let the hammers fall.

The noise was a screaming nightmare. Shotguns and rifles and pistols and the screamin' of scared horses and the screamin' of badly wounded and dyin' men.

Wong, he come out of his shop, some sort of funny-lookin' hatchets in his hands, and give them a fling, hittin' his mark both times; one rider fell to the dust, minus his head!

Luther Long come up the boardwalk, ridin' his horse

smack at me. I shot him between the eyes and emptied another saddle.

Johnny Bull was deadly with his Colts; I seen him drop Bitter Creek and Tulsa Jack, then turn and put lead into Kilby Jones. The foreman stayed in the saddle for a moment, then toppled over into the dirt.

George Waller come out of his store with a pistol in each hand, smokin' them Colts as he come. He took out Nimrod and Bob Clay before a slug took him in the leg and knocked him down.

Boardin' House Belle, she come chargin' out into the street, right in the middle of it all. She jerked Fox Breckenridge slap off his horse and dumped him on his butt in the dirt. I heard her squall, "Spurn my affections, will you?" Then she hauled off and slugged him, right on the side of his jaw. Fox dropped like he'd been hit with a sledgehammer and lay still.

Joe Coyle tried to make a run for it. Leo Silverman blew him out of the saddle, letting the gunfighter have both barrels from a goose gun.

Clay Dundee met his end when he tried to hightail it out through an alley and run into Rusty. Rusty, with a Colt in each hand, dotted Clay's eyes and put an end to another career.

De Graff was down on one knee, with a Henry, Martin Truby beside with another Henry. I seen them clear three saddles—Pete Clanton, Dave Tunsall, and Ike Burdette goin' down under the deadly hail.

Burtell and Dick Avedon was bangin' away at each other, from opposite sides of the body-littered, bloody, and horse-crap-filled street. Dick got lead into Burtell, but as he was goin' down, Burtell eared back the hammer and shot Dick through the chest.

Burtell's left arm was all bloody, but he wasn't about to give up the fight. He blowed a kid tinhorn out of the saddle, hurt but not dead, and then walked right out to him and laid his Colt up alongside that punk gunfighter's head.

Pen Castell ended the life of the feller who ran the leather shop, knockin' him off a roof. Liftin' my left-hand gun, I sighted Pen in and watched as the slug took most of his jaw away. He fell into a horse trough and was still.

From up past the end of the street, I heard a wild Rebel yell, the kind that sends chills runnin' up and down your spine, and here comes Jesse Bates and the whole Arrow bunch. They had busted through the blockade and was a most welcome sight. Miss Maggie and Miss Jean was right in the middle of it, reins in their teeth and a smokepole in each hand.

Lydell Townsend went down under the guns of Miss Maggie and Tanner Smith dropped to his knees, gut-shot from two rounds from Miss Jean.

A bullet hit the post I was standin' next to, sendin' splinters into my face, stingin' and drawin' blood, but not doin' no serious damage. Turning, I faced Waldo Stamps and we both fired at the same time.

I felt a tremendous blow in my right side that knocked me backwards and down to the boardwalk. I seen where my slug had hit Waldo in the shoulder, spinnin' him around.

Lookin' down, I first felt relief, then got pissed off.

The bastard's bullet had hit my fine new watch and ruined it.

"You no-good peckerhead!" I yelled at him. "You busted my watch."

"Hell with you!" Waldo snarled, and lifted his gun.

A bullet hit him in the right temple and exited out the left. Waldo dropped to the boardwalk. Turnin' my head, I seen Pepper acrost the street, a rifle in her hands.

We grinned at each other.

And then it got almighty eerie quiet. Gettin' to my feet, I looked around. The fight was over. I could hear the sounds of gallopin' horses, their riders whippin' them hard, gettin' the hell out of town.

Bernard Pritcher come walkin' up the center of the street, carryin' a shotgun that was near'bouts as big as him. He had him two gunhands marchin' in front of him, their hands held high over their heads.

"By the Lord!" the newspaper man hollered. "That was quite exhilarating! March, you heathens!" He poked one sorry-lookin' gunslick in the butt with the shotgun.

Jesse Bates rode up to me, and seen me holdin' my side. "You hit, Marshal?"

"Naw. Bullet busted my watch."

He grinned at me. "We secured the town's supply wagons. I left some hands with them 'bout a mile out of town."

"That'll be good news for the Doc. He's got some much-needed medical stuff in them wagons. Any of your boys hit?"

"Couple. They don't look too bad."

Miss Maggie and Miss Jean rode up, Maggie askin', "Do we form up a posse and take out after the rest of them, Marshal?"

I thought on that as Rusty come up, blood drippin' from a scalp wound. "Let 'em go," I finally said. "We'll clear out and clean up this mess in town and then see to the gunhawks that might be left out in the county."

I looked back at Jesse. "Any word on the smaller ranchers and the nesters?"

"Most of them are all right. A few got hit pretty hard, but it's better than I thought it would be."

Lawyer Stokes come up to me, a Colt in each hand. He smiled. "I have been a fool, Marshal. I wonder if the town will ever forgive me for representing the Big Three?"

"I 'magine so, Lawyer. Now that you've come to your senses. That was some fine shootin' on your part a while ago."

Stokes blushed.

Maggie, she swung down and stepped up right close to the lawyer. "You married, lawyer?"

"Why . . . ah, no. As a matter of fact."

"Is that right?" she asked sweetly.

Me and Jesse and Rusty, we vacated that area in a hurry!

Chapter Nine

The roads leading into and out of Doubtful was cleared of debris and the stages started runnin' again. We buried twenty-seven gunfighters in boot hill. I sent De Graff foggin' it south to wire the U.S. Marshal's office and tell them to send in some help to once and for all clear this mess up.

Nobody I talked with had seen hide nor hair of A. J. Lawrence, Matt Mills, or Rolf Baker.

On the next stage that come through, I got a letter from the U.S. Marshal's office.

Can't spare anyone. Handle it yourself.

The letter went on to state that I had several thousand more dollars comin' to me in re-ward money. Seems like Waldo Stamps and a couple more that I'd smoked had some old flyers out on them. That ranch in the valley was gettin' closer and closer to reality.

Miss Mary and her barkeep was back, and had reopened the saloon. The big ugly bruise on my side had disappeared, and me and Pepper was makin' firm plans for our weddin'. It was going to be a double weddin'. Rusty and Tina was gettin' hitched up, too.

There hadn't been no more nightridin', I hadn't seen no sign of my brother, Jack, and for the first time in a long while, the valley was peaceful. Wire was bein' stretched to connect Doubtful to the telegraph office south of us; gonna be a big party, a real one this time, when all that was completed.

Doc Harrison and Pritcher and some of the others, includin' George Waller, they thought it was all over and done with. But me and the boys, we knew better. Knew it 'cause there was still about a dozen gunslingers still around. And they hadn't taken no part in the assault on the town.

Fox Breckenridge, well, he was still around. I'd had me a talk with Fox, and the longer I talked, the longer and grayer his face got. Went something like this: "Now, Fox, you know you're lookin' at spendin' the rest of your life in prison. Maybe even a hangin'. So here's what I'm gonna do. I'm gonna hang onto all the charges I got agin' you. As long as you're a good boy and marry up with Belle and keep her happy, you're free."

Fox fainted. After I dumped a bucket of water on him, he said, "For God's sake, Cotton, kill me and have done with it!"

"Nope. Belle says she's in love with you and that's that. Y'all just start makin' plans for the weddin'."

When I left him, he was cryin' like a baby. Plumb pitiful.

We all knew the time would come when the Big Three would be forced to come to town for supplies, and at the end of the third week after Doubtful's Big Battle, as Pritcher had headlined it in the *Informer*, I looked up one mornin' and here they come.

In a way, it was kind of pathetic. The ladies was in their carriages, all tryin' to look like royalty, with their noses stuck up high. But it didn't come off. They had them a passel of gunfighters with them: Little Jack Bagwell, Hank Hawthorne, Jim Reynolds, the Springer Brothers, and the Sanchez clan, includin' goofy Fergus and his whacky sons, Tyrone and Udell, and the two remaining Long Brothers. And with Rolf and Martha and Jeff, there rode Buck Hargon and Doc Martin and Sangamon.

And then everybody in the town of Doubtful stepped out onto the boardwalk, armed to the teeth. They didn't none of them make any threatenin' gestures, they just stood quiet with their weapons. The Big Three got the message; as silent as it was, it was loudly given.

I walked over to the store when the parade stopped at Waller's, and looked at Rolf and A.J. and Matt. "I'll talk with you men in the Sheriff's Office. Right now!"

When they was seated, I gave it to them straight from the shoulder. Big Mike was there, and he was glarin' hate at me.

"Get rid of your gunhands. All of them. Rusty is talkin' to them right now. He's givin' them twenty-four hours to draw their time and get clear of the Territory. If you men don't do what I tell you to do, well, maybe I can't make them old warrants stick, but I'll damn sure cause you men a lot of grief."

They exchanged glances and Rolf said, "Consider it done, Marshal."

"Fine," says I. "Now then, the war is over. There's been too many dead, too much blood spilled." Then I told a big whoppin' lie. "I've contacted the Army at Fort Kearney. If there is any more trouble, they'll be sendin' the cavalry in. Do you all understand that?"

They did.

"There ain't but one thing left to do," Big Mike said, standing up.

"What's that?" I asked.

"This!" Then he hit me and knocked me plumb out the brand-new door of the jailhouse.

It took Big Mike about a half a minute to bull his way through the shattered door; he got all tangled up in the splintered wood.

But that give me time to get to my feet and splash water on my face from the horse trough. Then to get set for his wild rush at me.

And he was wild, screamin' and cussin' as he jumped off the boardwalk.

As he jumped he lost his balance and was unsteady for a couple of seconds. That give me time to haul off and bust him right smack on his big Roman nose. It busted and he squalled as the blood squirted. And it also knocked him backwards a few steps. He shook his head and I popped him again, this time on the jaw. Then I got all tangled up in my spurs and went down to the dirt.

He tried to fall on me, to crush my chest with his knees. I rolled away just in time and kicked out, my boot catching Mike on his side and bringin' a grunt of pain.

He tried to grab me in a bear hug, but a knee to his groin backed him up, pain all over his face. I hit him twice, a left and right to the jaw and it stunned him. He backed up, puffin' and blowin' and tryin' to clear his head.

He'd first hit me a hell of a lick, but anger and time had blowed away the clouds his fist had put in my head. Oh, I knew when the fight was over, win or lose, I'd be a mess of bruises from goin' through that jailhouse door, but for right now, I was just mad as hell.

And I had one more thing goin' for me: I'd been workin' hard for years and years, never once stoppin' for no vacation, and my muscle was packed muscle on top of muscle, while Big Mike had been barkin' out orders from the hurricane deck of the horse. He just wasn't in the shape that I was.

I tossed a fake at him and he knew it for what it was and brushed it away, gettin' set for what he thought would be followin'. But I fooled him again and stepped up and kicked him on the kneecap. He hollered and cussed and grabbed for his knee. That's when I let him have it. I hit him a combination of punches; to the head, to the belly, to the kidneys, then started all over again.

There was panic in the big man's eyes, all mixed up with desperation. He was losin' a fight and he just couldn't stand it. With a curse, he grabbed for his gun and had it out before I could push the leather off the hammer of mine.

"You saddle bum!" he hissed at me, and then eared back the hammer.

The slug took Big Mike in the head, and blowed out a bunch of yukk as it came out the other side. Mike toppled over on his side and was still, the pistol slippin' from his hand.

I turned and looked at my brother standin' there, his pistol barrel smokin'.

"Thank you," says I.

"Don't thank me yet." His eyes was hard and cold. "You don't have no idea what I come here for."

Then he just turned and walked away.

The killin' of Big Mike put the damper on anybody else who might have had ideas of causin' more trouble. A.J., Matt, and Rolf sent their gunhands packin', just like they promised they'd do. The wires was strung up connectin' us with the outside world, and we had us a whale of a town party.

Fox danced ever' dance with his beloved Belle.

Jack Crow had disappeared, and no one seemed to know where he'd gone. Personal, I didn't much care. I just wanted the valley peaceful.

Me and Pepper, Rusty and Tina, we got all hitched up proper. I knowed Pepper was hurt 'cause her folks didn't show up, but she didn't let it ruin nothing.

For our honeymoon, Pepper chose the spot, and it was some kind of lovely. It was in the high-up country; snuggest little stone cabin you ever did see.

"Who owns this?" I asked.

"We do," she said softly, her fingers busy at the buttons of my shirt. "We'll talk about property lines later."

Like I said, someday I was gonna have to speak to her about being so brazen. Someday.

Rolf had give it to her for a birthday present, and it was all legal. She'd told me it was just a little spread, and by some standards, it was. Ten thousand acres. But it was prime cattle and horse country.

After a time up in the cabin, me and Pepper took our time gettin' back to Doubtful. Everybody who seen us just grinned at us. Made my ears red.

Pepper, she just laughed and waved at them.

I turned in my U.S. Marshal's badge while Pepper spent some time over to Doc Harrison's place. The ladies was givin' her some sort of tea, or something like that. I sure was glad I wasn't invited. Makin' me drink tea might have been grounds for a divorce.

George Waller, he stopped by and had some coffee with us. Grinnin' like a fool, slappin' me on the back, kiddin' me about the honeymoon. I took it right well. Wasn't a whole lot I could say about it.

I'd run out of tobacco up in the cabin, so I excused myself and started across the street to get something to smoke.

"Cotton!" the voice stopped me and turned me slow in the street.

Jack Crow was facin' me, about forty yards between us. My mouth went all dry, for his hands was all over the butts of his guns.

"Jack. What's on your mind?"

He didn't believe in beatin' about no bushes—"Killin' you!"

Chapter Ten

I was conscious of people linin' the boardwalks; maybe they was talkin', but I didn't hear them.

"Why do you want to do that, Jack?"

He laughed that cold laugh at me. "'Cause I got the word that people are sayin' you're better than me. That hurt me, brother. I make my livin' at this. This is the only way I know how to prove them wrong."

"You're crazy, Jack! Plumb loco. We're *brothers!*"

"Don't make no difference."

"You're lyin', Jack. Who hired you to gun me?"

"Nobody, Cotton. And I'm tellin' you the truth. It's a business, Cotton. That's all it is. I'd kill Pa if he was around and got in my way."

"Jack. Don't draw on me. I'm better than you are, Jack."

"No way, kid. See you in Hell!"

He was quick; snake-quick. Like I said, I never wanted the title of gunfighter. But I knowed in all the west, there wasn't but two or three better than me. And Jack Crow wasn't one of them. Smoke Jensen, Louis Longmont, and maybe one more.

I walked slow toward my brother Jack, layin' on his side in

the bloody dirt. He grinned up at me, his mouth all bloody from his chest wound; I must have nicked a lung.

"Now you're a gunfighter, Kid. Now you can't never run away from it. I've marked you, Cotton. Like Cain. You're marked. You won't never live it down."

I squatted down beside him. He was fadin' quick. "Our brothers and sisters, Jack. Where are they all?"

"Gone. Scattered all to hell and gone. I never kept up with none of them."

"Anything special you want on your marker, Jack?"

If there was, he never got around to tellin' me. He jerked once, and then was dead.

Pepper come to me and touched my arm. "Maybe you can't ever live it down, Cotton. But we can sure try, can't we?"

I smiled at her. "We sure can, honey."

Then she kissed me right on the mouth! Right there in front of the whole damned town!

I'm just gonna have to speak to that woman. Brazen!

Well, Grandson, that's the story, all of it. You may be wondering why I go by the name of Cotton in the story and nothing else. Truth is—and I ain't never told anyone this before, not even your daddy—that I never much cared for my given name. Someone, either my ma or my pa, had themselves a real sense of humor when they named me Throckmorton Thaddeus Wheeler. (For a while, the family referred to me as T.T. but it sounded too much like "titty" and that was even worse than Throckmorton Thaddeus!) Then one day when I was fifteen a feller said to me, "If I was you, I wouldn't cotton to a name like Throckmorton Thaddeus, neither," so from then on I called myself Cotton and the name just sorta stuck.

Anyway, now when you talk about your old grand-daddy to your teachers and friends about them olden days in Doubtful, you'll be speaking the gospel truth. Cause it all happened just the way you read it. I ain't proud of some of the things I done, but sometimes you got to break some eggs if you're wantin' to bake a cake. (Not that I'd ever be caught dead bakin' a cake, but you know what I mean.)

I hope, now that you know the truth, you don't think any less of your granddaddy. I know a lot of it ain't too pretty, but those were some rough times in Wyoming Territory and we all done what we thought was right. Sometimes you gotta bend the law to keep from breakin' it.

Your Grandma Pepper is calling me to supper now so I reckon I'll put down my ink pen and have me some roast chicken and biscuits. Your grandma and me are looking forward to see you and your folks come Fourth of July. Grandma Pepper plans to bake you one of them peach cobblers you fancy so much—only this time don't eat it all at one sittin' like last year and get the runs agin.

Your loving grandfather,
Throckmorton Thaddeus "Cotton" Wheeler
Cheyenne, Wyoming

Turn the page for an exciting preview of

PRIDE OF EAGLES

by William W. Johnstone with J. A. Johnstone

On sale now, wherever Pinnacle Books are sold.

PRIDE OF EAGLES by William W. Johnstone
with J. A. Johnstone
Pinnacle Books
ISBN 0-7860-1736-8

www.kensingtonbooks.com

Chapter One

Distorted by shimmering heat rays, the town of Picacho, Arizona Territory, lay baking in the sun as Falcon rode into town. To the side of one of the houses a woman was washing clothes while two children played on the ground beside her. A dog walked up for a closer examination of Falcon, but it was too hot for him to offer any challenge, so he turned and withdrew to the shade of the building.

Picacho was built along the Southern Pacific Railroad, the steel ribbons that gave it life. In fact, it was the railroad that brought Falcon to Picacho. He was coming back from his silver mine, located in the Cabibi Mountains, near Oro Blanco. He had bought the mine from Doc Holliday, but his friend neglected to tell him that, in order to make the mine productive, he would have to deal with some hostile Apache Indians.

He took care of that, and was now on his way back to his home in MacCallister Valley, Colorado. He was in Picacho because it was the nearest place he could catch a train.

The largest structure in town had a big picture of a golden mug of beer painted on the false front of the building. Alongside the mug of beer, in large red letters, outlined in black, was the name of the saloon: The Brown Dirt Cowboy.

Dismounting in front of the saloon, Falcon tied his horse off at the hitching rail, then stepped up on the porch to go inside. If anyone happened to be looking in this direction at that point in time, they would have seen a big man, standing a little over six feet tall. His shoulders were wide and muscular and his waist was flat. Pale blue eyes stared out from a chiseled face. He had wheat-colored hair which he wore short and neat. He was wearing a long-sleeved red shirt, a buckskin vest, Levi jeans and tall black boots.

Falcon had been thinking about a cold beer for the last two days, and he could almost taste it now as he pushed his way through the batwing doors.

Hanging gourds of evaporating water made the interior of the saloon at least ten degrees cooler than it was outside. It was dark in the saloon, so dark that Falcon had to stand for a moment until his eyes adjusted to the lack of light.

He took out a long, thin cheroot and lit it by striking a match on the handle of his Colt .44. He took a few puffs, then, squinting his eyes through the cloud of smoke, surveyed the saloon he had just entered. The bar was made of unfinished, wide-plank boards, with an attached ledge at the bottom to be used as a foot rail. There was no mirror behind the bar, but there was a shelf with an assortment of liquor bottles. A bartender with pomade-slick hair and a waxed moustache was standing behind the bar, with his arms folded across his chest.

Over the last few years Falcon could almost define his life by places like this: flyblown towns, crude saloons, and green whiskey. Although he could easily afford the high life, Falcon had been wandering around ever since his wife, Marie Gentle Breeze, herself an Indian, had been killed by Indians. Sometimes the cold sweats and killing rages still plagued him but, for the most part, he was able to put that behind him now.

Falcon stepped up to the bar.

"What can I do you for?" the bartender asked.

"Is your beer cold?"

"Colder than a mountain stream," he answered.

"All right, I'll take a glass," Falcon said.

The bartender drew the beer and put it in front of Falcon. "Just passing through, are you?" the bartender asked.

"Yes," Falcon replied without elaborating. He picked up the mug and took a long drink before he turned to look around the place. Although it was mid-afternoon, the saloon was nearly full, the customers drawn by the fact that this was the coolest building in town.

As he stood at the bar, a tall, broad-shouldered, bearded man stepped in through the back door. At first Falcon wondered why he had come through the back door, then he saw that a star was barely showing from beneath the vest he was wearing. The sheriff pointed a gun toward one of the tables.

"I just got a telegram about you, Kofax," the lawman said. "You should'a had better sense than to come back to a town where ever'one knows you,"

"Let it be, Calhoun," Kofax replied. "I ain't staying here long. I'm just waitin' around for the train to take me out of here."

The sheriff shook his head. "I don't think so. You won't be catchin' the train today," he said. "You're goin' to jail."

Kofax stood up slowly, and stepped away from the table.

"Well now, you're planning' on takin' me there all by yourself, are you, Calhoun?" Kofax asked.

The quiet calm of the barroom grew tense, and most of the other patrons in the bar stood up and moved to both sides of the room, giving the sheriff and Kofax a lot of space.

Only Falcon didn't move. He stayed by the bar, sipping his beer and watching the drama play out before him.

"You can make this a lot easier by dropping your gunbelt," the sheriff said.

Kofax chuckled, but there was no humor in his laugh.

"Well now, you see, there you go. I don't plan to make it easy for you," he said.

"Shuck out of that gunbelt like I told you, slow and easy," the sheriff ordered.

Falcon saw something then that the sheriff either didn't see, or didn't notice. Kofax's eyes flicked upward for a split second, then back down toward the sheriff. Kofax smiled, almost confidently, at the sheriff.

"Sorry, Calhoun, but like I said, I don't plan to make this easy for you."

Curious as to why Kofax wasn't more nervous, Falcon glanced up and saw a man standing at the top of the stairs. The man was aiming a pistol at the sheriff's back. That was what Kofax had seen when he cut his eyes upward, and that was what was giving him such supreme confidence.

"Sheriff, look out!" Falcon shouted.

"Stay out of this, you son of a bitch!" the man at the top of the stairs shouted. He turned his pistol toward Falcon.

Falcon dropped his beer and pulled his own pistol, firing just as the man at the top of the stairs fired. The shooter's bullet missed Falcon and hit a whiskey bottle that was sitting on the bar. The impact sent a shower of whiskey and shards of glass.

Falcon's shot caught the shooter in the chest, and he dropped his pistol and clasped his hand over the entry wound, then looked down at himself as blood began to spill between his fingers. The shooter's eyes rolled up in his head and he tumbled forward, sliding down the stairs, following his clattering pistol all the way down. He lay motionless at the bottom, his head and shoulders on the floor, his legs still on the steps.

Although the sound of the two gunshots had riveted everyone's attention, the situation between Kofax and the sheriff continued to play out and, almost before the sound of the first two gunshots had faded, two more shots rang out. The sheriff's bullet struck Kofax in the neck, forcing him back against the cold wood-burning stove, causing him to hit it with such impact that he knocked it over, pulling down half the flue pipe.

As the smoke from four gunshots drifted through the saloon, only the sheriff and Falcon were still standing. Both were holding smoking pistols in their hands, and they looked at each other warily.

"I thank you for taking a hand in this, Mister," the sheriff said. "Most folks would have stayed on the sidelines."

"Yeah, well, I didn't really have that much choice in the matter," Falcon said.

The sheriff chuckled and nodded. "I guess you didn't at that," he said. He put his pistol away.

Falcon re-holstered his own gun.

"Can I buy you a drink?" the sheriff asked.

Falcon looked pointedly at his beer mug, which now lay empty, on the floor where he had dropped it when the shooting began.

"I guess I could use a new one at that," Falcon said.

"Two beers," the sheriff said.

The barkeep, who had dived to the floor behind the bar when the shooting started, now stood up, drew two beers and put them on the bar.

"Thanks," Falcon said, taking a swallow of his beer.

"The name is Calhoun," the sheriff said as he lifted his own beer to his lips. "Titus Calhoun."

"Glad to meet you, Sheriff. I'm Falcon MacCallister."

Upon hearing Falcon's name, Sheriff Calhoun coughed and sprayed beer. Slamming his beer down on the bar, he reached for his pistol, only to find his holster was empty.

"Are you looking for this?" Falcon asked, holding the sheriff's pistol.

Seeing that Falcon had his gun, the sheriff put his hands up.

"Put your hands down, Sheriff," Falcon said. He put the pistol back in the sheriff's holster. "Whatever you think you might have on me, it's wrong. I'm not wanted anywhere."

"I . . . I reckon, under the circumstances, I've got no cause not to believe you," the sheriff said.

"Good. Now, maybe you can tell me about these two men we just had a run-in with."

"That one's Rollie Kofax," Sheriff Calhoun said, nodding toward the one he had shot. He looked over toward the stairs where the other man lay, half on the stairs and half off. "The one you shot was Willy Cardis. I just got word today that they was the ones that held up a stagecoach last week, over near Perdition. There was three of 'em, but Gilly Cardis, got hisself caught.

"Gilly Cardis? You mean the two brothers, names were Willy and Gilly?" Falcon asked.

Sheriff Calhoun nodded. "They was twins," he said. "And I don't expect Gilly's goin' to be none too happy to hear that his brother got shot. I'd say it's a good thing he's in jail right now, otherwise, you'd probably wind up havin' another gunfight on your hands."

"Yeah," Falcon said drolly. "Seems like just about everyone I've ever run across had a brother somewhere. And those brothers all want to make things square."

"What are you doin' in Picacho, Mr. MacCallister? That is . . . if you don't mind my askin'."

"I don't mind at all," Falcon said. "I have some property down around Oro Blanco. I was just down seeing to it."

Sheriff Calhoun shook his head and clucked, quietly. "That's not a place that's too healthy to be, right now. What with the Indian problem and all."

Falcon finished his beer. "Let me buy this round," he said. "That is, if you'd care for another."

"Don't mind if I do," Calhoun said.

"There's no Indian trouble now," Falcon said. "I had a nice meeting with Keytano and . . ."

Calhoun snapped his fingers and smiled, broadly. "I know where I heard your name now," he said. "You and Mickey Free brought in Naiche a few years back, didn't you?"

"Yes."

"And Keytano? You had a . . . I believe you called it a nice meeting . . . with Keytano?"

"Yes," Falcon said.

Calhoun chuckled, and shook his head. "Only someone like you could call a meeting with Keytano nice."

"Keytano is a good man," Falcon said. "He's a man of honor, and I like men of honor."

Falcon finished his second beer, then set the empty mug down. He glanced toward the two dead men who had been dragged to the back of the room and covered with a tarpaulin.

"I don't have to stick around for any kind of an inquest, do I?" he asked.

Calhoun shook his head. "No, but I'm sure there's a reward for Cardis. If you wait around a couple of days, I can get it approved and get the money to you."

"Do you have a volunteer fire department in town?" Falcon asked.

"Yes," Calhoun replied, puzzled as to why Falcon would ask about that.

"Give any reward money I might have to the volunteer fire department," he said. "I've never known one, anywhere, that couldn't use a little extra money."

The sheriff nodded. "You're right about that, Mr. MacCallister, and I'll do that for you," he said. "Speaking for the town, I'll tell you that we are grateful."

Falcon stuck out his hand for a handshake. "I need to get down to the depot to make arrangements to catch the train," he said. "Maybe I'll see you again, sometime."

"It would be my pleasure," Sheriff Calhoun said.

"Who is that fella MacCallister, anyway, Sheriff?" the bar-tender asked when Falcon left the saloon.

"He is the kind of man people tell tall stories about, Sam," Sheriff Calhoun replied. "Only in Falcon MacCallister's case, they're all true."

When Falcon arrived in MacCallister the next afternoon, he stopped by the post office to pick up his mail. One of his letters was from his brother Andrew in New York, asking him again why he didn't just cash in everything and come to New York.

Falcon chuckled as he read the letter. He knew it was more than just brotherly love that made Andrew invite him. Despite his footloose lifestyle, Falcon was the wealthiest of all his siblings.

The other letter was from Conrad Kohrs.

Falcon held the letter for a moment or two before he opened it, wondering what the wealthiest cattle baron in America wanted with him.

Chapter Two

A rat, its beady eyes alert for danger, darted out from one of the warehouses onto the dank boards of the pier. Finding a piece of sodden bread, it picked up its prize, then darted back to the safety of its hole. Falcon MacCallister stood on the same pier, looking out over San Francisco Bay. He pulled the collar of his coat up against the damp chill air as he listened to a bell buoy clanging out in the harbor, its syncopated ringing notes measuring the passage of the night. From somewhere close, a bosun's pipe sounded a shipboard signal, incomprehensible to landlubbers but fully understood by the ship's crew.

Gossamer tendrils of fog lifted up from the water and swirled around the pilings and piers so that the steel girders and wire cables of the dock loading-cranes became ethereal tracings. Long gray fingers of vapor had San Francisco trapped in its grasp.

There was no breeze.

The gaslights of the street lamps were dimmed and all sound was deadened by the heavy blanket. There was a dreamlike quality to the scene that made it hard to distinguish fantasy from reality. Figures moved along the streets and sidewalks, but they were no more than apparitions gliding through the fog, appearing then disappearing as if summoned and dismissed by some prankish wizard.

Falcon was in San Francisco to take delivery of a horse for Conrad Kohrs. But it wasn't just any horse, it was a very special horse, bred by King Abdul Aziz of Arabia.

"A king's horse have I bought and for it a king's ransom have I paid," Kohrs said in the letter he had sent to Falcon.

Kohrs chose Falcon as his emissary, not only because the well-known cattle baron was Falcon's friend, but also because he knew Falcon would be coming to Montana to attend the Montana Stockgrowers Association meeting.

The horse had been brought to America onboard the *Sea Dancer*, a tall-ship that plied the Pacific Ocean. Because of the value of the horse, it was shipped under special circumstances, not sharing a stall with other horses, but enjoying a private suite, constantly looked after by its own groomsmen.

Falcon had made arrangements to take delivery of the horse even before dawn because he intended to put it on the morning train.

The *Sea Dancer* lay at anchor alongside pier number seven, flaunting its half-naked dancing-girl figurehead, the long, sleek, gilded black hull glistening in its own running lights. Someone was standing on the dock alongside the ship as Falcon approached. The man was wearing a dark peacoat and a billed cap. The sleeves of the coat, as well as the bill of the cap, were decorated with gold braid.

"Captain MacTavish?" Falcon asked.

"Aye, Captain Sean MacTavish at your service," the sailor answered. "And you would be Falcon MacCallister, I take it?"

"Yes."

"Well, 'tis a fine horse my old friend Connie is getting," Captain MacTavish said.

Falcon chuckled. "Connie?"

"Aye, it was Connie we called him when he sailed with us," MacTavish said. "I was a midshipman when first we met." TacTavish chuckled. "Connie and I went ashore in Calais. Ahh, the French girls. We were just boys, mind you, but we'd been around the world a time or two, so we were pretty worldly for our age. But it turns out the Captain didn't think so. We got a caning we did, the both of us."

MacTavish paused before he spoke again. "But the French girls . . . ah . . . the French girls. I tell you true, 'tis three canings I would have taken for the lessons those French girls taught us." The captain turned toward the ship.

"Mr. Peabody!" he called.

"Aye, Cap'n," a voice returned from the deck.

"Land His Highness."

"Aye, aye, sir."

MacTavish turned back to Falcon. "I don't know what Connie will call the horse, but we've been calling him His Highness, for true it is that he lived better than anyone did on the voyage, myself included."

A wide gangplank was lowered from the side of the ship, then a sailor came down the plank, leading the horse. Falcon walked over to examine the animal when it reached the dock.

The horse had a distinctive muscular profile with large, lustrous, wide-set eyes on a broad forehead; small, curved ears; and large nostrils. Falcon whistled softly.

"He's quite a beauty, isn't he?" MacTavish said.

"Yes, he is."

"T'was said, when we took him abroad, that he was the King's favorite."

"Then why did the King part with him?"

"'Tis said he wanted the bloodline to start in America," MacTavish said. He rubbed his hands together. "Well, m'boyo, 'tis your responsibility now. Do give Connie my best."

"I'll do that," Falcon said.

* * *

"You sure he's pickin' up that horse this early, Dingo?" Cyrus asked. "Hell, it ain't even light yet."

"Yeah, He's getting' him early so he can put 'im on the eight o'clock train."

"How do you know this?"

"'Cause I met some fella off the ship that brung the horse over," Dingo said. "We was drinkin' together. He got drunk and the next thing you know, he was tellin' me about this here ten-thousand-dollar horse."

"You know that's a load of bullshit," Cyrus said. "There ain't no horse worth ten thousand dollars. And even if there was, who would you find to pay you that much for it?"

"This here horse is worth that much. He's one of them special breed of horses that kings and the like have," Dingo said. "But we ain't goin' to try and get that much money for him. If we sell him for five hunnert dollars, well, that's five hunnert we don't have now."

"Yeah, well somethin' else we don't have now is the horse," Cyrus said.

"Shhh," Dingo said. "Here he comes now."

Falcon was riding a rental horse, and leading the Arabian. Suddenly there was a flash in the darkness and the sound of a gunshot echoed back from the line of warehouses. Falcon felt the impact of the bullet as it hit his horse, then the horse went down under him.

"I got 'im!" Dingo said.

"You got the horse," Cyrus corrected.

"It's the same thing."

"No, it ain't the same thing. If you hadn't kilt the horse, we could'a had both of the horses. You should'a aimed at the rider."

"I *was* aimin' at the rider," Dingo said. "Come on, let's check him out."

The two men moved up, cautiously, toward the fallen horse. They could see the rider lying, perfectly motionless, pinned to the ground by the horse that was on his leg.

"I think he's dead," Dingo said.

"What makes you think he's dead?"

"Look at the way he's lyin' there. His eyes is open, but they ain't movin'. He don't look like he's breathin'."

"Check 'im out, Dingo. See if he's dead," Cyrus said.

Holding his pistol beside him, Dingo leaned over the motionless form of the rider, then reached out with his other hand to check for a pulse.

Falcon remained still until Dingo got close enough. Then, reacting quickly, Falcon reached up and grabbed the assailant's gun, jerking it away cleanly.

"What the hell?" Dingo shouted, taking a step back in surprise.

Falcon's leg only appeared to be trapped. In fact, it was under the soft belly of the horse, so it was very easy for him to pull it out.

"Shoot 'im, Cyrus, shoot 'im!" Dingo shouted.

Falcon sat up then cocked his pistol. The deadly, double click of the sear engaging the cylinder sounded exceptionally loud in the still morning darkness.

"I wouldn't listen to Dingo if I were you, Cyrus," Falcon said.

"Dingo, the son of bitch knows our names," Cyrus said. "How does he know our names?"

Falcon chuckled. Were these two so dumb that they didn't even realize they had just given him their names?

"Unbuckle the gunbelt," Falcon said to Cyrus.

"You goin' to shoot us, Mister?" Cyrus asked, his voice cracking with fear.

"I might," Falcon said. "I don't have time to take you to jail."

"If you're goin' to shoot someone, shoot him," Cyrus said. "This here wasn't my idea."

"Shut up, Cyrus. We was both in on this."

"But you was the one that come up with it," Cyrus said. "You said there was this here real valuable horse and we could steal him and sell him. That's what you said."

Falcon chuckled. "Were you going to share in the money, Cyrus?"

"Well, yeah," Cyrus said.

"Well, there you go then. You are as guilty as Dingo."

"Yeah," Dingo said. "There you go, you're as guilty as me. So he's goin' to shoot both of us."

Falcon sighed. He really didn't have time to take them to jail, and he had no intention of shooting either one of them, even thought they were damn near too dumb to live. But he couldn't just let them go. Then he got an idea.

"Take off your clothes," he said.

"What?"

"Take off your clothes, both of you."

"Are you sayin' you want us to strip down to our long handles?" Cyrus asked.

Falcon shook his head. "No, I'm saying I want you to strip down to the skin. I want both of you butt naked."

"Mister, I ain't a'goin' to do that," Dingo said.

"All right," Falcon said. "Cyrus, you strip while I kill Dingo."

"Yes, sir, I'll strip," Cyrus said. "You go ahead and shoot him."

"No, wait!" Dingo said, holding his hands out in front of him. "Don't shoot, don't shoot! What's the matter with you, Cyrus, tellin' him to shoot me?"

"Well, if you won't take offen your clothes like he said," Cyrus said as he pulled off one of his boots.

"All right, all right, I'll strip," Dingo said.

Lifting up first one foot, then the other, the men started removing their boots.

"Mister, this ain't natural," Dingo said. "It ain't right, you makin' us strip like this."

"It wasn't right for you to shoot at me, either."

"I didn't shoot you, I shot the horse."

"But you said you was shootin' at him," Cyrus said.

"Cyrus, will you shut up?"

A moment later, both men stood naked, shivering in the morning chill.

"Now what?" Dingo asked.

"Take your clothes over to the edge of the dock and drop them in the water." Falcon shifted his gun to his left hand, then threw the gun he had grabbed from Dingo toward the bay. It made a little splashing sound as it went into the water. "Drop your holsters in there too."

Glaring in anger, the two men scooped up their clothes, then padded, barefoot, across the board dock. They looked toward him in one last, fruitless appeal. He waved his gun to tell them to go through with it.

Both men dropped their clothes into the water, then looked back at Falcon.

"Now what?" Dingo said.

Falcon shrugged. "Now nothing," he said. "I'm through with you. You can go on your way."

"Go on our way? Where are we going to go, naked like this?"

"I don't care," Falcon said. "Just get out of my sight. I've never seen anything uglier than you two naked jaybirds."

Dingo and Cyrus hurried away, disappearing into the morning gloom. They continued arguing with each other and Falcon could hear them, even after he could no longer see them.

Falcon laughed out loud, then looked at the Arabian, who through it all, had stood quietly.

"Well, horse," Falcon said. "I hadn't planned on riding you, but I guess I've got no choice now. We've got a train to catch."

Falcon took the saddle from the rental horse, put in on the Arabian, then mounted and rode off. Even in a ride like this, he could tell that this was some horse. Maybe not a ten-thousand dollar horse, but it was some horse.

Lowell Spivey, the guard at the maximum security blockhouse of the Yuma Territorial Prison, settled back in his chair and looked at the clock. It was 2:30 in the morning. Spivey had just switched to the night shift and was having a hard time adjusting to it. He was tired and wanted to go to sleep. And though he could close his eyes and grab a quick nap in the chair, it was frowned upon.

"Hey, Spivey?" one of the prisoners called.

"What do you want?" Spivey answered.

"You better come have a look at Cardis."

"What's wrong with him?"

"I don't know, but he's back there moanin' like he's hurtin' real bad."

"It can wait till mornin'," Spivey replied.

"Then if you ain't goin' to do nothin' about it, at least come back here and tell 'im to shut up. He's keepin' the rest of us awake."

"Yeah," one of the other prisoners shouted. "Or open up his cell and let one of us shut 'im up."

A couple of the other prisoners laughed.

With a sigh, Spivey got up, opened the outer door, and walked down the cell-flanked corridor toward the cell that was Cardis'. When Spivey reached Cardis' cell, he saw the prisoner doubled up on his bunk, both arms wrapped across his stomach.

"What is it?" Spivey asked. "What's wrong with you?"

"I think it was somethin' I et at supper'." Cardis grunted.

"Everybody else ate the same thing," Spivey said. "How come you're the only one complaining?"

"Maybe 'cause I'm the only one that got sick," Gilly Cardis replied.

"Yeah, well, try and keep quiet, will you?" Spivey asked. "You're keeping the others awake."

"I'll try," Cardis said. Suddenly he gasped, and grabbed his stomach again.

"All right, all right," Spivey said, pulling out the keys. "Come on, I'll take you to the dispensary so the Doc can take a look at you."

"Thanks," Cardis said.

Spivey put the key in the lock, but before he opened the door, he looked at Cardis.

"Don't just sit there, you know what to do."

"Yeah, I know what to do," Cardis answered, though he didn't change from his doubled-over position.

"Well, do it, Cardis, I'm not going to stand here all night," Spivey said.

"Don't get all in a huff, I'm doin' it," Cardis grunted.

Cardis stood up and leaned against the wall. Spivey walked over to him, then pulled one of Cardis' arms into position and started to cuff his hands behind his back. Cardis let out a cry of pain. "I can't get my arms behind me," he grunted. "It hurts my gut too much."

"You know the rules. If I let you out of our cell at any time other than when it's authorized, you have to have your hands cuffed."

"Can't you cuff 'em in front?"

Spivey hesitated for a long moment, then he sighed. "Alright, I'll cuff 'em in front. But I ain't supposed to be doin' this, so don't give me any trouble."

Cardis held his hands together in front while Spivey put the manacles on him. The manacles were held together by a short length of chain so that when his wrists were bound, Cardis could hold his hands about twelve inches apart.

"Okay, tough guy, let's go," Spivey said. "You lead the way; you know where the dispensary is." He pushed Cardis roughly to get him started.

Procedure called for Spivey to inform one of the other guards any time he took a prisoner from the cell, but he didn't see any of the other guards around.

"Collins," Spivey said to the prisoner who had told him about Cardis, "if you see Kane, tell 'im I took Cardis to the dispensary, will you?"

"Yeah, I'll tell 'im," Collins called back from the dark of his cell.

"All right, you wanted to go to the dispensary, let's go," Spivey said, poking Cardis with his nightstick.

"I ain't the one asked to go to the dispensary," Cardis said.

"No, you didn't. You was just gonna lie in there an' moan all night. Come on, let's go." He jabbed Cardis with his night-stick again, this time in the small of the back, hard enough to make the killer gasp.

They left the cell block and stepped out into the still, dark night. Cardis looked up at the sky. It was a desert-clear night, with stars so bright that he felt as if he could almost reach up and pull one down.

Cardis's eyes scanned the prison yard, going immediately to the guard positions on top of the wall. None of the guards were watching. He grasped the chain with his fingers and waited until he and Spivey were around the corner from the dispensary.

"Ohh!" he suddenly said, stopping and bending over, almost as if he were about to fall.

"What is it now?" Spivey asked, the tone of his voice reflecting his irritation with the prisoner.

"My belly's on fire," Cardis gasped.

"Well, the quicker you get to the dispensary, the quicker you can get somethin' done about it," Spivey said, taking a step closer to him. "Come on, let's go."

Whirling around quickly, and using the small length of chain as a club, Cardis hit the guard and Spivey went down.

Cardis's rifled through Spivey's pockets until he found the key. Then, unlocking the cuffs, he put on Spivey's hat and coat and started toward the front gate, walking as confidently as if he fully expected the guard to open the gate for him.

Cardis' bold move paid off. The guard at the gate barely looked up from his newspaper as he pulled the lever to unlock the gate. With a little wave, Cardis, who kept his head down for the whole time, simply stepped through. He continued to walk slowly until he disappeared into the dark; then he broke into a run.